DEADLY CHRISTMAS

Rachel McLean writes thrillers that make your pulse race and your brain tick. Originally a self-publishing sensation, she has sold millions of copies digitally, with massive success in the UK, and a growing reach internationally too. She is the author of the Dorset Crime novels and the spin-off McBride & Tanner series and Cumbria Crime series. In 2021, she won the Kindle Storyteller Award with *The Corfe Castle Murders* and her last five books have all hit No1 in the Bookstat ebook chart on launch.

ALSO BY RACHEL MCLEAN

Zoe Finch series

Deadly Wishes
Deadly Choices
Deadly Desires
Deadly Terror
Deadly Reprisal
Deadly Fallout
Deadly Christmas

RACHEL McLEAN

DETECTIVE ZOE FINCH BOOK 7

DEADLY CHRISTMAS

Copyright © 2022, 2024 by Rachel McLean

All rights reserved.

No part of this book may be reproduced in any form or by any electronic or mechanical means, including information storage and retrieval systems, without written permission from the author, except for the use of brief quotations in a book review.

This is a work of fiction. Names, characters, businesses, places, events and incidents are either the products of the author's imagination or used in a fictitious manner. Any resemblance to actual persons, living or dead, or actual events is purely coincidental.

Ackroyd Publishing

ackroydpublishing.com

Printed and bound in the UK by CPI Group (Uk) Ltd, Croydon CR0 4YY

CHAPTER ONE

At Christmas time, Brummies could be split into two groups.

The first contained those people who loved the Frankfurt Christmas market.

They adored the cheesiness of it all. The little wooden cabins. The abundance of lebkuchen. Gluhwein on tap twenty-four hours a day, and the fact that for six brief weeks of the year the currywurst replaced the Balti as Birmingham's traditional dish.

On the other hand, there were people like Wendy.

Wendy hated the Christmas market.

To be fair, it was Wendy's job to clean up every morning. So it wasn't really surprising that she looked forward to the day the German stall holders packed up their lorries and headed back across the Channel.

Today was a particularly bad one. It was getting closer to Christmas and, as happened every year, the crowds had built up over time. Saturday nights were always the worst, too, and if the amount of puke Wendy was pressure washing off the pavements was anything to go by, about fifty thousand glasses of gluhwein and a hundred thousand steins of fizzy German beer had been drunk. Worse, there were a few currywursts still identifiable.

She closed her eyes and wished she could close her nostrils with them as she blitzed away the tenth pavement pizza of the morning. It was only 6am and already she was counting down the days until Christmas Eve.

Her colleague Manjit was across the street doing the same thing. The two of them did this four days a week, working their way along New Street, winkling out the remains of last night's festivities before any commuters or shoppers were around to see what had happened.

Yes, Wendy hated the Frankfurt Christmas market.

They reached the top of New Street and paused for a breather, as they always did. The steps leading up to the famous fountain, the floozie in the jacuzzi as she was affectionately known, were a popular spot for people to hang out on in the summer, eating packed lunches or drinking coffees from the New Street Gregg's. Wendy and Manjit liked to pause here and catch their breath.

Images from the pavements Wendy had worked her way through from the Bullring kept flashing in front of her mind. She shook her head to clear them away.

"Rough today, isn't it?" muttered Manjit.

"You can say that again."

Wendy's stomach felt heavy. She never ate breakfast before these shifts, knowing she'd struggle to keep it down. In fact, she couldn't even face lunch till about three in the afternoon, and by that time she was usually ready for bed.

"All downhill from here," Manjit said. "Gets easier after Sunday."

"You reckon? I think it gets worse every day from now on." Wendy leaned back on the steps, stretching out the muscles of her neck.

Manjit shrugged. "At least they give us overtime for a Sunday morning."

Wendy yawned. Working for the council did have some perks. It was a solid job with holiday, sick leave and a pension, if she made it that far. And in return for working on a Sunday morning, she got triple time. This way, she could give her kids a decent Christmas.

She heaved herself up from the steps, glad her waterproof uniform kept out the damp from the ground. She stretched her arms above her head. "Sooner we get on with it, sooner it's done."

Manjit nodded her head, her expression blank. "What now?"

"Victoria Square," Wendy replied.

Manjit grimaced. Victoria Square was beer-and-gluhwein central. It was lined with bars, as well as alcoves for people to stand in while they drank. At each end of the space was a sign: *This is a restricted alcohol area*. Wendy wondered if the person who'd installed those signs had any sense of irony.

"Which side first?"

"Town Hall," Manjit replied, glancing towards the Council House and grimacing.

So today they were leaving the worst till last. Wendy trudged over to the spot that Manjit indicated and started to clean. She tried to get herself into an absent zone when she was doing this, her mind miles away, singing Christmas songs in her head. When the Christmas songs became too much, she switched to Duran Duran, her favourite local lads, even if they were a bit old school.

"Shit."

Wendy looked up. She frowned at Manjit, who was round the side of one of the cabins that served as stalls. "You OK? What you stepped in?"

"It's not that." Manjit beckoned furiously. "Get over here."

Wendy frowned. "D'you want me to bring my machine?"

"Leave it. Come over here, Wendy, please." Manjit sounded scared. Wendy had never heard her friend speak with this urgency.

"What's up?" Wendy hurried over to Manjit, whose face had paled. "What have you found?" As Wendy approached, Manjit pointed towards the ground. She waggled her hand and looked at Wendy, and then back at the ground.

"Where did he come from?" Manjit asked.

Wendy looked down. A man was slumped on the ground, tucked around the back of the cabin. He was dressed in a shabby coat, holes at the elbows and cuffs and a thick layer of dirt. His jeans were frayed at the ankles and worn thin at the knees. If Wendy's nose hadn't already checked out in preparation for work today, she was confident he'd smell pretty bad.

She poked him gently with her toe. They wore steel-capped boots so she knew she had to be careful.

"He's not moving," Manjit said.

"No." Wendy nudged him again. *Oh shit*. Was she going to have to bend down? Slap his face to wake him up. She shivered.

This wasn't the first time this had happened. Normally it was drunk stag dos, the revellers intending to get back to a hotel but falling asleep in one of the drinking booths. And she'd found plenty of rough sleepers stretched across the benches in Pigeon Park.

Wendy looked away and drew in a breath. Bending down, she put a hand on his shoulder, giving it a gentle jiggle.

"Is he...?" asked Manjit.

"I don't know." Wendy knelt on the floor next to the man. His head was twisted to one side, his face pointing towards Chamberlain Square behind him. She put her hand on his chin and gave it a pinch. No response.

"This is all we need," she breathed.

She looked up at Manjit, who was blinking. Manjit was ten years younger than she was, no kids, more... delicate. *Don't faint, mate.*

Manjit muttered under her breath. A prayer, maybe. "Dead, isn't he?"

Wendy stood up. She slapped her hands together, trying to erase the smell that was already sticking to her.

"Dead as my great granny," she replied.

CHAPTER TWO

Detective Inspector Zoe Finch parked her green mini on double yellow lines by the side of Birmingham Town Hall. This was as close as she could get to the crime scene, and it was still a building site.

The city centre was a constant building site, although not as bad as it had been a year ago. A city without construction is a stagnant city, her dad used to say.

She went to the boot of her car and grabbed her duffel coat. It was chilly this morning and her normal leather jacket was nowhere near enough. She slammed the boot shut and headed past the Town Hall towards the crime scene.

The area had already been taped off. Two layers of protection: an inner cordon for the scene itself, and an exclusion zone outside it to keep the public at a distance. It was half past nine in the morning, and the punters wouldn't be flocking to the Frankfurt Christmas market this early, thank God.

Zoe had once loved the market. In 2004, when the market had been running for just three years, she'd taken

Nicholas. He was just three months old, excited by the fairy lights, the carousel and the stallholders who wanted to pinch his ruddy baby cheeks. But now she was one of those Brummies who was sick of the thing. Not as sick of it as her uniformed colleagues, though: they hated the thing. What with all the drinking and puking and fighting it was like an FA Cup final every day for six weeks on the trot.

Zoe spotted DC Rhodri Hughes near the inner cordon, talking to an FSI in a white suit. Probably Adi Hanson. A case like this, he'd always be on the spot.

She approached them. "Rhodri." He turned and straightened. She nodded at the FSI and was rewarded with a grin. It was Adi alright.

"Hi, Adi. You been here long?"

A shrug. "Half an hour. Forty-five minutes, maybe. Where were you?"

She raised an eyebrow. "It's supposed to be my day off."

He laughed. "Weekends don't exist for Crime Scene Managers."

"Nor for DI's," she replied. "At least not this weekend." She pulled her coat tighter. "What have we got, anyway?"

Adi and Rhodri both looked towards the tent behind the stall.

"One IC1 male. Early seventies, by the look of him," Adi said, "but he could be younger. Looks like he's had a tough life."

"How so?"

"Pockmarked face, swollen nose, scars on his wrists."

"Suicide attempts?"

"Possibly. I'm not the expert."

"How did he die?"

"Not sure. No sign of injury."

Zoe nodded. "Exposure?"

"It was just above freezing in the city centre last night. Two degrees. It's a possibility."

"Uniform wouldn't have called FSI and CID out for natural causes."

"No."

"So what's up?"

"There are marks on his hands. Writing, I think. Can't read it, though."

"A message?"

Adi shrugged. "Come and take a look."

Zoe motioned for Rhodri to follow them. Adi pulled aside the fabric of the tent and Zoe ducked her head to go inside. The man was in the centre of the space, his body twisted so that his feet faced New Street but his face looked toward the Town Hall. Or it would have done if his eyes had been open.

His skin was dirty and his clothes ragged, but there was no visible sign of trauma.

"Looks like exposure to me, boss," said Rhodri.

"There's writing on his hands," said Adi.

"Oh."

Zoe bent down. The man's right hand was twisted and lay partially under his body. She could make out markings on the back of his hand. His left hand rested on top of his coat. The wrist was circled with a line that looked like it had been drawn with biro.

"That's all?" she asked.

Adi shook his head. "Come round here. The left hand, there's more."

She stood up and shuffled round to stand behind Adi, then squatted down again.

Adi lifted the man's hand slightly. "See?"

Zoe cocked her head. There was what looked like writing on the fleshy part of his palm, near the base of the thumb.

"I can't read it."

"I don't think it's English." Adi lowered the man's hand.

"Have you got photos?"

"I don't want to disturb him too much until the pathologist has taken a look. But yes, we have some."

"And photos of his face? Ones I can show to potential witnesses?"

"Of course."

Zoe stood up. "I assume there's no ID on him."

"Nothing. All he had in his pockets were some sweets and 53p in loose change."

"Poor bastard," muttered Rhodri. Zoe nodded.

"OK," she said. "Give me a shout when the pathologist gets here. Who are we expecting?"

"Dr Adebayo," Adi told her.

"Good." Adana knew her stuff.

"Sure it wasn't exposure, boss?" Rhodri asked. "It'd have been freezing round here last night."

"Not quite," she replied. "Two degrees above."

"Still... you wouldn't catch me sleeping around the back of one of those stalls at this time of year."

Zoe frowned at him. "I don't imagine he had much choice in the matter."

Rhodri stiffened. "No. I s'pose not." He looked down at the man's body, lying between them.

"Right." Zoe sighed and pulled her phone out of her pocket. She dialled the office.

"DC Williams."

"Connie," Zoe said, "I'm at a crime scene. Possible suspicious death. Unidentified male, in his sixties or seventies."

"OK, boss. What d'you need me to do?"

"I'll send you some photos, and a description. Or rather, Adi will. We need to get started on finding an ID."

"Is it a murder?"

"We don't know yet. Could be natural causes." Zoe tightened her grip on the phone. "But my gut is telling me otherwise."

"Send me the photos and I'll start trawling mispers."

"Thanks." Zoe hung up and turned to Rhodri.

"Er, boss?"

"Yes, Rhod?" They were outside the tent now, having left Adi behind. There was no sign of Adana.

"If this turns out to be a murder enquiry..."

"Yes, Rhod?"

"You know I built up some leave? Planning to visit my folks in the valleys, like."

"You know what happens to leave when there's a murder, DC Hughes."

"Yeah. Sorry."

She stopped walking and turned to face him. "When does your leave start, Rhod?"

He bit down on his bottom lip. "The twenty second, boss."

"That's four days away."

He nodded. "Yes, boss."

"Well, you'd better do everything you can to help get this case wrapped up in time, hadn't you?"

"Yes, boss."

CHAPTER THREE

CONNIE SCREWED up her nose and scratched her chin. She was itching a lot lately. She hoped she wasn't getting some sort of skin complaint; finding time to see the GP was impossible when you were a member of CID.

She gave her chin one last scratch, then bent over her computer.

The boss had sent her an email with a description of the man, and Adi Hanson had forwarded photos. The guy looked like a rough sleeper, so the best place to start was homeless shelters.

She'd spoken to Rhodri after getting off the phone from the boss, knowing she could rely on her colleague to tell it like it was. "Scruffy old bastard," he'd told her. "Stinks to high heaven." And the boss's email had described tears in his clothes and dirt around the hems of his trousers and noted that his shoes were worn thin.

The boss had also said that the man didn't smell as bad as she might expect.

Connie wished she could get down there and find out for herself. God knows, she'd had enough experience of homeless people in Uniform. Back then it had seemed like every day she was called out to help someone who was sleeping rough.

If he didn't smell so bad, maybe the guy had only recently become homeless.

Connie felt a shiver run across her skin. Poor man. He'd never reach the stage of neglect that most rough sleepers attained. But it didn't matter when you were dead. His body would decompose like anyone else's.

She scrolled through Google Maps. There were four shelters in the city, one of them not far from Victoria Square where the body had been found.

She dialled the boss.

"Connie, got anything for me?"

"There's a shelter near you," she said. "Newhall Street, just outside the ring road."

"Send me the address."

"D'you want me to call the others?"

"Please. Have you had the photos from Adi?"

"I have."

"Are they presentable?"

"Just about."

"Shelters are used to all sorts. Ask if they know who he is. If they've seen him come through their doors in recent weeks."

"Will do."

"Good," said the boss. "Rhodri and I will do the Newhall Street shelter. Then we'll head back into the office."

The line went quiet.

"Boss?" Connie said.

"Sorry. Pathologist is here. Rhodri's going to head to that shelter. Let him know if you get anything."

"Of course."

CHAPTER FOUR

Freya Garside didn't like it when people let her down.

She'd spent her life honing a reputation for efficiency and reliability. If she said she would do something, then she'd damn well do it regardless of the consequences. And she expected other people to live by similar principles.

Today, however, she was disappointed. Mr North, her neighbour five doors along, had promised to take on the Santa role for the children at the local primary school. The school's Christmas fair was taking place at two o'clock this afternoon, and the two of them had agreed to meet at her house at 10 am.

It was 10.30 now, and there was no sign of Mr North.

Freya glanced again at her watch. She clicked her heels in a gesture of irritation and pulled on her coat, one of three hanging on the four hooks in her hallway. The fourth hook, always empty, was reserved for visitors.

Sighing deeply, she pulled open her front door, restraining herself from yanking it too hard and slamming it behind her. She turned left at the end of her path and

CHAPTER FOUR

clipped her way towards Mr North's house. All of her neighbours were on the same side of the road; opposite was Kings Heath Park. The park was the best thing about living in Avenue Road, even if it did attract too many teenagers.

Freya pulled her shoulders back as she reached Mr North's house. She stared up at the windows before turning into his path. Her house, and this one, were two of only five along here that still had the original paths and front gardens. The rest had been converted into driveways.

The curtains in the front bedroom window were closed. There were no lights on downstairs, despite it being dull today.

She cleared her throat. "Are you even at home, Mr North?" she muttered.

A woman with a pushchair passed, trailing a grubby-faced toddler. The woman gave Freya a smile. Freya responded with a wrinkled nose and a nod. The toddler had chocolate around its mouth and was wailing. Wailing toddlers, almost as bad as rowdy teenagers and unreliable neighbours. Thank God her two children had decided not to have offspring of their own.

She allowed her gaze to roam over the house one more time, then marched up the path. Mr North's front door had a knocker. She rapped it three times and stood back to wait.

Thirty seconds passed by, and no response.

She rapped the knocker four more times and stood back, moving towards the road to get a better view of the house.

If a curtain twitched in that top window she wanted to know about it.

He'd promised to act as Santa for the local primary school; had he changed his mind? Was the man hiding from her?

Unreliable, and a coward. She tutted.

Freya licked her lips and looked at the houses on either side. The one on the left was in disrepair, the front door scuffed and rubbish hanging out of the wheelie bin. She wrinkled her nose. Residents of The Avenue were not supposed to leave wheelie bins in front of their houses. They were supposed to pull them through the alleyways to the side and store them at the back, to avoid an unsightly street scene.

But not all residents were created equal.

She looked at the house on the right. Good. This one was tidier, even if the ornate curtains suggested its occupants might not be her kind of people.

Steeling herself, she walked back to the street and squeezed past a chunky hatchback car to reach the front door of the house. This one had a doorbell. She pressed it heavily.

An Asian woman in her mid-thirties answered the door. Her hands were clad in oven gloves. Freya looked down at them, wondering why the woman hadn't thought to take them off before opening the door.

"Can I help you?"

"I'm looking for your neighbour, Mr North."

"Albert? What d'you want him for?"

That's my business, Freya thought. "Can you tell me if he's in?"

"No idea." The woman pursed her lips. "Come to think of it, I haven't seen him for a little while."

How could she not have noticed? Freya would know at once if her neighbours strayed from their regular routine.

"Does he have a habit of disappearing?" she asked.

The woman laughed. "I don't spy on him. Sorry, I've no idea." She reached up to scratch her nose, then realised she was wearing an oven glove, removed it and scratched again.

"But Albert doesn't really have a regular routine, not like most." She hesitated, looking Freya up and down. "Have you tried around the back?"

"Not yet."

"He sometimes goes in that way. You might find he answers his back door."

Freya stared at her. Round the back? Trespass on the man's land just to find out if he was in?

Freya liked to watch her neighbours. She was concerned for them, wanted to be available if they needed her. But she would never access someone's house via the back door.

Someone had tried to do it to her house once, a delivery driver. She'd been horrified.

She swallowed, her mouth suddenly dry.

"Thank you for your help."

Freya turned and walked away from the woman. Back on the pavement, she looked up at Mr North's house.

Where are you, you old bastard?

The poor children were going to be disappointed. Children were good at being disappointed.

What would she do? The PTA would be disappointed in *her*. And all because she'd trusted her neighbour.

She would be letting people down. Something that Freya Garside never did. She pulled in a breath, running through her mind for alternative Father Christmases.

Her mind landed on a possible candidate and she felt the tension in her shoulders drop. She would spend the morning making calls. She would sort it all out and she would never ask Albert North to help her out again. And he could rot in hell for all she cared.

CHAPTER FIVE

Zoe eyed the pathologist, who was approaching the body with her heavy bag in one hand. Rhodri stood to one side, watching.

"Rhod," she said. "Connie's given me the name of a shelter in the city centre. Can you get over there and see if they know anything about our victim?"

"You're definite he was a rough sleeper?"

"Not definite, no. But judging by the state of his clothes, it's a fair assumption. And I want to get started on *something*. Just get a couple of the most palatable photos from Adi and take them over there. Maybe he had some mates who can identify him."

Rhodri grimaced.

Zoe clenched her teeth. "There a problem?"

"You think a bunch of homeless guys are going to talk to us? They're not exactly keen on chatting to the police."

"I know it's sensitive, but we need to try. Speak to the staff at the shelter first. They'll give you a pointer on the best way to proceed."

He nodded. "Boss."

Zoe watched as Rhodri approached Adi, who glanced over the DC's shoulder at her. She gave him a tight smile and he turned to Yala, his deputy. At least something was finally happening.

Zoe straightened up and walked towards the tent. It was attached to the back of the stall, its roof tied to the gabled roof of the wooden structure.

She pulled the curtain aside and Adana turned to look up at her.

"Zoe. Thanks for bringing me out here on a Sunday morning."

"I know. Sorry."

Adana waved a hand. She was bent over the body, her back to Zoe. "I'm joking, Detective. It's the nature of the job. These poor sods never pick the most convenient time to die."

"No." Zoe watched Adana pull the man's clothing aside and examine the skin of his chest. "What do you think?"

Adana leaned back on her heels. "Not sure."

"Can you tell us if it's natural causes?"

Adana stood up and pulled down her face mask. "Is it ever natural causes, with people like these?"

Zoe pulled in a breath. Even if this man had died naturally, it was hardly a natural death. Hypothermia, the flu, even tuberculosis... any one of a variety of causes could claim someone of his age sleeping rough, and not one of them a significant risk for those with a roof to sleep under.

"Nothing's natural about this," Adana muttered. She crossed herself, surprising Zoe. Adana gave her a sidelong look. "Yes, Zoe. I'm a woman of faith as well as science. The two aren't incompatible."

Zoe said nothing. Her dad's untimely death and her

mum's alcoholism had drummed any potential belief in a higher being out of her.

"So how are you?" Adana asked.

"Me?"

"You. Can't be easy without Mo."

Zoe swallowed. DS Mo Uddin, her best friend and second in command, had been in Scotland for four months now, settling into his new role in the Complex Crimes Unit.

"I'm fine."

"You haven't replaced him yet."

"There's a process."

"Oh, I know that. But I also know about secondments."

"Can we just focus on him?" Zoe gestured towards the man on the ground. Adana raised an eyebrow, aware that she'd touched a nerve, then pulled up her mask and bent back down to the victim.

Zoe hadn't seen any sign of injuries on the man. His skin was grey, but unbroken. No sign of infection or trauma. The only oddity was the pen marks on his hands. But then, she hadn't removed his clothes. Anything could be hiding under the layers.

"So when you ask if this is natural causes..." Adana began.

"Yes?"

"In this context, you're talking about heart attack or hypothermia. Especially at this time of year."

"Possibly. TB, too."

"I'd need to look at his lungs to be sure, but it doesn't look like TB to me. The skin would be paler."

"What about heart attack or hypothermia?"

"It's not hypothermia. Extremities aren't showing signs of it. It could be a heart attack, though. But it might not be."

CHAPTER FIVE

"Can you tell without a post-mortem?"

"I'll need to bring him into the morgue, get a proper look." Adana craned her neck to look up at Zoe. "Just because there's no bleeding or visible bruising, doesn't mean this wasn't done *to* him."

"I know." Zoe sighed. "Can you give me a time of death, at least?"

Adana pulled her phone out of her pocket and opened a weather app. "It was two degrees above freezing last night. That would have afforded some preservation, slowed down the natural process."

"And?"

"At what time would this stall have been closed up last night, Detective?"

Zoe shrugged. They still hadn't managed to trace the stall owner. "Midnight, I'd imagine." The German market stayed open till eleven, and then they would need time to clean up.

"In that case, I'd say he died around that time."

"How so?"

"I'd estimate time of death as yesterday between late evening and early hours. He was brought here after he died."

Zoe felt her skin shiver. *Don't jump to conclusions.* Just because someone put him here, didn't mean they killed him.

Not necessarily.

She looked up and past the roof of the stall towards the CCTV cameras on the side of the Council House. "In that case, Dr Adebayo, my team and I will be examining CCTV very carefully."

CHAPTER SIX

THE SHELTER WAS anonymous and almost impossible to find. Eventually Rhodri spotted a scuffed green door between two shop fronts, but not until he'd spent five minutes on Google streetview checking for the location.

How were the punters supposed to find this place, he wondered. Or was it deliberate? He knew how overstretched facilities like this were.

He pressed the buzzer next to the door and a latch clicked. He pushed the door open to find himself in a cramped hallway, another door in front of him. It was locked. No buzzer this time.

There was a sign on the door, printed on A4 paper.

Welcome to Greenfields Shelter. Please wait a moment and someone will let you in.

Not many green fields around here, Rhodri thought.

He looked around the space. There would be a camera somewhere, sussing him out before they sent a human being to greet him.

Sure enough, there it was in the corner over the door. He

CHAPTER SIX

made eye contact, resisting the urge to give a little wave. He wondered what they would make of him, whether he looked anything like their usual visitors.

Rhodri knew his suit needed dry cleaning and there was a stain on his coat following a hot dog incident on his lunch break last Tuesday, but he also knew he looked every inch a copper.

He straightened, cleared his throat, and shifted his gaze to the door in front of him. At last it opened and a short, plump man who looked like he'd been scrubbed to within an inch of his life emerged.

He held out a hand. "Detective."

"How did you know?" Rhodri offered his hand and felt it being pumped vigorously.

The man smiled, his eyes twinkling, then dropped the smile as if he'd suddenly remembered it was inappropriate.

"We have our sources. Little birds that tell us what's going on in the city. We heard there were a bunch of you crawling all over Victoria Square and we thought you might come knocking on our door."

The man's accent was Scottish, although which part of Scotland Rhodri had no idea. He wondered if the sarge had reached the point where he could spot the difference between different Scottish accents.

"Why? D'you know who he is?"

The man shook his head. "Sorry, no. We just..." He frowned. "Why don't you come in? I'll make us both a cup of tea and we'll see if we can help you."

"It's alright. I—"

The man raised a hand. "Come on. I don't like standing down here." He glanced at the outer door behind Rhodri. "Let's go inside."

Without waiting for Rhodri to respond, he turned and walked through the inner door. Rhodri followed. No choice, really. How did he find himself in these situations, with members of the public telling him what to do? It wasn't how these things panned out for the boss. Or even for Connie.

He followed the man along a corridor and through another door into a large office. The office had three desks. One was piled high with paperwork, files and books. The other two were neat.

The man leaned against the messy desk. "I'm sorry, Detective. My name's Jimmy Kirk. I'm the manager of this place, for my sins. And you are...?"

"DC Hughes." Rhodri dug his ID out of the inside pocket of his jacket and held it up. Kirk gave it a glance then cocked his head at Rhodri.

"You'll be wondering if my parents were Trekkies."

"Err..."

A smile. "My dad was. My mum didn't know why he picked the name. But there you have it. James Tiberius Kirk is my full name. Mum thought maybe Dad was classically educated when he suggested the middle name. She didn't twig till it was too late."

"Mr Kirk, I need to talk to you about—"

"Sorry. I'm waffling on. You need my help to identify the fella you've found at the market, I imagine."

James Tiberius Kirk certainly seemed to know a lot about this investigation. Rhodri resisted the urge to ask him how. "I was hoping to show his photograph to some of your... service users."

"Service users. Don't call them that to their faces, they'll think you've lost the plot." A pause. "But no."

"No? *No what?* Rhodri was getting confused. Was it

deliberate? Did this seemingly friendly man have something to do with the crime?

"No, you can't show his photo to our fellas."

"One of them might be able to—"

Kirk put a hand on Rhodri's arm. "Have you had dealings with homeless men, Detective?"

"Of course." No police officer hadn't, in one form or another.

"Well, our guys are hard core. We take in people no one else will have. Street drinkers, chronically ill. Our licence means we have to kick them out every morning, but they come back the next night. Same fellas, often in the same bed. We get to know them."

"I don't see how that's—"

"They have trust issues, Detective. If you or one of your colleagues tried to talk to them, they'd clam up."

Rhodri pursed his lips. This, he understood. "In that case, I can share our photos with you and ask if you'll show them to your... fellas."

Kirk smiled. "You're catching on, lad. That sounds like a fine plan." He pulled out a mobile phone that looked at least four years out of date. "Here. Have my email address, and forward me the images. I'll run them past a few people and let you know if we get a match."

"When will you be able—"

"This evening, Detective. That good enough for you? It's the best I can do."

"Fair enough." Rhodri took out his phone and held up the clearest of the photos that Adi had given him. "Before I do, can you take a look?"

"Of course." Kirk held out a hand and Rhodri gave him the phone. He frowned as he looked at the photo. Something flickered across his face, but was quickly replaced by the same frown.

He looked at Rhodri as he handed the phone back. "Sorry. Never seen him here."

"You're sure?"

"Sure. I know all our fellas well. Just send me that email, and maybe one of them will know your guy."

CHAPTER SEVEN

Connie had already pinned half a dozen crime scene photos to the board. Zoe stood in front of it, hands on hips, trying to imagine their victim's last hours.

Of course, he might not be a victim at all. Adana hadn't ruled out natural causes. But if he'd been put behind that stall after he was dead, then it was a good bet that whoever had put him there had also killed him.

She shouldn't make assumptions. People who lived on the streets often went to significant lengths to avoid coming into contact with the authorities. And even if their lives hadn't taught them to be wary, they often simply didn't know what the process was when a death happened. If someone came across a friend who'd died on the streets, then they might just have gone for the easy option and hidden him.

But how easy would it be to hide the body of a grown man? Sure, he was skinny, but even then, he must have weighed at least twelve stone.

It would take some determination to carry a body from wherever he had died to that spot, and to manage it without being spotted by the stallholder or a member of the public was an achievement that, in different circumstances, she might have applauded.

Once they had the CCTV footage, they'd know.

She turned at the sound of the door to the outer office opening and closing. The board was out here, next to Mo's old desk. Zoe often used her own office for team briefings, but since Mo had gone, she'd started making use of the extra space out here. She still missed him.

Rhodri stood next to her at the board, surveying it in silence. She wondered how long it would be before he couldn't stand the silence any longer.

"He's a weird fish," the DC said, finally.

Zoe smiled. Less than a minute. "Who is?"

"The manager of the shelter I just visited. Named after Captain Kirk on Star Trek, called himself Jimmy. Seemed to think the whole thing was amusing."

"In what way?" She didn't shift her gaze from the board. Connie had also written the names of the shelters and homeless charities they'd identified. Three of them had crosses next to their names.

"He thought it was inappropriate that I might try to talk to his 'fellas', as he called them. Told me there was no way they'd speak to me."

"That follows. The homeless often don't have a lot of trust for the police."

"No," said Connie, who'd joined them at the board. "Zaf had a mate who dropped out after school, lived on the street for a few months. If ever he spotted a squad car, he scarpered."

"Despite the fact we spend more time helping rough sleepers than arresting them," Rhodri pointed out.

"Not always," Zoe replied. "Anyway, was he any help in identifying our man?"

"Not yet. Said he'd show them the photo himself, later. But..."

"But what?" She turned to the DC.

"He was... oh, I don't know, I'm probably imagining it. But it felt to me like he did recognise him. He said he didn't, though."

"In that case, he probably didn't," Connie said.

"Or maybe he had something to hide," Zoe suggested.

"Why would someone who runs a shelter be involved in the death of one of his clients?" asked Connie.

"Why does anyone do anything?" Zoe shot back. "It's probably nothing, Rhod, but I don't see why you shouldn't pop round there again later, when he's had a chance to speak to his clients. It is a potential murder enquiry, after all."

"We don't know that yet," Connie said.

"Jimmy Kirk doesn't know we don't know that."

Connie sniffed.

"So what about the other places?" Zoe asked her. "You've put crosses by some of them."

"Those ones have closed down."

"OK. You speak to the others?"

"I did. Sent photos to them all, they've said they'll come back to me if they recognise him."

"Follow that up by phone in a couple of hours. They might have been able to circulate the photos a bit by then. Probably get more people around later on, though, when the cold starts to bite. Meanwhile we've got the CCTV to examine."

"That'll tell us what happened," Rhodri said.

"Let's hope so." Zoe turned to the two DCs. She was

painfully aware of how small the team was without Mo. "I took a look around when I was there. There are cameras on the walls of the Council House, plus the Town Hall directly behind the crime scene."

"There are some on the shops at the top of New Street, too," Rhodri added.

Zoe nodded. "Can someone print off a map of the area, and we'll work out where there are cameras and what the angles are?

"I'm on it," Connie said. "And I've left a message with the council about their cameras."

"That stall'll block the view from a lot of them," Rhodri said. "He was hidden round the back of it."

"Not on his way in," Zoe replied. "The cameras will have caught him being put there."

Rhodri scratched his nose.

"You got any idea how long they'll take, Connie?" Zoe asked.

"Tomorrow. No one's working today."

Zoe clenched a fist and rapped her lips with her knuckles. "Bloody hell. A man's dead. I know it's the council but for once, can't they just pull their finger out?"

"I'll try again, boss."

"No. I'll put in a call with a member of the cabinet. In fact, I'll get Frank to do it."

"Boss." Connie's tone was clipped. Neither of the DCs had had much contact with DCI Frank Dawson since his permanent promotion to Lesley's old job. Too many people she trusted were leaving, Zoe thought. Maybe she'd be next, if her boyfriend Carl got his way.

"Right." She stretched out her hand. "We still need to wait for the pathologist's report, but our priority right now is to identify our man and get at least some of the CCTV footage. Connie, get that map and we'll make a start. The CCTV control centre can help us."

"Boss."

The door opened and Zoe turned towards the sound. In the doorway stood a middle-aged man in a creased grey suit and a tie in a shade of green that made his face look even more sallow than usual.

"Frank," she said.

His cheek twitched. He still didn't like her not calling him *sir* or at least *boss*. But Frank Dawson had been her equal in rank for many more years than he'd been her senior.

His gaze passed over the two constables, who she knew were looking at the ground or the board. *Meet his eye*, she thought. Neither of them would be promoted if they acted like wallflowers.

"Zoe," he said. "I see you've made a start."

"Our priority is to identify the body," she told him. "And to get hold of CCTV footage from the area. There are at least six ca—"

He shook his head. "I need a word. In private." He jerked his head backwards.

Zoe pursed her lips and looked at the two DCs in turn. "You know what to do." She smiled at the DCI. "No problem, Frank."

CHAPTER EIGHT

THEY STOPPED IN THE CORRIDOR, Zoe's hand still on the door.

"What's up?" she asked, her breathing tight. She was annoyed that Frank had pulled her out of a briefing. It might have been Sunday, but that didn't mean things couldn't be run professionally, and that was all the more important with just three of them on this investigation.

He glanced over her shoulder. She didn't turn to follow his gaze.

"Frank," she said. "I need to get on with this investigation. What's happened?"

He leaned towards her. He smelt of breathmints. Frank was trying to give up smoking and she knew he was chewing at least a pack of chewing gum each day.

"Three of you isn't enough," he said.

She felt her shoulders relax. "Tell me something I don't know. But you know how long it's taking to—"

He shook his head. "I'm bringing in another officer."

"Right. Don't I get a say i—"

"It's temporary, Zoe. For the duration of this investigation. I've found someone who's available, and beggars can't be choosers. Besides, she's experienced."

She. Zoe tried to think of the female CID officers who might have applied for Mo's job. She couldn't think of anyone.

Unless...

"Is Connie going to be acting up?" she asked.

Frank snorted. He leaned back. "Why would I do that? You'd be short a DC."

True. "Who is it, then?"

The last time Zoe had been allocated a temporary DS, it had been Ian Osman. A disaster from start to finish. His secondment had begun with the kidnapping of his children, and ended with him on trial for corruption.

"Who, Frank?"

"You've met her."

Zoe frowned. "Sheila?"

"No."

No. Sheila Griffin wasn't looking to move from Organised Crime, as far as Zoe knew. And if she did, it would be a loss.

"Layla Kaur," Frank said.

Zoe's breath caught in her throat. "DS Kaur from PSD?"

"You know any other DS Kaurs?"

"No. But she investigated me. She and I don't exactly get along."

"She's a professional, Zoe. Her team has been disbanded and she was looking for something better than local CID. Your team in Force CID is perfect for her."

Perfect for Layla, maybe. Not perfect for Zoe. Layla Kaur had interviewed Zoe when Ian was on trial. She'd suspected

Zoe of being involved with organised crime, like Ian had been. In reality, Zoe had been observing Ian, knowing exactly what he was up to and helping the Professional Standards Division, or PSD, identify corruption higher up in the ranks.

"I'm not happy about it," she said. "You know as well as I do it's not a good idea to put a former PSD officer into a team they've investigated in the past."

"I know protocol, Zoe, and to be honest this time it's not my priority. You've got a murder enquiry, your team will be champing at the bit to get it wrapped up for Christmas, and I've got to show top brass we're taking this seriously. And with your victim being homeless, there'll be political pressure to show we give him just as much attention as any other murder victim."

"We don't know yet that he's been murdered."

Frank cocked his head. "You've got a board set up in there. Your team are digging out CCTV footage and visiting shelters. You're working on the basis that this is suspicious."

She shrugged. "It is. But we can cope on our own."

A snort. "No, you bloody well can't. Just do as you're told, Zoe, and accept Layla into your team. I want to see her with the same level of responsibility that DS Uddin had."

"To be fair, Mo was an experienced DS and someone I'd—"

"Layla Kaur is an experienced DS. You might not like what she did, but—"

"I have nothing against PSD. You know I was helping them."

A smile flickered on his lips. "Maybe by the time you've wrapped up this case, DS Kaur will believe that too."

Zoe said nothing. She didn't really care what Layla Kaur

thought of her. Or she hadn't, until she'd found out she was going to have to work with the woman.

"Play nice, Zoe. I want to see her getting a warm welcome and the opportunity to make a full contribution."

Zoe ran a hand through her hair. "Of course, Frank. Just as you say."

CHAPTER NINE

Freya had to admit that Mr Khaled was doing a good job in the role of Father Christmas. She'd knocked on his door, five along from Mr North's, when she'd realised she was in urgent need of a stand-in, and he'd come to her rescue.

He'd even toned down his accent, not that he was fooling anyone. Still, this was Kings Heath, the last place anyone would comment on an ethnic Santa.

Santa. The very word made her shiver. Another one of those Americanisms that she'd observed creeping into British life over the last seventy-three years. Hallowe'en was her least favourite. Money for menaces, that was what it was.

She had an eye on the entrance, watching people entering the school. If Mr North appeared, she wanted a word. Letting her down like that, it was... well, it was downright rude. She didn't see why he should be allowed to get away with it. And of course, it wasn't Freya he'd let down. It was the children.

Thank goodness for Mr Khaled. He was doing a marvellous job, despite everything.

CHAPTER NINE

Two small brown-skinned children emerged from the grotto the PTA mums had built and grabbed parcels from a basket held by Gwyneth, one of the elf helpers the teachers had roped in. A woman came out behind them, straightening as she came out of the low doorway. It was the woman Freya had spoken to earlier, Mr North's neighbour.

The woman smiled as she recognised Freya.

"Mrs Garside, isn't it?"

"Miss." Freya gave her a thin smile. "*Miss* Garside." She hesitated. "But feel free to call me Freya, since we're neighbours."

The woman's smile widened. "Freya. I'm Ruti. Did you manage to track old Albert down?"

Freya sniffed. She hated that casual way the young had of reminding elderly people just how damn old they were.

"No. I had to rope Mr Khaled in for Saint Nick duty."

Ruti frowned. "Saint...?"

"Saint Nick. Saint Nicholas." No one knew the traditions any more.

"Ah." The woman looked back towards the grotto. A small girl and her dad were emerging, full of giggles. "Yes," she said, "my boys were very happy with him. It's nice for them to see an Asian Santa."

Freya felt her neck stiffen. An Asian Santa? Did the woman think she'd done it deliberately?

Ruti touched Freya's arm. "Thank you. They appreciate it. Makes them feel more... part of it."

"Oh. Good." Freya was thrown. Did Ruti's family even celebrate Christmas? Didn't they have their own festival? What was it, Eid?

Snap out of it, she thought.

"So you haven't seen Mr North, then?" she asked.

"Sorry. D'you want me to send him up to you if he reappears?"

Freya shook her head. It was too late now. "When did you last see him?"

"Like I said, Albert's not exactly regular with his habits. But I think it was over a week ago. He wasn't around last weekend, I remember there was a parcel delivered for him. My husband took it in."

"Did Mr North come to pick it up?"

A frown. "It's still next to my front door."

Freya felt her stomach dip. Was Mr North ill? Could he be lying in his house, while she was here, focused on the festivities…?

She put a hand on her chest, suddenly feeling like she might faint.

"Ruti," she said, swallowing hard to regain her composure. "Do you mind if I impose on you?"

One of the boys was tugging on Ruti's arm. She bent to whisper in his ear, then looked up at Freya. "Of course not. How can I help?"

"Has Mr North – Albert, as you call him – did he by any chance let you have a key to his house?"

CHAPTER TEN

"Everything alright, boss?" Connie asked as Zoe stepped back into the office.

Zoe forced a smile. "Fine, Connie. Good news."

"Oh?"

Connie was at the board, writing up names of shelters. Rhodri was at his desk. He looked up.

"Er, yes," Zoe continued, shifting from foot to foot. "The DCI's identified someone to fill DS Uddin's role."

Connie and Rhodri exchanged glances.

"Who?" Rhodri asked.

Zoe looked at him, trying hard to keep her face still. "DS Kaur."

Connie dropped the post-it note she was holding. "DS *Layla* Kaur?"

"That's the one."

"From PSD?" Once again, Connie exchanged looks with Rhodri. *Stop it*, Zoe thought.

"She's a competent sergeant," Zoe said. "With plenty of experience. She'll be an asset to the team."

Connie's brow was furrowed. "Are you sure you're OK with that, boss?"

Zoe drew herself up. "Having a DS on board will help us clear this case up quicker." She looked at Rhodri. "More chance of getting this done and dusted in time for Christmas leave."

Rhodri blushed. "Yes, boss."

Was it her, or had his Welsh accent dialled up a notch or eight?

Zoe sighed. "I know what you're both thinking. DS Kaur interviewed me when she was looking into links with Organised Crime. But you both also know that she found nothing, and that PSD later acknowledged our role in bringing those officers who *were* corrupt to justice."

Connie stared at Zoe. Rhodri's gaze dropped. Not *all* officers, they would be thinking. They'd taken Detective Superintendent Randle down. But the force had never acknowledged that he'd been working for Assistant Chief Constable Bryn Jackson. Who'd been not only retired by the time it all came out, but dead, too. No point in besmirching his memory, the high-ups had clearly decided.

Zoe knew how these things worked. So did Connie and Rhodri, although they were less adept at hiding their feelings.

"She starts tomorrow morning," Zoe told them. "And I want her to receive a warm welcome and be provided with all the resources she needs to do her job."

"Yes, boss," Connie replied.

"Rhod?" Zoe raised an eyebrow at DC Hughes.

"Course, boss. Whatever you say."

"Good. I'll oversee the strategic direction of this investigation. DS Kaur will be the link between us and external

CHAPTER TEN

teams. So if you need to speak to Forensics, Pathology or Uniform, you square it with her first."

"Even if we need to talk to Adi?" Rhodri asked.

"I just said Forensics, didn't I? DS Kaur will be the link to the FSI team."

"Right," Rhodri muttered.

"OK," Zoe said. She stepped towards the board and put a hand on a post-it that Connie had added. "Where are we?"

"I've got a lead," Connie said.

"What kind of lead?"

"A shelter, in Chelmsley Wood. They think they might know him."

"Excellent. Rhodri, you stay here. Carry on trawling through HOLMES. Call me if you hear from Adi or Adana."

"I don't need to speak to DS Kaur?"

Connie stifled a smirk.

"She hasn't started yet," Zoe said. "So, no."

"Ah. Right. Of course, boss. I'll let you know if I find anything."

"Good. Connie, they given us a name?"

"Bob."

"Bob?"

Connie shrugged. "Just Bob."

"Which may or may not be his real name."

"Exactly." Connie didn't look as if she held out much hope.

"OK, Connie. Let's head over to the shelter."

CHAPTER ELEVEN

"Hey, Rhod."

"Hey, Geet. How you doing?"

"Counting down till Christmas. How about you?"

Rhodri grimaced. If they didn't get this case solved soon, he was going to miss Christmas in the valleys. Including his mum's famous Christmas pudding.

He hadn't made it back last year, and there'd been hell to pay. He knew his mum would never forgive him if he missed it two years in a row.

"Same," he said. "I'm working on a possible murder inquiry."

"Possible?"

"Post mortem hasn't come in yet, but we're assuming it's suspicious."

"OK. So how can I help you?"

"You guessed."

"Rhod. It's a week before Christmas, you're on a murder case and you call me up out of the blue. You need my help."

"Yeah. You cover the city centre, don't you?"

CHAPTER ELEVEN

Geeta Harris was a uniformed PC, one of Rhodri's colleagues from before he'd joined CID. Some of them were sniffy with him now, but not Geet. "Yeah. City centre, Digbeth sometimes. Ladywood if I'm really lucky. That where your body was found?"

"You've not heard about it?"

"Only just come on shift, mate. What have I missed?"

"Street cleaners found a body round the back of one of the stalls in the German Market. Early this morning."

The sound of teeth being viciously sucked came down the line. "Poor bastard."

"I've got some photos of him. D'you mind taking a look, let me know if you've seen him around?"

"He a rough sleeper, then?"

"Judging by the state of his clothes, probably."

"OK. Ping them over."

Rhodri held up his phone and sent two of the photos across to Geeta. They were the clean ones, the ones the boss was happy for the team to share.

"You got them?"

"Just opening the first one. Oh." Her voice had dropped. "Yeah."

"You know him?"

"Wouldn't say I know him, but... yeah."

"Where have you seen him?"

"New Street. Hanging around the station, trying to get warm. A woman complained about him... three nights ago, I think it was. We had to ask him to move on. I think he headed over to Brindleyplace."

"You know where he went after that?"

"Sorry, mate. Haven't seen him since."

"You seen him before that?"

"I think I did. I can't be sure, but..."

"But what?"

"There was a bit of an altercation last Saturday. Down by Moor Street station, under the bridge. Two guys were making a hell of a racket. They scarpered soon as we got there like, but yeah, judging by these clothes I think one of them was him. He seemed familiar when we spoke to him at New Street."

"What kind of altercation?"

"Yelling. A guy who was passing said he'd seen another guy punching your bloke."

"Did you get a look at the other guy?" Rhodri frowned. There was no sign of bruising on the crime scene photos. But then, the amount of dirt on the fella, it might have been hidden.

"Not much of one. But he was white, medium build, rough sleeper too by the state of him."

"So there were witnesses, then?"

"Just the one. Hospital porter on his way home from a late shift. He said he heard shouting, went to see what was happening but didn't get any closer."

"Did he hear what they were shouting about?"

"No. It wasn't in English."

Rhodri scratched his chin. "Not in English? Geet, I don't suppose your witness knew what language it was, did he?"

"Sorry, no. Said it might be Russian."

Russian. Was their victim Russian?

That might change things. Or then again, it might not.

"Did the witness approach the two men?"

"They saw him, then ran. In opposite directions, apparently. Hang on a minute." Rhodri heard the clattering of keys. "Yeah, your man headed towards New Street, the other guy into Digbeth. We didn't manage to find either of them."

Of course not.

Rhodri took a breath. "No other witnesses? You're sure?"

"Sorry. I took the number of the guy we spoke to, though. I'll send it across."

"Thanks, Geet. You've been a massive help."

CHAPTER TWELVE

The shelter was in a modern building with high windows and graffiti-strewn walls. Zoe grimaced as she and Connie approached it.

"Not the most welcoming of places."

Connie gave her a shrug. "They rarely are, boss."

"I suppose you've got more recent experience than me," Zoe replied. Connie had been in CID for two years. Before that, she'd have been in regular contact with the homeless.

Another shrug.

"You ever come here, when you were in Uniform?"

"Not that I can remember. It's in Solihull. My patch was the west of the city."

Zoe nodded. Chelmsley Wood was an area Force CID had found themselves visiting regularly. A year earlier, they'd uncovered an organised crime gang just a five-minute walk from here. By the look of the buildings and the amount of litter adorning the pavements, you'd never know it was part of the leafy town of Solihull.

CHAPTER TWELVE

"OK," she said. "I'd like you to ask the questions. I'll observe."

"Any reason, boss?"

Zoe shook her head. "It's experience for you. And you're good at this kind of thing."

"OK. Thanks." Connie didn't sound grateful.

Zoe hung back and waited for Connie to press the buzzer next to the door. The two of them waited, Zoe looking up at the camera above the door. Maybe they'd be lucky and there'd be CCTV of their victim.

She glanced at her watch. One in the afternoon. She needed to call Adana, find out when the preliminarily postmortem report would be ready.

An indistinct voice came through an intercom and the door buzzed. Zoe nodded in the direction of the camera and followed Connie inside.

The shelter's reception area was an open space with no features apart from another camera and a glass-paned door ahead of them. After a few moments, a woman came through it.

"DI Finch, DC Williams. Sorry to keep you waiting."

The woman was young, maybe thirty, with a large frame and an efficient manner.

"I spoke to you earlier, I believe," Connie said. "Ms Dean?"

"Jane Dean, that's me. Come on up, I'll put the kettle on."

Connie gave Zoe a nervous look then turned back to Ms Dean. "It's OK. We haven't got long."

Zoe put a hand on the DC's arm. She hadn't eaten or drunk since leaving the house at 8.30am. *Take it where you can find it,* she thought. "It's fine. A cuppa would be most welcome."

Ms Dean smiled at her. "Good. Follow me, then."

They followed her through the doors and up a flight of stairs. Ahead of them was an open set of double doors. Zoe could make out a serving hatch and tables. There was the sound of voices and the smell of institutional cooking.

At the top of the stairs was a tiny hallway with three locked doors. Ms Dean brought out a key on a chain and unlocked one. She stood back, ushering the detectives inside.

"Take a seat. I'll just get those drinks. What would you like?"

"Tea please, two sugars," Connie said.

"Coffee, black. No sugar," Zoe added.

"It'll have to be instant."

Zoe resisted the urge to cancel her order. "That's fine." She needed caffeine, whatever the source.

The door banged shut and Zoe looked at Connie, who was surveying the room. Zoe wanted to get this done quickly, but at the same time she didn't want Jane Dean to feel rushed. A witness in a hurry was a witness who didn't remember key information.

"You think we've found him, boss?" Connie asked.

Zoe shrugged. She drew her coat tighter around her shoulders; it was cold in here. "Let's hope so. But if they don't have a surname..."

"Bob isn't exactly an unusual name."

"Nope."

The door opened and Jane Dean entered, carrying two mugs. She placed them in front of the detectives and leaned against the wall. A shelf of books shifted next to her, and Zoe found herself worrying that the whole thing was about to come crashing down.

"So," Dean said. "You're wanting to know about Bob."

"I'm really hoping you've got more information than just the name Bob," Zoe replied. She sipped her coffee. Bitter, but warm. And it would keep her awake.

"You got that photo?"

Connie frowned at her phone for a few moments before holding it out. She'd picked one of the crime scene photos, a close up which made the victim look like he was in a very deep sleep. Not dead.

Dean grimaced. "Poor chap. Yeah, that's Bob alright. He came here five times in the last fortnight."

"Is it common for rough sleepers to move back and forth between Solihull and the city centre?" Zoe asked.

"You'd be surprised. Moving keeps them busy. Keeps them active and warm, too. Most of our clients move around in search of somewhere better."

"Better?" Connie asked.

"A better spot for begging. A better pitch to sleep in."

"Did Bob sleep here?"

A shake of the head. "We don't offer overnight accommodation. We just provide food and somewhere warm to come during the day. Some of our clients travel in and out of the city centre, there are more overnight shelters there."

"How?" Connie asked.

"Sorry?"

"How do they travel? It's nearly ten miles."

"They beg for bus fare. A few walk, not many though."

"So when did you last see Bob?" Zoe asked.

"Three days ago. Thursday."

"During the day?"

A nod.

"Do you have his full name?"

"Sorry. We don't pry. We just ask clients for a name we can address them by. Some of these men are scared of the authorities. They believe that if they give us their full name, we might hand them into the police, or the tax man."

"You never overheard him using his full name? Or anyone else using it?"

"Sorry. He was just Bob. Might not even be his real name. Plenty of rough sleepers adopt a street name."

Zoe sighed. All they had was that their victim had been here on Thursday, and that he went by the name of Bob.

"Did he have anyone else he would hang out with?" Connie asked. "A mate?"

"He kept himself to himself. Preferred to eat on his own when he was eating." Dean raised an eyebrow. "He didn't always have a choice in the matter, though. We get busy, and some of our guys are... outgoing, shall we say. But no. There was no one else who I think would be able to tell you anything about him."

Zoe pursed her lips. She thought of 'Bob' lying behind that stall in Victoria Square.

"What was the state of his health?"

Dean shrugged. "OK, as rough sleepers go. He had a cough, some bruising on his arm. Nothing unusual."

"Nothing that might have been chronic? Nothing that might have killed him?"

"I'm not a medical professional."

"If your clients do have serious health issues, what d'you do?" Connie asked.

"We have a friendly GP who comes over about once a

month. It used to be more often but he can't spare the time now, his regular practice is short-staffed."

"Has he visited recently?"

"Not in the last two weeks. He wouldn't have seen Bob."

"No?"

"Bob only started coming here two weeks ago."

Zoe straightened. "You hadn't seen him before that?"

"Never. I assumed he was new to the streets. His clothes were in pretty decent condition two weeks ago."

Zoe exchanged glances with Connie. She turned back to Dean. "By decent condition, what do you mean?"

"Clean. Intact. A little shabby, but from regular wear. He looked like he'd had access to a washing machine and a regular change of clothes. That went downhill fast."

"I don't suppose you talked to him about how he became homeless?"

"Like I said, we don't pry."

Of course. Zoe sighed. "Thanks for your time, Ms Dean. You've been very helpful."

CHAPTER THIRTEEN

RHODRI HAD TRAWLED the mispers database three times. He'd hunted through HOLMES. He'd searched Google, and he'd rung the number that Geeta had given him. No answer, of course.

Should he call Geeta again, find out if there was another way of getting hold of that witness? Her team would have an address, surely.

He was stumped. And he needed to make progress. Not only because he wanted this case solved, but because he wanted to show the boss he wasn't as useless as she seemed to think he was.

He shouldn't have reminded her of his trip to the valleys. Yes, it was important. His mum was going to bloody kill him if he didn't make it. But that wasn't the boss's problem. He'd made himself look unprofessional.

He'd never make sergeant if he carried on like this. He knew the boss had talked to Connie about the sergeant's exam, and he'd failed it once himself. He'd been in CID longer than she had, but it looked like she was going to

CHAPTER THIRTEEN

leapfrog him. He couldn't be angry at her, though. Connie was a mate. She'd got him out of plenty of scrapes, and never looked at him the way the boss sometimes did.

He missed the sarge. DS Uddin would give him a steer, come up with a way past this blockage. DS Uddin was such a good sarge that he wouldn't just find a way through, he'd guide Rhodri towards finding it himself.

It sometimes felt like when the sarge had gone, he'd taken ten of Rhodri's IQ points with him.

Still. IQ wasn't everything in this job. He was bloody good with witnesses. He had a knack for putting people at their ease and getting them to open up. The sarge had mentioned it at his last review meeting.

That was what he needed to be doing now. Talking to that witness of Geeta's, finding out what there was to know about the last few days of their victim's life.

He grabbed his phone just as the office phone rang. He frowned and dropped his own phone back onto the desk.

"Force CID, how can I help you?"

"Is that Rhodri?"

"Who's calling, please?"

"It's alright, Rhod, you don't have to be so formal."

"Oh. OK." He cleared his throat. *Who was this?* "Can I help you?"

"Is Zoe there?"

"She's gone out to interview a wit— who is this, please?"

"Sorry, Rhodri. It's Adi."

"Oh." Adi Hanson. Crime Scene Manager. Why wasn't he calling the boss on her mobile? "She not picking up her mobile?"

"It's going to voicemail. Thought I'd try this number, just in case."

"Anything I can help with?" Rhodri straightened in his chair.

Silence.

"Adi?" Rhodri said. "If you can't get hold of the boss, maybe I can help."

"OK. Yeah, go on then."

Rhodri nodded, waiting.

"Rhodri?"

Rhodri frowned. "Still here."

"We've found something that might help you identify your victim."

"What kind of thing?" A wallet, Rhodri hoped. With a driving licence and credit cards. The sooner they knew who this guy was, the sooner they'd be able to figure out who'd killed him.

"A letter. It was stuffed right down inside the lining of his coat. Almost like he'd wanted it hidden."

"Who's it from?"

"Not sure. It's handwritten, but not in English. Looks like the same language as the writing on his hands."

Rhodri felt his heart rate pick up. "Which language?"

"Nothing I recognise. I'm sending it back to the lab. They'll work it out."

"Fine." Rhodri gripped the phone. "Can you send it over here, though? A photo?"

"Course. It'll be in your team inbox any second."

"Cheers." Rhodri pressed a key on his keyboard to wake it up and clicked through to email. Sure enough, there was a message from Adi with an image attached.

He opened it and looked at the image. He turned his head to one side and the other. He squinted.

None of it helped.

"What language is that?"

"No idea, mate," said Rhodri. "Looks Eastern European to me, though. Not Russian."

"No?"

"That's a different script."

"Ah." Rhodri knew nothing about Russian. "Are all the Eastern European languages in different scripts, then?"

"Not all of them, I don't think. Like I say, the lab will get to grips with it."

Rhodri thought back to his conversation with Geeta. The other man in the altercation. Geeta had said the argument had been in Russian.

But it might not have been Russian. The witness might not know the difference between one Eastern European language and another. Rhodri wouldn't have done, so why should some random hospital porter?

"Thanks Adi. Can you let us know when you've got a translation?"

"Of course I will, mate. You'll tell Zoe about this, yes?"

"I will."

Rhodri hung up and stared at the image, licking his lips.

This was an opportunity.

He picked up the phone and dialled. But not the boss.

CHAPTER FOURTEEN

It was eight pm now and the roads were quiet. Sunday nights in Birmingham weren't quite what Zoe remembered from her childhood in the nineties, but they were still nothing like Saturdays. Everyone hunkered down, preparing themselves for the week ahead. Trying to get a decent night's sleep.

She felt her chest tighten as she thought of the week she had in front of her. A week till Christmas. Six days now, really. Her son Nicholas was due home from Stirling University the next day and she was looking forward to being able to spend some time with him. She'd not managed to book time off – the needs of her team had put paid to that – but she was hoping to be able to get off work early and take him for a drink.

Nicholas would understand. He'd grown up with this life. A single mum at the age of twenty-three, she'd had no help from his dad, who'd denied even being Nicholas' father until the poor boy was eight. Her own dad had died when she was pregnant and her mum had been no use.

CHAPTER FOURTEEN

Her mum. Zoe swallowed the lump in her throat. Annette Finch, alcoholic and general nuisance in life, was now in Lodge Hill cemetery.

Zoe shook her head. She didn't have time to think about her mum.

"So," she said to Connie as they approached Robin Hood Island. "Did you believe her?"

"Believe her, boss?"

"All that business about client privacy and not wanting to pry. D'you think she really has no idea who any of her clients are or how they came to be homeless?"

"Well..."

Zoe scratched the back of her head. "Sorry, Con. I'm being cynical."

"Connie," Connie replied in a low voice.

Zoe turned to her then back to the road. "Sorry?"

"I... I don't like being called Con."

"But Rhodri does it."

Connie raised her eyebrows. Zoe laughed.

"What does Rav call you?" Rav was Connie's boyfriend, one of the Forensics team.

She shifted in her seat. "Er... not Con."

Zoe laughed again. "I'm sorry, Connie. I won't do it again. Poor Rhod, he likes to put his foot in it, doesn't he?"

Rhodri had frequently put his foot in it with Zoe, back when she'd been a DS and he'd felt more comfortable around her. Now she was a DI, and his boss, he trod more carefully. And he knew that if he was going to make DS himself, he needed to act professionally.

"So are you putting yourself forward for next year's sergeant's exam?" she asked.

Connie flinched. "I'm thinking of it."

"You know I'll support you."

"That didn't make much difference last time." Connie's hand went to her mouth. "Sorry boss, that sounded ungrateful."

Zoe reached out and squeezed Connie's wrist. They were in Zoe's green Mini, Zoe at the wheel. "Lighten up, Connie. I know it's the exam itself that counts. Your record is unimpeachable. The way you've conducted yourself in the last year, showing you can take on extra responsibility and that you have the initiative to lead a team."

Zoe flicked a glance sideways to see that Connie was blushing. She smiled.

"Don't be embarrassed. It's true."

Connie nodded her head, her eyes on the road. "I was going to ask you something, boss. But it's a bit late now."

"A bit late for what?"

"It's OK."

"No." Zoe passed Sarehole Mill on their right and headed towards Harborne. "Tell me."

"Well, with a murder investigation on and the team short on bodies..."

"Yes..."

"I was hoping to have the opportunity to act up. But you'll have DS Kaur in place now, so there's no point."

Zoe frowned. She blipped her brakes as a lorry in front of her shifted from side to side on the road. *Slow down.*

"I'm sorry, Connie. It didn't occur to me. And if you were acting up, we'd be short a DC."

"I know. But if I pass the exam, that would be an issue too."

"That's your plan? If you pass, you want Mo's old job?"

Connie licked her lips. "I do."

Zoe shot her a smile. "That's very loyal, you know. But if you want your career to progress, your best bet is to find a posting in another team."

"I enjoy Force CID."

"I know you do. And you're bloody good at it. But moving from DC to DS in the same little team doesn't give you the breadth of experience you need if you're ever going to make DI."

Connie pulled in a breath. "I think it's a bit soon for—"

"If you want to progress, you need to be planning. Considering your next move with half an eye on the one after it."

"Is that what you did?"

Zoe barked out a laugh. "Afraid not. I just found any posting that would take me after I told them I was a single mum. And not with..." she stopped herself finishing the sentence. She didn't want Connie to know she'd spent her whole career avoiding DCI Jim McManus, Nicholas's dad.

They crossed the Bristol Road. The office was just over a mile away now. "Think about it, Connie. Look around at other teams, talk to some colleagues. See what's out there."

"I don't want to leave you even more short-staffed than you already—"

"You need to be selfish for once. Don't worry about me. I'll be fine." She didn't tell Connie that Carl had been suggesting the two of them might transfer to another force. He was in line for a promotion, but it meant a move north.

"OK. And yes," Connie said.

"Yes what?" They stopped at the entrance to the Force CID offices and Zoe waited for the barrier to lift.

"Yes, I think she was telling the truth. Jane Dean. I went on a forensic psychology course last month. They taught us things to look out for in witnesses' behaviour. It's not what everyone assumes."

"Quite the opposite, sometimes."

"Yeah. And I think she was being honest. She had no more idea than we do who our victim really is."

Zoe sighed as she squeezed into a parking space. "Then we're back at square one."

CHAPTER FIFTEEN

"Rhod."

"Hey, Brid. How's things?"

"Fine. And it's Bridget. What d'you want?"

"Who says I want something?"

There was a sigh down the line. "The only time you ever call me is when you're working on a case and you think it's got a connection to my team. Not everything is organised crime, you know."

"I do know that."

"Why isn't DI Finch talking to my boss?"

Rhodri knew that the boss had a close relationship with DS Sheila Griffin, who led one of the organised crime teams. He also knew that if he had a concrete reason to suspect a link to organised crime, he should be telling the boss and letting her deal with Griffin.

But he didn't have a concrete reason. Just an accent and a letter he couldn't read. And he wanted to prove himself.

"This is just a hunch. I didn't want to trouble the boss with it."

Another sigh. He could sense the eye-rolling even if he couldn't see it. "So you're troubling me instead."

"I've leave you alone, Bridget, if it's too—"

"No. Hit me with it, Rhodri. You never know, we might be about to break a major case."

"We might."

"I was joking."

"Oh."

"Just tell me what you're calling about, yeah, and I can get on with my day."

Rhodri was beginning to regret this. He and Brid had got on well when they'd both been in Uniform. He'd have even described her as a mate.

But now he thought about it, he'd been the one acting matey, not her. Even back then.

He licked his lips.

"OK. So a body has turned up in Chamberlain Square. Homeless guy."

"Tell me something I don't know. Everyone's talking about your German Market murder."

OK. He didn't know that. "Anyway, Forensics have found a note inside the lining of his coat. Looks like he hid it, like."

"Hmm."

Rhodri took a breath. "The note's in Russian. Or something like it."

"And?"

"And that's it. Well, maybe not Russian. I'm not sure about the alphabet. It might be another Easte—"

"Let me stop you there, Rhodri. First off, it's not an alphabet. It's a script. And secondly, are you seriously telling me you've found a note in an Eastern European language and automatically assumed an organised crime connection? You got any other evidence to back up a conclusion like that?"

"Err..."

"Thought not. It ever occurred to you that you might be just a little bit racist, Rhodri?"

Rhodri felt his chest fill with air. "Come on, Brid, that's a bit—"

"It's OK, Rhodri. I know you're not a racist, not really. But what you just assumed is."

"But most of the—"

"*Some* organised crime involves Eastern European gangs. Not all. And there are plenty of Eastern Europeans who are no more involved in organised crime that you and me. Less so, in fact."

"I know that." Rhodri was aware that his voice had gone small. He knew he shouldn't let Bridget intimidate him. He was working a case, using his initiative. Nothing wrong with that.

But yeah. Maybe his assumption had been a little bit racist.

He could feel heat spreading up his neck. He was glad Connie wasn't here to see this.

"Yeah, you're right," he said. "I'm sorry I called you. You have a good Christmas, yeah?"

"Just send it over."

"What?"

"You've gone to the trouble of calling me. Might as well finish the job, ruin my day good and proper."

"Oh. OK. I'll email it to you."

"You do that."

"And you'll tell me if it looks familiar? Is there anyone in your team who might able to translate it?"

"I can't answer that, can I? Not without knowing what language it's in. But you never know, you might get lucky."

"Thanks."

"Despite being a moron."

Rhodri clenched a fist. He wanted to protest, but knew there was little point.

"Thanks, Bridget. I owe you."

"You do. Rhod. You do."

CHAPTER SIXTEEN

FREYA TOOK a sniff as they entered the house. Not a deep sniff – she was far too cautious for that – but a thin, shallow one.

Just in case.

She needed to know whether Mr North was in here somewhere. Slumped dead in a chair perhaps, or in his bed...

It didn't bear thinking about.

But no. The house smelled of boiled vegetables and aftershave. And whilst her experience of dead bodies was limited, she didn't imagine they would smell of cabbage.

Ruti was ahead of her, making her way through the narrow hallway towards the kitchen at the back. The hall had muted yellow paint on textured wallpaper, with photos peppering the walls. Family photos, going back many decades by the looks of them.

"Hello?" Ruti called. She looked back at Freya, her face full of concern. She'd insisted on coming in with Freya, given it was she to whom Mr North had given the key, but was clearly uncomfortable here.

"He's not here," Freya said, trying to reassure the woman. "We'd smell him."

Ruti shook her head. "Not if he's fresh."

Fresh.

Freya shuddered.

"If he *were* in here, he'd have been here for a while," she said. They'd had to push aside a pile of post when they'd opened the door. "Not fresh."

The house was cold, traces of damp on the wall near the kitchen door. It felt like the heating hadn't been on for a good few days. Not that that told her anything; Mr North was a pensioner like her, and would be equally frugal.

Ruti was in the kitchen now. Freya followed her, bracing herself for abandoned food or sour milk. The room was the mirror image of Freya's own kitchen, narrow, with a door to the side and windows looking out over the garden. Unlike many of the residents of Avenue Road, she'd never seen the point in knocking down walls or building extensions. And it seemed Mr North hadn't either.

The kitchen was tidy. The small table under the window held a neat pile of envelopes and an alarm clock. The worktops held nothing more than kettle, toaster and bread bin.

Ruti opened cupboards. Tins were stacked in neat rows. In the fridge was a carton of milk that had Freya gagging when the smell was released. Ruti grunted and closed the door quickly.

Freya pushed out a breath. "We need to search the rest of the house."

"He's not here. You said so yourself."

"He might be ill. We should check."

Ruti shrugged her shoulders and gestured towards the kitchen door. "I'll take downstairs, you go up."

Since when was the younger woman in charge here? It was Freya who'd asked for the keys, Freya who had reason to be looking for Mr North. If it had been left to Ruti, his absence would never have been noticed. What kind of neighbour lived on the other side of a person's bedroom wall and didn't realise they'd been missing for up to two weeks?

"I'll look at the post," Freya said, heading back to the door. That might tell them how long a period they were looking at.

She bent to the pile of post. Circulars, a copy of the local free sheet dating back ten days. She sifted through the envelopes. The postmarks went back to the first of December.

"Judging by the post, I'd say he's been missing two weeks."

Ruti was upstairs, having ignored her own instructions. "Or he's still here, but not picking up his post," she replied, her voice indistinct.

Freya shook her head. If Mr North was here, he was alive, at least. And if that were the case, he would have answered them.

Unless he was unconscious...

She approached the stairs. "Any sign of him?"

Ruti emerged from a bedroom and stood at the top. "Nothing. The beds have been made, and it looks like there are things missing from the bathroom. No toothbrush, that sort of thing."

"So he didn't leave in a hurry."

"It looks like he meant to leave."

So why didn't he warn me he would fail to fulfil his Father Christmas duties? Freya resisted voicing her irritation, aware that Ruti would find her uncharitable.

Ruti came down the stairs, her footsteps echoing in the empty house. Her fingertips left a trail on the dusty bannister.

"What do we do?" she asked.

Freya sniffed. She was a busy woman. She didn't need this.

But still. Mr North was a neighbour. And he could be in trouble, or lying in a ditch somewhere.

"We call the police," she said.

CHAPTER SEVENTEEN

"OK, SO WHAT HAVE WE GOT?" Zoe threw herself into her chair. It was gone six and she'd been working for almost twelve hours. Everyone was keen to get this one solved in time for Christmas, but with the victim's identity still a mystery, that was looking less likely with each passing minute.

"I spoke to some mates," said Rhodri. "And Adi."

Zoe sat up. "Adi? Why didn't he call me?" She saw the look on Rhodri's face. "Sorry."

A shrug. "'s OK, boss. He tried to get your mobile but there was no answer, so he called the team number."

Zoe nodded, impatient to know why Rhodri hadn't told her Adi was looking for her. "What did he have? Any evidence that might help us work out how our victim died?"

"Nothing like that. But he found a note, stuffed into the lining of the victim's coat."

"Tell me it had his name and address on."

Connie sniggered. Rhodri glanced at her and smiled. "Sorry, no. But it might help us."

"How?"

"It's in Russian. Well, not Russian probably."

"In Russian but not in Russian?" Connie asked.

Rhodri frowned at her. "An Eastern European language, Adi reckons. He's sent it to the lab. And I've given it to my pal in organised crime. I thought there might be a link."

"Just cos he's Eastern European, doesn't mean he's a gang boss," Connie muttered.

"Hang on, Connie," Zoe said. "You're right, but it doesn't do any harm to check it out. Being a murder victim does make you about a thousand more times likely than the average member of the public to be mixed up in organised crime. Did your mate have anything useful, Rhod?"

"Sorry. But she's taking a look at the note. Or one of her colleagues is. Depends on the language."

"Let me see this note."

"Adi emailed it through." Rhodri went to his desk and bent over his computer. Zoe followed him.

"Means nothing to me," she said. "Get this printed off and up on the board, will you?"

"Sure." Rhodri sat at his desk and clicked a few computer keys. He stood up and headed for the door.

"You OK?" Zoe asked him.

"Just getting the printout."

She pointed at the printer in the corner of the office. "What's wrong with that?"

Rhodri raised an eyebrow. "On the blink. Again."

Zoe sighed. "Typical. Go on, then. I don't want anyone else picking up what could be sensitive material."

"Boss." Rhodri all but ran out of the room.

As the door shut behind him, Zoe noticed Connie smirking.

"Don't mock him, Connie. He's keen. And he wants to get to his mum's for Christmas."

Connie straightened her face. "Yes. Sorry."

"What are your Christmas plans, anyway?"

"Zaf's already home from Uni." Connie blushed, no doubt remembering that Zaf had dumped Nicholas in November. "Mum's all over him like a rash."

"Pleased to have her boy back?"

"You bet. I'm happy to work late hours on this case, if you want me to."

"Don't avoid your family. You'll regret it in the long run."

A cloud passed over Connie's face. "Whatever."

Zoe laughed. "Annabelle's a good mum. She'll spoil you too, I bet."

"It's a bit much, sometimes. I envy Zaf." Connie scratched her head. "You don't want to hear about my family. Especially with Zaf and Nick..."

"Water under the bridge, Connie. I think Nicholas has found someone else."

"Good. I mean it. That's good."

"It is."

The door burst open and Rhodri hurried in, his breathing shallow and a sheet of paper in his hand. "Got it."

"Well done, Rhod. By the state of you I don't imagine anyone else had the chance to clap eyes on it, let alone pinch it."

"It was coming off the machine just as I got there."

"Hand it over."

Rhodri shoved the paper in her direction and sank into his chair. Zoe surveyed the letter. It wasn't in Russian. The script was the same as English but the words were unfamiliar. Zoe passed it to Connie.

"I don't suppose this means anything to you?"

Connie turned the sheet around in her hands. "Sorry."

"No." Zoe held in a breath. "OK. So we have this note and we have the fact that our guy liked to frequent a shelter in Solihull where he used the name of Bob."

"And that he'd only been going for two weeks," added Connie.

"Jane Dean said he looked clean when she first saw him. Like he'd only just found himself on the streets. Do we think maybe two weeks ago he had a home?"

"That fits with what Geeta told me," Rhodri said.

"Geeta?"

"PC Harris. Works the city centre. She says there was a fight a few nights ago. Might have been our guy. And some other bloke who was Eastern European."

"You didn't think to mention this earlier, Rhod?"

"Sorry."

Zoe slapped her palm onto the desk in front of her. "It's coming together. Not as fast as I'd like, but we know more about him now than we did yesterday. I don't suppose PC Harris had any witnesses? Or the details of the other guy in the fight?"

"There was a hospital porter who saw some of it. The other fella ran away."

"Of course he did."

There was a knock on the door. Zoe turned to it. "Come in!"

Sergeant Jenner, on reception duty today, entered, holding a sheet of paper. "Sorry to interrupt."

"It's OK. What's up?"

Jenner looked from Zoe to Connie and back again. "A woman phoned in. A Freya Garside."

CHAPTER SEVENTEEN

"And?" Zoe said.

"She reported her neighbour missing. And she sent us a photo."

"Is that the photo?"

A nod. Jenner handed it to Zoe.

The man in the image looked better fed and healthier than their guy, but he had the same long nose and pointed chin. The same bright blue eyes and long eyelashes.

It was their victim.

CHAPTER EIGHTEEN

"Well I must say, they were most ungrateful." Freya sipped at the tea Ruti had made for her. It was too strong and the milk tasted as if it were about to turn, but it would have to do.

"What did they say?"

They were in Ruti's front room. The TV was on in the corner and two boys knelt in front of it, eyes not leaving it for a second. Probably for the best. This topic of conversation wasn't for young ears.

Freya gritted her teeth and drew in a breath as she set the cup down on a side table. "Well, they said thank you, of course. That's the least you'd expect. But when I offered to go into the house and see if I could find anything that might be of use to them, they told me not to set foot in it again."

"Set foot where?" A man opened the door to the room carrying a plate of biscuits. He smiled at Freya and held it out.

Rich Teas. That would do. Freya took one and thanked him.

"Next door, love. Albert's place," Ruti told him as he settled into the armchair to Freya's left. One of the small boys turned to grab a biscuit, then went back to his TV-watching.

"What's happened? He was supposed to do Father Christmas, wasn't he?"

"He's missing," Freya told him. She swallowed and licked her lips, hoping she wasn't getting crumbs on Ruti's sofa. The room wasn't decorated to Freya's taste but it was immaculate. And contrary to her expectations, the house didn't smell of curry.

"Missing? Definitely?"

Freya sniffed. "He hasn't been in his house for two weeks, judging by the pile of post. And your wife spoke to the neighbour on the other side."

"Olive."

"Yes, Olive." Freya had no idea what the woman's name was, only that she'd arrived home as they were leaving Mr North's house.

"Olive saw him in the garden two weeks ago," Ruti said, looking at her husband. "She chatted to him over the fence."

"Was he ill, maybe?"

"He seemed fine, apparently. Talking about how he'd harvested the last of his parsnips and was planning to get the garden ready for winter."

"And did he?"

Ruti looked at Freya. "I don't know."

"We didn't check the garden," Freya said, tutting. They should have looked out there, in case he'd gone out that way. Maybe someone had dragged him.

"Too late now," said Ruti's husband. He'd introduced himself when they'd entered the house but Freya hadn't caught his name and it felt rude to ask now. She was hoping Ruti might address him by name.

Freya stood up. "Not necessarily."

Ruti looked up at her. One of the boys, the one without a biscuit, turned and looked at her as if he'd had no idea she was in the room.

"How so?" asked Ruti.

"All of the gardens along here can be accessed via the alleyway at the back."

"But the police said not to go anywhere near th—"

"They said not to go back into the house."

"I think the garden counts as the house," Ruti's husband said. He stood up. He was a few inches taller than Freya but she wasn't going to let him intimidate her.

"It's publicly accessible. I'm going to have a look."

Ruti and her husband exchanged glances. Freya knew that look; they were silently wondering why they'd allowed a mad old woman into their home.

Let the young people mock. Freya had an old man to worry about. She'd known Mr North better than any of those police officers or crime scene people would have done. Unlike them, she cared.

"Don't worry," she said. "I'll be careful. If the police arrive, I'll leave."

"I don't think that's the kind of careful they mean," Ruti told her. "What about if you leave things behind? Footprints, fibres from your coat, that kind of thing. It could contaminate the scene. Place you under suspicion."

"My wife has been watching too many American crime series," Mr Ruti said.

Freya smiled. "And good for her. I'll let you know how I get on."

CHAPTER NINETEEN

"Did she say how long he's been missing?" Zoe asked PS Jenner.

"She wasn't sure, but she reckons about two weeks."

"Did she give us a name? For the neighbour, not her own."

"Albert North, Ma'am."

"I don't suppose she happened to say that he was Eastern European?"

"Sorry, Ma'am. She didn't."

"Ah well. Can't have everything. Thanks."

Jenner left the office and Zoe walked to the board. She pinned up the photo and grabbed a pen, writing the name 'Albert North' above it.

She ground her finger into it and turned to face the two DCs.

"We have an identify, folks. Now all we need to do is work out who wanted him dead."

"I'll look him up on HOLMES," Connie said. She hurried to her desk and sat down.

"Thanks. Rhod—"

"I'll Google him."

"Fair enough. See if you can find anything that might be linked to this altercation your mate was talking about."

"Will do." Rhodri sat at his desk and started typing.

Zoe returned to the board and stared at the name she'd just written there.

Albert North. It wasn't Russian, or Eastern European. And nor was it Bob.

So what was with the letter? Maybe it wasn't in an Eastern European language at all, but something...

Something what?

Albert North, that was as British as names got, wasn't it? It certainly wasn't from Eastern Europe. But maybe he'd migrated to Britain some years ago and changed his name. It wasn't uncommon, back in the days when immigrants faced even more discrimination than they did now.

There was only one thing for it.

"Rhod, I want you to come with me."

Rhodri looked up from his screen. "Boss?"

"Connie, you can handle Google as well as HOLMES, can't you?"

"Of course."

"Good. You keep trawling. Call me if you get anything helpful."

"Will do. Where are you off to?"

"Albert North's house. We're going to have a chat with his neighbour."

CHAPTER TWENTY

Mr North's garden had been well tended. There were a few weeds sprouting between the cracks of the crazy-paved patio, but that was to be expected after the place had been left empty for two weeks.

Other than that, the space was immaculate. A bed on each side of the garden held a few shrubs and between those, bare, well tilled soil. It looked like Mr North had been in the habit of planting annuals, and cleared his plot every year in between seasons.

Freya had been hoping for more signs of decay. A broken down shed, a pile of logs. Somewhere a body might have been hidden. Or at least a clue.

But there was nothing.

She worked her way around the perimeter of the garden, easing shrubs aside so she could take a proper look at the fences and the earth in front of them. There was no rubbish, no discarded garden tools, not even a stray plant label left behind. At the end of the garden was what looked like a vegetable plot. It was bare, just a few canes remaining from the year's harvest.

Why didn't the young look after their gardens like this? The young couple on the left of her house had allowed their plot to descend into weed-strewn chaos. When she'd gently challenged them about it, the young woman (whose name was Flower, not that Freya ever stooped to using it) had replied that it was deliberate, to benefit wildlife.

It had taken all of Freya's resolve not to scoff in the woman's face.

Wildlife. There was plenty of wildlife in Kings Heath Park. Well, maybe not as much as there had been once, but still. That was the point of living right opposite the park, wasn't it? Enjoy the wildlife over there so you didn't need to have it in your own garden.

Freya reached the end of the garden and turned the corner to walk along the back fence. The fence was slightly less sturdy here, probably managed by the people behind in Highbury Road. But there was nothing that might help her determine what had happened to Mr North.

"Everything alright over there?" came a voice.

Freya turned to see a woman peering over the fence she hadn't yet investigated. A white woman in her thirties, with messy hair and a t shirt celebrating some band Freya had never heard of. Olive, she presumed.

"Yes, thank you." Freya continued her progress along the back fence.

"Albert's missing, I hear. Are you police?"

Freya straightened up. "No. I am a concerned neighbour. That is all."

"I haven't seen you before. How do I know you're not trespassing?"

"Because Ruti – Mrs Sandhar – let me use her key."

"Oh. Where is Ruti?"

Freya chewed her bottom lip. *So nosey*.

"She's at home, with her children."

"Ah. Good kids. So how do I know she let you in?"

Freya approached the fence. The woman backed away a few steps.

"Look," Freya said. "I'm the one who reported Mr North missing to the police, and I'm worried about him. I'm hoping that by searching his garden, I might be able to—"

"Shouldn't you leave the police to do that?"

"They aren't here. I thought I might get a head start."

A laugh. "They won't thank you for that."

Freya said nothing. Instead, she returned to the back fence and tried to work out how far along she'd progressed before she'd been interrupted.

"Anyway, good luck," the woman said. "I hope the police don't do you for interfering in an investigation."

Freya stropped in her tracks. They wouldn't, would they?

She stepped back onto the grass. Maybe she should stop.

"Er, excuse me?"

Freya turned. *Shut up and leave me alone*. "I already told you. I—"

A woman stood at the other end of the garden, on the patio that Freya had already examined. She was tall with long red-brown hair, and she wore a duffel coat.

Freya hadn't seen a woman in a duffel coat for many years.

"Who are you?" Freya asked.

"I could ask the same of you."

Freya pulled herself up to her full height. She was glad she was some distance away from the woman, as she was probably four inches too short to be anything close to as formidable as she'd like to be.

"My name is Freya Garside. I live five doors down. Mr North, my friend who lives here, is missing, and I'm checking the garden in case there's any—"

"I think we can take it from here, Ms Garside."

"It's *Miss* Garside."

The woman pulled a police badge from her pocket.

Freya felt her mouth fall open and quickly shut it. "Oh. Sergeant...?"

"Detective Inspector Finch. Force CID. I'm Senior Investigating Officer on this case and you're disturbing a potential crime scene."

"Oh." Maybe the woman next door had been right. "I'm so sorry."

"I suggest you walk back towards where I'm standing, slowly and carefully, and then leave via the side alleyway."

"Yes." Freya started walking.

"And give me your address. We'll need to interview you."

"Yes. Of course." Freya was level with the woman now. She really was very tall. She gave the detective a nod and a hesitant smile. She could only hope that the police understood she was just trying to help.

The detective gestured towards the alleyway. "That way. Please."

"Yes." Freya walked in the direction indicated, almost crashing into a scrawny man carrying a holdall.

"Oh."

"Oh indeed," the man replied. "Who are you?"

"A neighbour. Are you with...?" Freya gestured backwards with her head.

CHAPTER TWENTY

A smile. "I'm DC Hughes." His accent was Welsh. "I'm with DI Finch. You alright? You look a bit pale."

"I'm fine. Thank you."

This was all too confusing. The first detective had been angry with her. Now this one was worried about her. Or was that just how they operated?

She swallowed. "I'll be at home if you need me. I'll put the kettle on."

Without turning to see the detective's reaction, Freya scuttled home, hoping none of the neighbours would notice her.

CHAPTER TWENTY-ONE

"Who was Miss Marple in there?" Rhodri asked.

"Freya Garside. The woman who reported him missing," Zoe replied. She pulled in a breath and surveyed the garden. It was neat and tidy. There might be clues here, but she'd need Adi's team if she was going to find them. "And I'd rather you didn't talk about witnesses like that."

"Sorry."

Zoe turned to him. "You get a key from the next door neighbour?"

"Yeah." He held it up.

"Good. How did they react?"

"It felt like she'd been expecting me."

"Maybe they've all been talking to each other."

"Maybe."

Zoe shook her head. That was all she needed, the neighbours comparing notes.

"Rhod," she said. "Uniform are on their way. I want all the neighbours within five doors either side interviewed. But first I want to make sure they aren't talking to each other.

Can you start knocking on doors, tell them we'll be with them shortly and remind them not to confer before they've spoken to us?"

"No problem, boss. You got a key to the back door?"

"No. I'll come with you round the front."

They walked along the alleyway to reach the front garden. A small group of people had gathered opposite, Miss Garside at their heart.

"She's going to be trouble, that one," Zoe said.

"She looked like she was about to faint," Rhodri replied.

"Women like that are made of sterner stuff than you give them credit for."

"Right. You want me to...?"

"Yes. Start with Freya Garside. Send her home, tell her to shut the fuck up. If the others are neighbours give them the same spiel."

"Without the 'shut the fuck up', I s'pose?"

Zoe cocked her head at Rhodri. "What do you think?"

"I'll be polite."

"Thanks."

Rhodri glanced at the front door to the house then crossed the road, pulling on his tried and trusted smile as he approached the group of onlookers. He'd disperse them with the minimum fuss, Zoe knew. Rhodri might not be the brain of Britain, but he knew how to deal with people.

As did Connie, in her own way. Zoe knew she was going to lose one of them soon, and her team would be weaker for it.

"Right." She looked at the keys Rhodri had given her. One Yale and one deadbolt. She approached the front door and knocked.

No reply. She pushed open the letterbox and peered

through. Ideally she would have uniform with her for this, but Rhodri had spoken to the Control Room while they'd been driving here, and learned that Miss Garside had already been in the house and found it empty.

Helpful Miss Garside. Thoroughly contaminating the scene of crime.

Zoe couldn't rule out the possibility it was suspicious. Act like an idiot to cover up involvement in the crime. The woman didn't look like a murderer, but then, who did?

"Hello?" she called through the letterbox. "Is there anyone here? It's the police."

She still didn't know if Albert North had relatives, or maybe a lodger.

No response. As she'd expected.

Zoe took a pair of overshoes from her pocket, and some gloves. She lifted the key and turned it in the lock.

Beyond was a dingy hallway with mustard yellow wallpaper. A pile of post had been shoved aside.

"Police," Zoe called. "Anyone here?"

She continued walking, towards a narrow kitchen. The space was tidy, no sign of abandoned food. It looked like their victim hadn't left in a hurry.

This was a perfectly good house, in a nice neighbourhood. Why would someone leave it empty to live on the streets?

She opened and closed drawers. Knives appeared to be in their correct place, and there were no more notes or letters. The table was empty save for a small clock and a pile of envelopes.

This room would need to be combed in detail by the FSIs, but there was nothing jumping out to explain why

Albert North had left his home to sleep rough, or why someone had killed him.

Zoe walked back into the hall and through to the back room, which had a table in its centre. This room was cold, with shelves in the alcoves and dusty books. She doubted anyone ever came in here.

She approached the shelves and scanned the books.

History books, mainly about British military history. Nothing with an Eastern European link.

She took one of the books from a shelf – something on the Boer War – and opened it. The book smelled of ink and there was no sign of damage to the spine or pages.

She replaced it and pulled out another one. D-Day landings. This one, too, was as pristine as it would have been when it left the shop.

She tried ten more books, and found them all in the same condition. Either Albert North had been a fastidious reader, or the books were for show.

Frowning, she left the room and entered into the final downstairs room, at the front. Net curtains were closed in the bay window and the room had a faded, yellowing air, not helped by the fact that those curtains looked like they hadn't been washed for some time.

This room looked lived-in. There was a small pile of books on a side table and an armchair with a dent in it from regular use. The sofa across from it looked less worn.

She picked up one of the books. An Alistair MacLean novel. Thumbing through it, Zoe couldn't help but notice its pages had been folded down and its spine bent back. The other two novels were the same.

So the books in the dining room *were* for show. But why?

She heard footsteps in the hall and left the room, half-expecting to see Freya Garside standing there.

It was Rhodri. "You left the door open, boss."

"I'm expecting Adi. And Uniform. Any news on that score?"

"They'll be here in four minutes. And I've sent all the neighbours packing. You find anything useful?"

"Not yet. Just some suspicious books. And the fact that he didn't leave in a hurry. Albert North's decision to go onto the streets was planned."

"Who'd plan a thing like that?"

"No idea, Rhodri. But if we can work that out, we might get a better idea of why he died."

CHAPTER TWENTY-TWO

Zoe sat in her car, watching the street. Rhodri was with Uniform, working their way from house to house and conducting interviews with neighbours. Hopefully someone would help them pin down the day on which Albert North had left his house. *Hopefully* someone would have witnessed something that might lead them to a suspect.

She couldn't help but be suspicious of Freya Garside. The woman had entered the house, albeit with a key, and gone back to the garden after being told to leave the house by the police. Was she trying to cover up traces of her own earlier presence in the house, or maybe add extra traces to the scene to disguise those she'd left there earlier?

But Miss Garside was in her seventies. She was an elderly spinster living opposite a park in Kings Heath. Hardly murderer material. And Albert North had been killed in the city centre, two weeks after leaving his home five doors up from Freya.

No, Freya wasn't a suspect. But Zoe wanted to find out if the woman knew more about Albert's movements in the last few weeks. She was the curtain twitching type, the sort who would log comings and goings as efficiently as a crime scene manager.

She started at a rap on her window. She turned to see Adi stooping over her car, wearing his customary smile.

Zoe fumbled with buttons for a moment and eventually opened the window.

"Zoe," Adi said. "How's it going?"

"Better than it was," she replied, nodding in the direction of Albert's house. "The victim from the Christmas Market lived in that house over there. Looks like he left it two weeks ago."

"Why?"

She shook her head. "No idea. That's one of the things we need to find out. Meanwhile, can your lot start work on the house? See if you can find anything that might tell us why he decided to disappear, or who might have wanted him dead."

"You're saying he decided to disappear? He willingly left his house to sleep rough?" Adi looked towards the house. "There someone else living there? A wife, kids? Someone he was trying to get away from?"

"As far as I know, he lived alone." Zoe got out of the car and Adi stepped back onto the pavement. It was fully dark now and the park looked eerie in the dim light of a few overhead lamps.

Adi screwed up his mouth. "People are odd. Glad I don't have to work out his motivation."

"No. You just find me the piece of evidence that lets *me* work out his motivation. Please."

Her phone rang, a mobile number Zoe didn't recognise.

She raised a finger, closing her window and watching as Adi zipped his lips.

"DI Finch." Hopefully it would be another lead.

"Ma'am, it's DS Kaur."

Zoe felt her chest sink. Layla. She'd been hoping to put this conversation off until morning.

"Layla. How are you?"

"I'm very well, Ma'am. Looking forward to starting with your team in the morning."

I bet you are. "Layla, please don't ma'am me. Call me boss. And can I phone you back? I'm at..." Zoe sighed. She should bring Layla in on this; her new DS would have to take an active role the next day. "I'm at the residence of our victim from the German Market."

"Oh. That's a breakthrough."

"Means we know who he is, and where he lived. If nothing else."

"Any family? Do you need me to organise a Family Liaison Officer?"

"My DCs could do that, but no. He lived alone."

"Why di—"

"Layla, I'm sorry, but I need to interview a witness. Can we pick this up in the morning, maybe? 8am, Rose Road office?"

"Yes, boss. You sure you don't want me in earlier?"

Zoe yawned. It was a Sunday, and she'd been working more than twelve hours so far. "No thanks, Layla. I'll see you at eight."

"No problem, boss." The line went dead, and Zoe opened the window again.

"Everything OK?" Adi asked.

Zoe gave him a smile. "That was my newest team member. DS Kaur."

His eyes widened. "DS Layla Kaur? From PSD?"

"No longer from PSD. She's Force CID now."

"Well, yes, but... why is she in your team?"

"I need a DS, she needs a team. But let's just get on with this case, shall we? I want to go home and feed my cat, if it's all the same to you." She saw his face drop. "I'm sorry, Adi. You're knackered too. You don't need to start the hard work on this till morning. It's not like any of it's going anywhere."

"We need to seal the scene and make sure it's protected. Once I'm happy with that, only then can I go home."

"Right."

Adi was thorough, and wouldn't leave his team to work when he'd gone home. It was one of the things Zoe liked about him.

"OK. You crack on with that, and I'll do this interview." Zoe crossed the road, trying to push Layla Kaur out of her mind.

CHAPTER TWENTY-THREE

Freya opened her door to find the redheaded detective standing outside. She was young, probably no more than forty, but had the air of a woman who'd lived longer than her years. She gave Freya a tight smile and showed her ID again.

"I'm Detective Inspector Zoe Finch," she said. "We met earlier. In your neighbour's garden."

"Yes. Please forgive me, I was trying to help."

There was a twitch of the detective's nose, so slight that a less observant person might not have noticed it. "Yes. Well, if you could stay away from the house from now on, we'd be grateful."

We. Freya looked past the woman to see whether she had a colleague. A more senior man, perhaps. But no, she'd said she was the senior officer. Police were barely out of nappies, these days.

"Come in," Freya said. "Can I get you a cup of tea?"

"A coffee would be good. Black, no sugar."

"Certainly." Freya gestured towards her living room.

Like Mr North's, it was at the front of the house. Overlooking the street, where she could keep an eye out for her neighbours. Somebody had to.

The detective followed Freya's gesture into the living room. Freya resisted the urge to follow her in and check she wasn't disturbing things. Detectives, she imagined, would be exceptionally nosey.

Tea. And coffee.

She hurried into the kitchen and turned off the radio – Radio Three, Vivaldi – so she could hear if there were any sounds from the living room. The house was quiet, the only noise the ticking of her late father's beloved grandfather clock at the top of the stairs.

Quickly, she put just the right amount of water in the kettle and set it to boil. She brought tea, the strainer, and a jar of coffee down from a cupboard. Within a few minutes, she had a tray with two cups and a plate of digestives and was heading back into the living room. If the detective had decided to exercise her curiosity, she wouldn't have had much time for it.

In the living room, the young woman was sitting in Freya's favourite armchair, in the window. Freya glanced at the side table beside it, her reading glasses and book with its leather bookmark. The detective would have realised this was her favourite chair, and taken it deliberately, to unsettle her.

Clever. But it wasn't going to work.

Freya set the tray down on the coffee table in the centre of the room and placed coasters beside it. She placed her own tea down and then took the detective's coffee to the side table and placed it on the coaster that lived there.

CHAPTER TWENTY-THREE

"Thank you," said the detective. She picked up her coffee and sniffed, her expression wary. Clearly satisfied, she nodded, sipped and placed it back down.

Freya used instant – she would never have one of those new-fangled pod coffee machines – but she prided herself on buying the good stuff.

Freya took her place in the centre of the sofa. She picked up her own cup and saucer, placed a biscuit in the saucer, and leaned back. She was determined to relax. The detective would have questions for her about Mr North and their relationship. She would ask why Freya had been searching the back garden. She might even be suspicious of her for doing so.

Freya had good answers to all these questions.

She smiled over her cup. "So have you found him yet?"

The detective raised an eyebrow. "Mr North?"

Freya nodded. "He's been missing for two weeks. I'm hoping he's turned up. But then, after all this time..."

She shivered. She should have turned the heating up.

The detective licked her lips and leaned forward. "Miss Garside, I'm sorry to tell you that Mr North is dead."

Freya's breath caught in her throat. Had he been in that house, all along, lying there dead?

She knew she should have searched upstairs herself.

"How? Was he...?" Her gaze darted towards the wall, in the direction of Mr North's house.

A shake of the head. "He was found in the city centre early this morning."

"Oh my goodness." Freya put her cup down, clattering it against the saucer. Her hand went to the chain she wore around her neck. "How?"

"We don't know, yet. But in the meantime, we're trying to find out more about Albert, when he left his house and who he associated with on this street."

"Well, judging by his post, he left two weeks ago. Ruti – that's Mrs Sandhar who lives next door to him – she said she hadn't seen him for at least a week. And the woman who lives on the other side, Olive, she says she spoke to him two weeks ago. About his garden."

"His garden."

Freya felt her face grow warm. *Control yourself, woman.* "His garden. Yes."

"Which you were so keen to investigate."

"Ruti and I had already been inside the house. I felt it only right and proper that we should be thorough."

The detective leaned back in her chair, making it creak. Freya winced.

"Please, leave the investigating to the police next time, if you don't mind."

Freya nodded. She knew how overstretched the police were these days. Budget cuts and political correctness taking up all their time. If they weren't up to their job, she would make no promises.

"If you need to take a DNA sample from me, I'd be happy to oblige." She worked her tongue into the inside of her cheek. She'd had cells scraped before, as part of a medical procedure. It didn't hurt.

"We will, thank you. I'll send my colleague Adi Hanson or one of his team round here."

"Of course." Freya sniffed. "So what questions do you need to ask me?"

A smile flickered on the detective's lips. Freya took

another gulp of her tea. Her mouth was dry; why hadn't she brewed a pot?

"Firstly, how well did you know Mr North?"

"Not very. We spoke occasionally, when we passed in the street. There aren't so many old folks along here now as there used to be." She forced a smile. "They keep dying on us."

"When did it occur to you that you hadn't seen him for a while?"

"I went to his house this morning. He'd promised to take on the role of Father Christmas at Kings Heath Primary School. The Christmas Fayre. I like to help out, my role is to make sure there's a suitable St Nick."

"You haven't tried to make contact at any point in the previous two weeks?"

"I've been busy with Christmas preparations. I may not have children of my own, but my sis—"

"It's OK, Miss Garside. I appreciate that there are many reasons why you might not have noticed that your neighbour was missing."

"How did he die? Was there an accident?"

"We haven't determined the cause of death yet, I'm afraid. But I can tell you that we found Mr North in the vicinity of the German Market."

Freya felt like she was about to fall off her chair. Her heart rate suddenly picked up and she could feel her palms grow clammy. "He's the man on the news?"

"He is. I'm sorry."

Freya swallowed. The lump in her throat was so big she thought it might choke her.

"But that man was murdered."

"We haven't determined the cause of death yet."

"That man was... he was a tramp."

"It appears that Mr North was living on the streets during the last two weeks, yes. When you last saw him, did he say anything about leaving? Or about any problems he was having?"

"We spoke about the Father Christmas role." Freya tried to remember. It had been three weeks. She should have tried to contact Mr North in the last few days, she knew, to check everything was alright for today.

If she had done so, she'd have been able to report him missing. He might be alive now.

No. You can't think like that. It wasn't her fault.

"Detective, I think I need to take my pills. This is all very..."

The detective leaned forward, her face full of concern. "Of course. I'll wait."

Freya felt her pulse pick up further. "Please. Can't this wait?"

The detective sat back. "Of course. We'll come back in the morning, if that suits you."

Freya nodded, her throat dry.

Poor Mr North.

Lying there in the night, behind the stalls of the market. It was no way for anyone to end their days. And Mr North had been the kind of man who cleaned his kitchen and tidied his garden.

That made it worse.

"I'm sorry," she croaked.

The detective stood up. "Thank you for your time. Do you need anyone to sit with you? I can get a Family Liaison Officer."

"No. I'll be alright. Once I've taken my pills."

She'd have some supper and go to bed. Try not to dream. It would be fine.

The detective was at the living room door. "You don't have to get up. Take care of yourself."

Freya nodded. She slumped back in her chair, her mind racing.

CHAPTER TWENTY-FOUR

Rhodri was leaving a house two doors along when Zoe emerged from Miss Garside's front door. She gave him a tired smile.

"How are the neighbours holding up?"

He shook his head. "They're freaked out, boss. It's not good having one of your neighbours killed, like."

"No – but you haven't been telling people he was murdered, have you, Rhodri? Cause of death hasn't been determined yet, remember?"

"Course not, boss. But people have their own ideas. And they're probably right, aren't they?"

Zoe nodded. "Has anyone provided any useful information?"

"Not yet. But Uniform have still got two more to do."

Zoe looked along the street. She should stay, but she was exhausted. And Rhodri had the energy of a much younger man.

Besides, he wanted to prove himself, didn't he?

"I'm leaving you in charge. Wait here till all the interviews are done, and call me if there's anything I need to know. Then go home."

"What about Connie?"

"Give her a call too. I'm assuming she hasn't found anything, or she'd have been on the phone. Tell her she can head home."

"Right." Rhodri pulled his phone from his pocket and Zoe turned towards her car.

Her house in Selly Oak was only a ten minute drive from Kings Heath at this time on a Sunday. She pulled up outside, glad to see a light on in the downstairs window. It meant Carl was waiting for her.

The front door opened as she brought her key up to the lock. He stood in the hall, wearing an apron and wiping his hands on a tea towel.

Zoe smiled. "Cooking?"

"Christmas pudding. A bit late, I know."

Zoe heard a sound behind her and turned to see her cat Yoda rubbing against the back of her leg. She picked the cat up, pretending to groan.

"This one is so heavy now, I think I'll collapse under her weight."

"She was hassling me for Dreamies before."

Zoe let the cat burrow its face into her cheek and rub its cheek against her. She stroked the top of its head then set it back down on the carpet.

"I hope you didn't give her any."

Carl held his hands up. "I wouldn't dare."

Zoe approached the hob. "Home-made Christmas pudding is fine by me at any time." She kissed him and walked back into the living room, slinging her coat onto a chair. Carl picked it up and hung it on a hook in the hall.

The kitchen smelled of spice and sugar. It was heavenly.

"I know you're supposed to make it in October," Carl said.

Zoe turned to him. "January, more like."

He shuffled towards her, placing the tea towel on a surface, and wrapped his arms around her. Zoe leaned her head on his chest, breathing in the smell of Christmas.

"Thanks for coming here and waiting for me," she said.

"I figured you'd be late, what with finding that bloke round the back of the German Market. I take it you're working that case?"

Zoe pulled back. "I'm SIO."

"Good choice."

Zoe took a breath, scanning Carl's face. He'd previously been Layla Kaur's line manager, until she'd left PSD for reasons unknown to Zoe. Layla clearly hadn't seen fit to tell him about her new role.

"I've got a new DS," she said. "Just for this case."

"Good. Who?" He picked up the tea towel, went back into the kitchen and lifted the lid of a pan that was rattling on the hob.

Zoe stood in the doorway. "Layla Kaur."

Carl turned to her. "*My* Layla Kaur?"

Zoe cocked her head. "I hope not."

"You know what I mean. They've assigned Layla to your team?"

"They have. Frank dragged me out of a briefing to tell me. She starts tomorrow."

Carl whistled. "How d'you feel about it?"

"Seeing as the last time I spent any time with the woman she suspected me of corruption, not all that great."

"You were cleared. She knows you were feeding me information about David Randle."

"Still. She was a bitch in that interview."

Carl put his hands on Zoe's arms. "She was doing her job. I've seen you interviewing suspects, and you're just the same."

Zoe shrugged his grip off. "Thanks." She turned into the living room.

"Oh come on, Zo. Don't be like that."

"I'm not Zo," she replied, sinking onto the sofa. "Not to you." That was what Mo had called her. Only Mo. She missed him.

Why did you have to move to Scotland, Mo?

Carl sat down next to her. He put a hand on her knee. "I'm sorry. Zoe. Look, it'll be fine, I'm sure. She's a good copper, she'll help you solve the case."

Zoe leaned back. She dragged her hands through her hair, snagging her fingernails. "I know. I need to put all that behind me."

"You know the best way to do that."

She pushed his hand off her knee. "I don't want to talk about it."

"They've offered me a promotion, love. You'd get a transfer easy."

"This is my son's home."

"He's at university. In Stirling. Cumbria is a lot closer."

Zoe closed her eyes. "Have you cooked anything I can actually eat now?"

"There's a pie in the oven."

"You baked pie too?"

"Don't be daft. It's from Sainsbury's. But stodge is what you need right now."

Zoe turned to him and stroked his face. He was right. "Thanks, sweetie. I know you mean the best. I'm tired. Let me eat, and maybe I won't be such a bitch."

CHAPTER TWENTY-FIVE

Layla was already in the office when Zoe arrived at 7.30 the next morning. She'd come in early, expecting to get a few minutes with Connie and Rhodri before the new DS arrived, but it seemed the woman was keen.

Layla had taken Mo's old desk, and while this was a perfectly reasonable and logical thing to do, still it felt odd to see someone else sitting there. Zoe shuddered at the memory of Ian Osman, who'd temporarily joined her team while Mo had been working for Frank, and turned out to be part of the web of corruption Randle had woven though Force CID. At least she could be safe on that score with Layla.

"Morning Layla. Welcome."

Layla swivelled round in her chair. She was dressed smartly and soberly, a dark trouser suit over a navy blue shirt. Her long dark hair had been scraped back into a ponytail and she wore the kind of makeup that was designed to look as if she wasn't wearing makeup at all.

"Morning, boss. I thought I'd get here early, give me time to get up to speed."

"Come into my office, won't you?"

Zoe led the DS into her office at the side of the room. She rarely ventured in here, preferring to be outside with the rest of her team, but it was useful for confidential conversations and for storing documents she didn't want just anyone waltzing in and having a gander at.

She had a feeling that with Layla on the team, she might be spending a bit more time in here.

Zoe gestured for Layla to sit down. She rounded the desk and took her own chair behind it, wishing she'd stopped for coffee on the way in. She needed the caffeine.

Should she ask Layla to fetch some?

No. That wasn't the job of a DS. Not unless she was already heading to the kitchen.

"Can I get you a coffee, boss? I hear you take it black."

Zoe felt her shoulders slump. Had Carl given Layla a pep talk?

She smiled. "Yes, please. Only if you're getting yourself one, though."

"I will." Layla stood and left the room. Zoe watched her pass through the outer office. Her footsteps were as neat as her clothes, her face registering no emotion. How did she feel about being assigned to this team? She'd have had no more choice in the matter than Zoe had.

Thanks, Frank.

Zoe fired up her computer and checked emails. There was one from Adi with his report from Albert North's house. So far, they'd found some muddy footprints in the garden but nothing inside. The footprints were probably Freya Garside's. Uniform were heading to her house this morning to pick up the shoes she'd been wearing yesterday.

CHAPTER TWENTY-FIVE

Bloody Freya Garside. Fancied herself as Miss Marple. But Zoe was no longer suspicious of her.

The outer door opened and Layla returned with two mugs. She stopped at the door to Zoe's office, unable to turn the knob. Zoe passed round her desk and opened the door for her.

"Thanks." She took the mug.

"My pleasure."

"I only expect you to get coffee for me if you're getting one yourself. And get one for the DCs while you're at it."

Layla closed the door and sat down, glancing through the glass partition to the outer office. "Where are they?"

Zoe checked her watch. "Not due in yet. They worked a long day yesterday. Got to cut them some slack."

Layla shuffled in her chair and focussed her gaze on Zoe. "So how do you want me to proceed?"

"Proceed?"

"In terms of roles. Do you want me to oversee the work of DCs Williams and Hughes, or will you continue to do that?"

"Where it concerns the day to day operation of this case, you'll be doing that. I'll have strategic oversight and I don't want any significant activity taking place without my say-so."

"Boss, if I might suggest..."

Zoe pursed her lips. "Go on."

"When I was working for Carl, I mean DI Whaley, he would assign me a specific aspect of each case to manage."

Zoe kept her gaze level on the other woman. "I'm not DI Whaley. I work differently."

"Of course."

Zoe waited for disagreement. There was none. Thank God for that.

She'd have a chat with Carl tonight, find out how best to handle Layla. If he was willing to tell her. The atmosphere this morning hadn't been warm, and she had the sense he was punishing her for not jumping at the chance to move to Cumbria.

"So where are we up to with the investigation?" Layla asked. "I took a look at the board, out there." She jerked her head sideways.

"We've managed to identify the victim. We don't have a cause of death yet, although we're confident it's suspicious. Rhodri may have come up with a lead concerning an altercation between the victim and another man last weekend. The other man apparently spoke with an Eastern European accent. And there's a note."

"A note?" Layla slurped her tea. Too loudly.

"The FSIs found a folded-up note hidden inside the lining of Albert's coat. It's being translated as we speak."

"Do we have any potential suspects?"

"We've spoken to Albert's neighbours. Nothing there yet. The next step is to piece together his history. He was retired, but where had he worked? Could there be some kind of professional grudge? And what about relationships? Was there a spouse, partner?"

"He lived alone?"

"He did. And that's the oddest thing about this case."

Layla leaned forward.

"He seems to have left home two weeks ago," Zoe continued. "Not been seen nearby since. From what we've gathered so far, it looks like he took himself off to live on the streets, and that's where he was killed. What I want to know is why he did that."

"Debts, maybe?"

"We'll need to talk to debt collection agencies. Check his

post. If someone was after him for money, that might be why he disappeared."

"It might not have been legitimate agencies or companies."

"Loan sharks are a possibility."

"Or organised crime."

Zoe rolled her eyes. "Not another one, please. Rhodri's got a bee in his bonnet about organised crime. But yes, see if you can rule it out. I don't want to end up going down a rabbit hole."

Zoe looked up to see the outer door opening: Connie. She smiled and beckoned.

Connie opened the door to Zoe's office and stepped inside, careful not to get too close to the new DS.

"Connie, have you met DS Kaur?"

"No." Connie held out a hand.

Layla shook it. "Pleased to meet you, Connie. I've heard good things."

Connie's gaze flicked to Zoe. "Thanks. Good."

"Right." Zoe stood up. "Rhodri will be here very soon. Let's get everyone up to speed, and then we can start work."

CHAPTER TWENTY-SIX

Connie felt uneasy about DS Kaur joining the team.

Last time they'd been blessed with a new DS, it had been Ian Osman. And he'd been a disaster from start to finish, ending up on trial for corruption.

DS Kaur was ex-PSD. She was trained to look at other coppers with a critical eye. To distrust them.

And now Connie was working for her.

She'd worked with DI Whaley before, when he'd been undercover. He'd been alright. But then, he'd been pretending to be one of them. Transferred down from Manchester to spy on Randle and the other high-ups, he'd hardly crossed Connie's path. Good job, seeing as the boss was going out with him and Connie secretly had a small crush on him.

Who could blame her? He was gorgeous.

Stop it.

She scrunched up her eyes and willed herself to concentrate. The boss was going over stuff Connie already knew. The fact that Albert North had left his home two weeks ago, and they didn't know why. The fight with some Eastern European guy. The note in his coat.

Once they had that translated, Connie hoped it would solve the case. Then she could make her mum happy and spend a bit more time at home.

Not that she wanted to.

The boss's phone vibrated in her pocket and she pulled it out.

"DI Finch."

DS Kaur was about to speak. The boss held up a finger to stop her.

"Hello Adi. Right. What does it say?" A nod. "Yes." Another nod. "OK." A fist thumped on her knee. This was good news. "Send it over."

The DI hung up and looked around the team. "Good news. The note has been translated."

Rhodri visibly slumped. Connie knew he'd been hoping to get a head start on that one, with his mates in Organised Crime. But the truth was, they'd probably have asked the Forensics lab anyway. And the boss had first dibs on their time, or rather, Adi Hanson did.

"What does it say?" DS Kaur asked.

"Hang on a minute. He's sending it over." Zoe looked at Connie. "Connie, check the team inbox."

Connie pushed her chair over to her desk and opened her emails. The message from Adi was already there. She clicked on the attachment.

She frowned. "It makes no sense, boss."

"They've translated it?" The DI strode to Connie's desk and leaned over her, peering at the screen.

"Yeah. But it's garbage."

The boss leaned in. "Kite tomorrow says hello landslip in the circus above Yonkers." She thumped the desk. "Shit."

"What?" Rhodri asked. His face had perked up, as if he thought he might still have a chance of getting the correct translation.

"It's some sort of code." The boss grabbed her phone. "Adi, have you read this thing?" A pause. "It's useless. I need it to go to— Good. Let me know when you've got something. Thanks."

She tossed her phone onto Connie's desk. "It's some sort of code. Useless to us until the nerds at the lab have scratched it."

"You think they will? DS Kaur asked. "It doesn't look like anything I've ever seen."

The boss looked at her. "You had a lot of experience with this kind of thing?"

"You'd be surprised. People who don't want you to find out what they're doing have a habit of using cyphers and codes."

"OK." The boss stood back. "Take a look at it, see if you can tell us anything."

The DS walked to Connie's desk. It was getting crowded. Connie wondered if she should move out of the way. But she could sense the tension flowing off the two senior women.

"It's a cypher," DS Kaur said.

"Oh, I've heard of them," Rhodri shifted in his chair. "Saw a film."

"Can you translate it?" the boss asked the DS.

"Sorry. I've not been trained."

The boss made a *hmpf* sound. "No." She straightened up. "OK, then let's work with what we do have." She pointed at the board. "Neighbours. Forensics, not that we have much of

CHAPTER TWENTY-SIX

those yet. Homeless shelters. And the Eastern European link."

"Adi says the note was in Croatian," Connie added, looking at the email on her screen.

"Croatian. So we need to find out *why* it's in Croatian. What links did Albert have with that country?" The DI looked at DS Kaur. "Rhodri has friends in Uniform who might be able to tell us if there are any Croatian rough sleepers in the city centre."

Rhodri spluttered, making Connie smile. The DS looked at him.

"Follow it up, then," she said.

"Right."

"DS Kaur, how else do you think we should allocate resources?" asked the boss.

DS Kaur licked her lips. "We also have the post-mortem today. I spoke to Dr Adebayo and she says it'll be this morning."

"Good."

"In which case I'll go to that. DC Williams, you work on the shelters."

"Rhodri went to one in the city centre yesterday," said Connie. "I think it'd be good to speak to the manager again, now we have a name."

"And the one in Solihull," the DI added.

"Yes," Connie replied.

"Good," said DS Kaur. "Rhodri, did you get much out of the manager you spoke to yesterday?"

"No," said Rhodri, with a shrug. "I don't think he trusted me, to be honest."

"Right. Connie, you work on the shelters. See if the name means anything to them. Ask for Croatian service users.

Rhodri, get onto your mates in Uniform. Ask about any incidents involving a Croatian man. And find out if anything came from the door to door in Avenue Road yesterday."

"Good," said the DI. "I'll follow up on Forensics. I'm heading over to the victim's house, via the crime scene."

"Is that the best use of your time?" DS Kaur asked.

The boss raised an eyebrow at her. "I like to see the scenes in the flesh. Talk to the FSIs. You let me know what comes back from the PM, yes?"

"Of course."

"And keep me updated on any progress Connie and Rhodri make. Guys, I want you reporting to DS Kaur, not me. Imagine she's Mo."

Rhodri muttered something indistinguishable. Connie flushed, imagining DS Uddin back in that chair.

"Yes boss." The sooner this case was solved, the better.

CHAPTER TWENTY-SEVEN

Layla looked up at the hospital entrance and drew in a breath. It had been some time since she'd done this – her work in PSD had rarely involved dead bodies. And when it did, the job of attending the PM would have been well above her pay grade.

The morgue was in the basement; weren't they always? She'd last been here six years ago, when she was working on the death of a man in Longbridge. Her last case in CID, before the high-ups had spotted her ability and moved her into PSD.

So what was she doing back in CID? OK, so it was Force CID, a step up from local, but even so... She knew that other coppers looked at her funny. Working in PSD tainted you for life. It was rare for officers to move out of it back to regular operations. Those that did often didn't thrive.

Get a grip, she told herself. DI Whaley had told her she was more than capable. He'd said that the myths were just that: myths.

She wondered whether the DI had talked about her with

DI Finch. No. He was much too professional. The very fact that she'd interviewed DI Finch when she'd been investigating corruption in Force CID meant that the two DIs would never discuss that case, or indeed her.

She found the morgue quickly, surprising herself. So much of the Queen Elizabeth hospital had changed in the last six years, but the morgue wouldn't be first in line when it came to cash for modernisation. You wouldn't find ministers visiting them or the press wanting to photograph them, so they were usually left well alone.

Dr Adebayo was in the reception area. Layla had never met her, but knew her by reputation. The pathologist was tall with high cheekbones, dark skin and cropped hair. The overall effect was of elegance and brusque efficiency, even when the woman was dressed in an overall and a pair of white wellies.

"You must be DS Kaur." The doctor held out her hand and Layla shook it. "I've been told to expect you. How are you getting on with Zoe?"

Layla licked her lips. *None of your business*. "Too early to tell." She smiled. "Is the body ready?"

A smile in response, equally insincere. "Follow me. We've done the PM itself, I'm running some additional tests."

"What were the results from the PM?"

"That's what I need the tests to confirm. Come this way."

Layla followed the doctor into a small room lined with lockers. Dr Adebayo opened one of them, slipped off her wellies and slid into a pair of heeled pumps.

"We don't need the boots?"

"Luckily no. I'd like you to put on a set of overalls, though. I don't want any risk of contamination."

"What is it we're testing?"

CHAPTER TWENTY-SEVEN

Dr Adebayo was bent over, adjusting her foot inside her shoe. She looked up at Layla. "Hair."

"There was something in his hair?"

"Not so much something *in* it, as the effect of the substance that I believe poisoned him."

Layla was partway through pulling on her overalls. She paused, surprised.

"Cause of death is poisoning?"

"The hair examination should confirm it. But yes, I believe it to be so."

That would explain why the photos Layla had seen of the body showed no signs of life-threatening injuries. There'd been some bruises and scars, but the man had been homeless. Par for the course, surely.

Layla followed the doctor into a white-walled room with a bench along one side. On it were some glass jars, plastic containers, computers and a microscope.

"OK." The pathologist drew a stool up to the bench in front of the microscope and grabbed a container. She brought out a slide and looked at Layla. "This slide holds one of your victim's hairs. If I'm correct, there'll be obvious effects."

She leaned over and peered into the microscope, slipping the slide onto it at the same time with practiced ease. Layla stepped closer, eyeing the equipment on the bench. She knew better than to touch. She wondered if Mr North's remains were being sewn up somewhere, the post-mortem itself having been completed.

"Have you done chemical analysis too?" Layla asked.

Dr Adebayo smiled, not looking up from the viewfinder. "Good question. Not yet, but with this particular substance, a hair examination is far more useful than chemical analysis. It's not easy stuff to detect, but its effects are clear."

Layla chewed her lip and waited. The room was quiet, the only sounds the doctor's gentle breathing and someone moving around in the next room.

At last the pathologist pushed back her chair. "Good." She looked at Layla. "Want to take a look?"

Layla moved towards the microscope. She leaned over it and peered in. She could make out the root of a single hair follicle.

"If you look closely," the pathologist said, "you'll see that there's atrophy of the hair bulb."

"Sorry?"

"The bulb is the part where the hair meets the root. It's damaged. There's also damage to the cuticles. Here." She adjusted the slide and the hair moved across Layla's field of vision. "See? It's not smooth. Rough, almost tangled."

Layla nodded. She'd never have recognised any of this if she hadn't been told what to look for. But now it made sense.

"And this is abnormal?"

"It is. Specific to thallium poisoning."

"Thallium?" Layla straightened up. "I've heard of that."

"Are you an Agatha Christie reader?"

"When I was younger."

"Before you became too busy. I know that feeling." The pathologist snorted. "The queen of crime fiction liked to use thallium. It's convenient, as it's odourless and tasteless. It can be administered in food. Small amounts lead to hair loss. Larger quantities result in death before the hair even has time to fall out. If quantities are large enough, unconsciousness can be almost immediate, death not long after."

"Which is what happened to Albert North?"

"That's my conclusion. I'll do some more tissue and blood tests, but I think they'll confirm it."

"So if this stuff has featured in detective novels, it'll be easy to get hold of."

"Not anymore. It's prohibited."

"Oh." That would reduce the choice of potential suspects, which in turn should make it easier for them to find the poisoner. "I don't suppose you know where a person might illegally get hold of thallium?"

"Sorry. Can't help you there. I do know that it's produced in China and Kazakhstan. Mainly Kazakhstan."

"Can you say how much of it was in his system?"

"Judging by the state of his hair, and the clear indications that he died quickly, enough to kill three people, at least. Or a large animal."

"Is it used to put animals down?"

"Not that I know of."

"OK. Well, thanks."

The pathologist nodded. "You'll get my formal report later in the day but I suggest you update Zoe."

"There was no other trauma? Could he have been drugged and then attacked?"

"I examined him externally at the scene, and then in more detail in my post-mortem. There are no injuries on him, at least none that would have killed him. There's some bruising on his upper arm and a minor cut to his shin. He's in a pretty good shape for someone living on the streets." She cocked her head. "Apart from having been given thallium, that is."

"Thallium. Could it have come from Croatia, by any chance?"

The doctor frowned. "I doubt it, but it's not impossible. Countries with a history of recent upheaval might be less effective in their regulation of these things. You're saying he was Croatian?"

"He had a note on him when he died. In Croatian."

"That might explain the poor dentition and the general state of his nutritional health. He's eaten well later in life, but his digestive system shows signs of near starvation some time ago."

"How long ago?"

"If I knew that, I'd be a miracle worker. But it wasn't recent, that much I can tell you."

"There was writing on his hands, said Layla. "Did you get a look at that?"

"I spoke to a colleague. It didn't seem to be anything coherent. Not a message, if that's what you're thinking. The pathologist licked her lips. "You going to report to your boss, then?"

"Yes." Layla didn't like being told what to do. She fumbled with her overalls, trying to reach beneath them for her mobile.

"Not in here. Go outside, take that off and call her. Tell her she'll hear from me formally within a couple of hours."

CHAPTER TWENTY-EIGHT

It was cold at the crime scene, icy rain threatening to turn to sleet. Still the German Market thrummed with activity around them. The cordon had shrunk to include only the stall behind which Albert North had been found, and the public was going about its Christmas as if nothing had happened.

As Adi was now in Kings Heath, his colleague Yala Cook was in charge here. Zoe approached her, her hands plunged into her pockets. Yala was bagging up evidence and placing it into a plastic crate, ready for a colleague to take to a van which was parked on Hill Street.

"Hello Ma'am," Yala said as she spotted Zoe.

"You're a civilian," Zoe replied. "Just call me Zoe."

Yala smiled. "You know I don't feel comfortable doing that." She gestured to the Uniformed PC on duty, logging visitors to the crime scene and any items that came in or went out. "You don't ask him to call you Zoe, so I feel odd doing it when I'm working with him."

"It's different," Zoe replied. "But if you can't bring yourself to use my name, just call me boss. Or DI Finch."

"Will do, DI Finch."

Zoe knew she wouldn't; the two of them had been working together for over four years and they had this conversation on a regular basis.

"How's it going?" Zoe asked. "Any new finds?"

"We've scoured the stall itself. But apart from a small amount of marijuana we found hidden at the back of the till drawer, there's nothing out of the ordinary."

"What nationality is the stall holder?"

"German."

"Any Croatian nationals working on it, or in the vicinity?"

"No idea, sorry. You'd have to speak to the other stall holders. Mr Kleinman, that's the guy who runs this stall, he's buggered off for a break. Says it's too depressing hanging around when he can't do business."

"Are the other stall holders helping him out? Is it that kind of community?"

"It seems to be." Yala shrugged her shoulders. "But to be honest Ma— DI Finch, I've been more focused on the forensics."

"Of course you have, sorry. There's me asking you to do my team's job for us." Zoe made a mental note to speak to Layla about assigning one of the DCs to speak to the nearby stall holders and find out if there were any Croatians in the market.

Her phone rang, and she glanced at the screen. Layla. "Sorry, I need to take this."

"Layla," Zoe said. "I need you to get one of the—"

CHAPTER TWENTY-EIGHT

"Boss, it's the PM. Formal result will be with you in the next few hours, but I knew you'd want to know."

Zoe turned away from Yala and cupped her hand around the receiver. She moved to the side of the stall, where the public wouldn't be in earshot.

"Go on."

"He was poisoned."

Zoe opened and closed her mouth. "Poisoned? What with?"

"Thallium, boss."

"That's a prohibited substance."

"In the UK. We don't know about its status in the Balkan states."

"I imagine it's outlawed pretty much everywhere. Did Adana say how much of it was in his body?"

"Enough to kill a cow, apparently."

Zoe blew out a thin breath, watching it turn into steam in the cold air. "OK. So we need to find out how it got into the hands of whoever administered it. And how that person was able to give it to Albert. I know it's not supposed to taste of anything, but that sort of quantity isn't something you'd be able to slip into a drink unnoticed."

"I suggest we talk to Counter Terrorism, boss. Find out if they're working on any leads with regard to thallium or substances like it."

"Or Organised Crime."

"Yes. I can follow both of those up."

Zoe nodded. Layla would have contacts in various departments, she realised. There would be people she would have had to bring in when she was investigating their colleagues. Not to mention people who'd been investigated and cleared.

Zoe wondered how hard it would be for Layla to win the trust of colleagues across the West Midlands force. Would it hurt the team, and this investigation? It was bad enough she herself was in a relationship with a PSD DI, but having one of them in the team... There were people out there who'd mistrust her, assuming she was associated with them in some way.

"OK," she said. "You start working on the poison. Try other units, and check HOLMES. Connie can help with that."

"Connie seems to like crunching data."

Zoe bristled. "She's more than that. She has a way with people. She's quiet, but some respond to that. Give her opportunities to work with the public. People warm to her."

"What about colleagues?"

"That too. OK, so she's not as chummy as Rhodri, but some people find that off-putting. The two of them have different styles, and they complement each other. Use it."

"You really want me directing the activity of DC Williams and DC Hughes?"

"I wouldn't have told you to if I didn't, would I? It's what Mo Uddin did, and it's what I want you to do. But if you don't think you ca—"

"Oh I can. I just wanted to be sure you were happy to trust me with that degree of responsibility."

"You're a DS, Layla. You worked in a unit where there wasn't a deep structure and I don't imagine you line managed anyone. And you're not line managing Connie and Rhodri. But direct them. Make sure they're being used on this case. They're both motivated. We can crack this."

"If you're sure."

CHAPTER TWENTY-EIGHT

Zoe thought over the leads they had. The thallium. The letter in Croatian. The identity of the victim, and the information about him they would surely find in his house.

"I'm sure of it, Layla. Rhodri will be in the valleys for Christmas, and his mum will be happy with him."

CHAPTER TWENTY-NINE

"Hello, is that Greenfields?"

"Aye. How can I help you?"

"I'm Detective Constable Williams. I work for DI Finch in Force CID, West Midlands Police, with DC Hughes. He visited your facility yesterday and spoke with Mr Kirk."

"*Facility*! That's a grand word. I wouldn't call it that, love."

Connie chewed her bottom lip.

"Can I speak with Mr Kirk please?"

"That'll be me. How can I help you, lass?"

"I'm calling because we have more information about the man found in Victoria Square on Sunday morning, and I'm hoping you might be able to tell us if he was a visitor to your... shelter."

"Aye, OK. What's the information?"

"We have a name for him. Albert North."

A pause.

"Mr Kirk?"

"Call me Jimmy, lass. Mr Kirk makes me sound like me dad."

"Jimmy. Does the name Albert North ring any bells?"

"Sorry, can't say it does. Is that all the information you have?"

"We believe that Mr North was a speaker of Croatian?"

"The language?"

"Yes. Do you have any Croatian people who come to your shelter?"

Another pause.

"Mr Kirk? Jimmy? Do you know if any of your regulars are Croatian?"

"Why would they be Croatian?"

"We can't disclose that right now. But it will help our investigation if we could find anyone he might have had contact with in the last two weeks who's a Croatian speaker."

"A Croatian speaker?"

"Do any of your regulars speak Croatian or come from the Balkan states?"

"Sorry, love. Can't help you there."

"Does that mean you don't have any Croatians who come to the shelter?"

"I wouldn't know, would I lass? I don't know Croatian from High Gallifreyan."

Connie smiled, despite herself. "This isn't *Doctor Who*, Sir."

A laugh. "I know that. All I'm saying is I wouldn't be able to tell the difference if someone spoke to me in either of those languages. Now Klingon, I could tell you if someone spoke to me in that."

"That's not much help to us, I'm afraid. Would you mind

asking around your service users, seeing if there is anyone who's a Croatian speaker and might have known Mr North?"

Another pause.

"Jimmy? Are you still there?"

"Sorry, lass. Of course. Can't say I'll have much luck, y'know. But I'll see what I can do."

"Thank you, Sir."

But the line was already dead.

CHAPTER THIRTY

"Miss Garside."

"Detective. I was wondering when you'd show up again." The woman gave Zoe a look like she was something Yoda had dragged in from the back garden.

Zoe responded with a warm smile. It didn't do any harm to be friendly, even with an interfering busybody like Freya Garside.

"How are you now?"

"I'm fine." The woman's tone was brusque.

"Can I come in, please? Or would you rather chat on the doorstep?"

Miss Garside looked past Zoe, up and down the street. From behind her, Zoe could hear children playing in the park opposite.

"Come on in." Miss Garside turned away from Zoe and walked into the house, leaving Zoe to follow and close the door behind her.

It was rare for a member of the public to do this. Normally they stood back to let the police enter, and then closed the door themselves. There was something about having the police on the doorstep that made people unnaturally aware of security. But Freya Garside, it seemed, was the confident type.

Zoe followed the woman through the hallway and into the kitchen at the rear of the house. Like Albert North's, it was narrow, not extended like so many of the kitchens in this type of house. Zoe's own kitchen hadn't been touched since she moved in – as someone who hated to cook, she couldn't see the point – but she did sometimes envy the spaces of those who were more imaginative with their homes.

Freya had already put water in the kettle. She turned to Zoe before switching it on. "Coffee, again?"

"If you don't mind."

"Why would I mind?" She flicked the kettle on and stood in front of it, her arms folded across her chest and her body upright. "So what else do you need to know from me?"

"I understand that you and Mr North weren't exactly close. But do you know if he had any connections to Croatia, or to anywhere else in the Balkans?"

"The Balkans? Oh, I know where you mean. Where they keep having wars. Why can't people just be happy with the borders that have been drawn on the map?"

Zoe didn't care what Miss Garside's views were on European politics, although she had a fairly good idea she could hazard a guess at some of them. The woman probably stood somewhere to the right of Oswald Mosley.

"Do you know if Mr North had any friends or acquaintances from Croatia? Did you ever see anyone from that part of Europe with him? Could he have maybe lived there at some point?"

The kettle clicked and Miss Garside brought two cups

out of a wall cupboard. The inside of the cupboard looked like it had been cleaned to within an inch of its life. Everything was neatly arranged, not a speck of dust in sight.

"I have no idea why you think I'd know such a thing." Miss Garside spooned a teaspoon of coffee into one of the cups and poured water over it. She then filled a small teapot, stirred it, and poured herself tea.

She bent over to open the fridge. "You sure you don't want milk?"

"No, thank you."

"No sugar?"

Zoe shook her head.

"It'll rot your insides, this stuff." The woman handed over Zoe's cup, rattling just a little in its saucer.

"Thank you." Zoe took the cup, wondering if Miss Garside intended for them to stay in here, standing in the kitchen.

Miss Garside picked up her own cup and took a long sip from it, eyeing Zoe as she did so. "Your officers have been bothering the residents."

"We need to find out what people might know about Mr North's disappearance."

"Old Mrs Farthing four doors down, she's terrified. The volume at which your men – women, one of them – knocked on her door."

Zoe knew that a police knock could be intimidating. Uniform weren't supposed to knock so loudly when conducting door-to-door enquiries, but she knew it was force of habit for many.

"I'm sorry," she said, sipping her coffee again. "But the more we're able to find out about Mr North's movements in recent weeks, the easier it will be to find out who killed him. People will be concerned for their own safety."

The older woman scoffed. "Rubbish. He died round the back of a stall in the German Market. He'd been away from home for two weeks. His death clearly has nothing to do with anyone around here, does it? If you ask me…" She drank her tea, her gaze on Zoe over the rim of her cup. "If you ask me, poor Mr North got confused and couldn't find his house. That's how he suddenly disappeared. Then he wasn't able to cope with life as a vagrant and got himself into trouble. Maybe he borrowed money, maybe he got into the middle of an existing conflict. I'm sure your officers will be able to get to the bottom of it."

Zoe resisted a smile. She wondered how many of the neighbours were discussing poor Albert's death, coming up with their own hypotheses, pitching competing theories. People might not be able to see into each other's houses along here, what with the park being opposite, but they clearly knew plenty about each other's lives.

"I can assure you, we're working on a number of leads."

"I know what that means. It means you don't have a clue what's going on."

That wasn't strictly true. OK, so there was no suspect yet and Zoe was stumped by the Croatian link right now, but she knew they'd get past that soon enough. Her next call would be Albert North's house, where she hoped Adi would have uncovered documentation or perhaps even a computer with information about why Albert had left home.

"So you're saying you've never been aware of Mr North having been connected with Croatia or the Balkans."

"Never. But like I told you yesterday, I hardly knew the

man." Miss Garside put down her cup. It rattled in the saucer.

No. But I bet you observed his movements.

"Can you tell me how long Mr North lived in this street?"

"He moved in on—" The woman's hand went to her chin. "Let me see." She looked up towards the ceiling, pretending to think. Zoe wasn't fooled. She'd been about to blurt out the exact date on which Albert had moved in. Zoe wondered if the woman kept a diary of her neighbours' movements. That would be like gold dust.

"He moved in in December 2014. Yes, it was around this time, because I remember we'd just had the fayre at the school."

"So he's lived here eight years."

"That would make sense."

"Did he happen to tell you where he lived before?"

"I'm sorry, Detective. Like I say, I hardly knew him."

Zoe nodded. Connie would be able to trawl through council records. If Albert had lived elsewhere in the city, they'd find him. If he'd lived outside Birmingham it would take a little longer, but wasn't impossible.

"Did he seem happy in the last few weeks?"

"Happy? How am I to judge if one of my neighbours is *happy*?"

"Did he seem concerned about anything? Had his behaviour changed?"

"I've already told you, I hardly knew the man."

Zoe slumped against the kitchen counter. Perhaps she should give up and go to Albert's house, see if Adi had uncovered anything useful.

"Miss Garside, I don't suppose you have any record of

comings and goings on Avenue Road do you?" Zoe had seen the armchair in the window. The notebook. "I know sometimes it can be helpful for a concerned neighbour to keep records." She tried to keep her tone light. "For security reasons."

"Hmpf."

"If you did, it would be extremely useful to us."

"I don't do that sort of thing."

Fine. Zoe put down her cup. "Thank you for your time, Miss Garside. If you do remember anything else about Albert's movements before he disappeared, please tell us. My colleagues are at the house, and here's my phone number." She handed over her card.

"Do you have a landline?"

"My mobile is the best one to get me on."

"Yes, but..." Miss Garside cleared her throat and placed the card on the counter, next to her discarded cup and saucer.

Zoe gave her a nod and headed for the door.

CHAPTER THIRTY-ONE

ADI HAD WORKED through the downstairs of Albert North's house and bagged up anything that might have been used as a weapon. Prescription drugs, knives... it was unlikely any of them would be linked to the man's death, but it never hurt to be thorough.

He'd also been searching for paperwork or letters. The link to Croatia, the letter... perhaps there would be more letters, from the same sender. Perhaps there would be documents explaining Albert's link to Croatia. Albert North certainly wasn't a name that sounded Croatian, but then, people changed their names. Maybe he'd emigrated, and worked hard to appear British? Changed his name, adopted a local accent. It happened.

There was a knock on the front door as he passed through the hall to the stairs.

"It's open!" he called. PC Battar was out on the front garden, checking people in and out. He didn't need to worry about security.

"Adi." It was Zoe, zipping up a forensic suit as she stepped through the door. "Anything interesting yet?"

"Sorry. Nothing. I'm looking for paperwork or letters, like you said."

She nodded. "I want to know if there are any other letters in Croatian. Or any in English that might be linked to the letter you found in his coat."

"I've checked inside the biscuit tins, back of kitchen cupboards, even in the wheelie bins. If he was hiding something downstairs or in the garden, then he took it with him when he left the house."

"You on your way to search upstairs?"

"Rav has already made a start, but yes. I'm just heading up. It'll take a while, though."

Zoe smiled, leaning against the wall. "I know."

Adi intended to be thorough. He wasn't to be rushed at a crime scene, and nor were his team. FSIs under stress missed things. Zoe, thank God, understood that. Not like Frank Dawson, who would stand over the FSIs, mouth-breathing, until he got a result.

"You want to hang around?" he asked.

She looked up the stairs. "I'll come up with you, have a quick look. I won't stay until you're finished. I need to get back to the team."

It was mid-afternoon now, and Zoe's team had worked late last night. They all had – all except DS Kaur, at least. Adi knew that Zoe would be concerned for them. That was one of the things he liked about her. But he was learning to ignore those feelings, now she was with Carl Whaley.

"Come on then." He headed up the stairs and Zoe followed.

Upstairs the layout was similar to the floor below. A large

bedroom at the front spanning the width of the house, over the living room. A second bedroom behind it, over the unused dining room. And a bathroom over the kitchen.

Adi made for the front bedroom first. It was clear this was the room Albert had slept in: the bed had a dent at its centre and there were marks around the doorknob where the man had fumbled for it in the night.

The room was all but empty. A double bed sat against the window, a bedside table on one side which looked like it might fall apart if Adi touched it. In one of the alcoves was a small wardrobe.

Adi opened the wardrobe. There were few clothes inside, just a suit in a bag that smelled of mothballs, and three pairs of formal shoes.

"Looks like he took his clothes with him."

Zoe was behind him, peering over his shoulder. "Looks that way. Are you sure he kept his clothes in here?"

Adi bent down to pick up a bundle of black material from the floor of the wardrobe. A sock. "Looks like it."

"So he abandoned his house, taking all his clothes, to sleep rough. We'll need to ask Uniform how much stuff he was carrying when they encountered him."

"There were no belongings with him when he died."

"No." Zoe looked pensive. Sad even. "Maybe whoever killed him took them."

"You think it was as simple as that? He was attacked for his clothes?"

She stared at the wardrobe for a moment then blinked as if resurfacing from somewhere far away. "Sorry Adi. You don't know. The PM says it was poisoning. Thallium."

"That's rare."

"Difficult to get hold of. This wasn't just a random attack by another street sleeper."

"No." Adi turned back to the wardrobe. He pulled out the bag with the suit inside and went to the bed. It had an old-fashioned eiderdown spread neatly across it. He wiped the surface of the bedside table; dusty.

He placed the bag down on the bed and unzipped it, easing out the suit. He went through the pockets and examined the linings. Nothing. He opened up the bag and checked inside that. Still nothing.

"What about the shoes?" Zoe suggested. "People sometimes hide cash in them."

"They do." Adi went back to the wardrobe and lifted out the shoes. Three pairs of men's dress shoes, hardly worn. None of them had money or anything else hidden inside.

"Sorry," he said.

Zoe sighed. "I'd best be getting back to the office. Let me know if you find anything in the other rooms, yeah?"

"Will do." He watched as she left the room. She was wearing a bulky duffel coat that made her look twelve years old, despite her height. Still cute, though.

Adi turned back to the wardrobe as Rav, the third member of his team, entered the room.

"Mate," he said. "Help me pull this wardrobe away from the wall."

The two men grabbed each side of the wardrobe and shifted it forward. Adi peered round the back. There was nothing there.

"Damn."

"What about the bed?" Rav asked.

Adi nodded, turning towards it. The two of them lifted the eiderdown. It was heavy and smelled musty. The more he disturbed things in this room, the more Adi felt the essence of old man. It made him sad.

What happened, Albert? Who would want to poison an elderly man?

They removed the eiderdown, folded it and placed it in an evidence bag. They lifted the sheet below it, and the one below that. It was a flat sheet, folded around the mattress with perfect hospital corners.

The mattress was stained to one side, but there was nothing under the bedclothes. And no sign of anyone tampering with the mattress to hide anything inside.

"Let's lift the thing," he said. He and Rav each took a side of the mattress and hauled it up. The damn thing didn't have handles. He wondered how old it was, then shuddered, imagining the generations of skin cells inside it.

They shifted the mattress towards the bottom of the bed and dragged it onto the floor, partially leaning it against the wall at the end of the bed.

"What's that?" Adi said. There was a brown envelope on the bed base. It had been concealed by the mattress.

He looked up. "Go get Zoe."

Rav hurried out of the room. Adi stood still, staring at the envelope. He needed to get the photographer up here before he disturbed it.

But there was one thing he was sure of.

A slight man in his seventies didn't hide an envelope under a heavy mattress like that unless there was something important in it.

CHAPTER THIRTY-TWO

The atmosphere in the office was starting to make Connie uneasy.

DS Kaur was still here, along with her and Rhodri. Rhod had spent the afternoon on the phone, chatting with his mates from other teams. The DS had returned from the post-mortem looking like the cat that had got the cream, and then proceeded to pore over web pages about poisons and previous incidents involving thallium.

Connie herself was working on identifying where the thallium might have come from. She'd trawled the system for cases where it had been seized or examples of it being used in the UK, and drawn a blank.

Thallium was used in glass and lens making, mainly in China and Kazakhstan. Especially Kazakhstan.

Connie had no idea where Kazakhstan was. She knew it was somewhere in Central Asia but apart from that, nothing. She'd been hoping maybe it wasn't too far from Croatia.

But no. Kazakhstan and Croatia might both have once

CHAPTER THIRTY-TWO

been part of the Communist bloc, but apart from that, there was no link. And they were thousands of miles apart.

She sighed.

The DS looked up from her desk. "All OK, Connie?"

"I'm trying to find any hint as to where the thallium might have come from. Not getting anywhere. Are there any other examples you know of where it was used in poisoning cases?"

"Not for decades." DS Kaur stood up and rounded the desks. She looked over Connie's shoulder at the screen, which had technical information on the properties of thallium. "Keep digging, though. I've heard good things about your research skills."

Connie rolled her neck. She was tired. Her mum had been nagging her to come home more often, to see more of Zaf. She wanted to see her little brother, but she had a job to do. Zaf would understand; her mum, not so much. And besides, Connie had her own place now, a flat in Ladywood. There was damp on the kitchen wall, but it was hers.

She felt a hand on her shoulder: the DS. She stiffened. DS Kaur had only been in the team a matter of hours and already Connie was convinced she wouldn't enjoy working for the woman. Her expectations had been low, she knew. But still...

"Keep digging," the DS said. The hand lifted from Connie's shoulder, and she felt about a stone lighter. DS Kaur went back to her own desk.

Connie had to think about something else for a while. That way, her subconscious might help her with the thallium research. Move away from the problem, refuse to shine a light on it, and sometimes it sorted itself out.

The letter Adi had found, the one in Croatian. It had been bugging her. The contents made no sense, and she wanted to see for herself what language it was in.

She brought up the photo of the letter and a website explaining the differences between the various Slavic languages. Poking her tongue between her teeth, Connie scanned it, picking out details. Specific letters. Accents.

She stopped.

Croatian, they'd said.

According to this website, it was impossible to tell the difference between written Croatian and written Bosnian. Not unless you were a native speaker who knew how fluent users wrote in the two languages. As far as the words and letters were concerned, they were identical.

She leaned back in her chair. Had the FSIs considered that the letter might be in Bosnian?

She thought for a moment, then brought up a photo of Albert North. This was one the FSIs had found in his house, a posed portrait from when the man was in younger. Not long after he'd moved into his house in Avenue Road.

She entered it into Google images and typed in *Bosnia*. She hit search.

Hundreds of results came up. Connie scrolled through them. Most of them were irrelevant, or indecipherable.

On the second page of results, she found one from a local news site. It had a photo of Albert. At least, it looked like Albert. In fact, it looked a lot like the photo she'd entered herself.

Connie scanned the page.

"Oh."

Rhodri looked up from his desk. "What?"

"I've got something," she said.

CHAPTER THIRTY-TWO

"What?"

The DS was at her desk. She looked up. "Connie. What's up?"

"It's..."

"What?" repeated the DS.

"It's Albert North. He isn't really Albert North at all."

CHAPTER THIRTY-THREE

"Zoe!"

Zoe turned to see Rav running out of Albert North's house. She'd paused to look across at the park and was wondering whether it might be a useful place to look for witnesses. If something had happened to Albert North that had made him abandon his home, then maybe someone walking through the park, or supervising their kids playing, might have seen what it was.

But it had been two weeks ago. No one would remember.

"Rav? What's up?"

"We've found something." He skidded to a halt beside her, out of breath. "There's an envelope hidden under the mattress in Albert's bedroom."

"What kind of envelope?"

"Brown, A4 or similar. Thick. Thick enough that he'd have felt it when he slept."

"Was it visible when the bed was made?"

"No. The mattress sags like hell and that eiderdown's heavy. And the mattress took two of us to move."

"Albert North was slim. Elderly."

"Exactly. A man like that doesn't go to that sort of effort to hide something without good reason. It's right in the middle, too: I don't think it's just been slid in."

"He could have used something to make it easier."

"Maybe. But either way, Adi thought you'd want to know right away."

"Thanks. Sorry." She started walking back towards the house, Rav at her side. "Have you opened it?"

"Adi'll be waiting for the photographer to capture it before he moves it."

"Good. It could be a significant piece of evidence."

"Or it could be an old guy being paranoid with his bank statements."

"I doubt it."

They reached the house and Zoe stopped to pull her forensic suit back on.

"Adi!" Rav called up the stairs. "I've got Zoe!"

"Bring her up."

Rav looked at Zoe, his face alight with the adrenaline of a find. She zipped up her suit and gave him a grin in response. "Go on, then."

He took the stairs two at a time. Zoe followed more slowly; she was fifteen years older than Rav. She knew that, because Connie had told her.

The photographer was at the end of the bed, taking shots of the envelope on the bed base. Adi stood to one side, his fists clenching and unclenching. He was eager to open it.

He raised his eyebrows at the photographer. She nodded and he approached the bed.

"Rav's right," Zoe said. "It's right in the centre." It wasn't only in the middle of the bed. It had been placed squarely there, all its sides parallel with the edges of the bed. If Albert had shoved it under the mattress and it had settled that way by accident, it would be quite something. Not to mention that their efforts would have moved it.

"Yeah," said Adi. He stopped, leaning over the bed. "Do you want to open it?"

"You do it." It was Adi's find. Zoe sensed the excitement pouring off him and his colleague.

Adi gave the photographer a glance and she nodded again. He reached out to pick up the envelope.

"It's stuck."

"What?" Zoe asked.

"It's been stuck down."

"That would explain why it's so perfectly aligned."

"And why it stayed put. It means he would have had to move the mattress out of the way to do it. He couldn't have just slid it in."

"No mean feat," added Rav.

"No," said Zoe. She thought of Albert North at the crime scene. Maybe he'd had more bulk before he'd gone on the streets. But he wasn't a tall man. And even if he had been stronger, it still meant this was important.

"What's it stuck with?"

Adi held out a hand. "Rav, I'll need a scalpel." He looked over his shoulder at Zoe. "It's glued down."

Rav opened a tool box, then handed a scalpel to Adi, who looked up at the photographer. She moved round him to get a better angle, firing off shots as he started to work.

Adi slid the scalpel beneath the envelope and began to ease it away from the bed. He moved slowly and carefully, his brow furrowed.

At last he'd loosened the entire layer of glue. "It wasn't covering the whole thing," he said. "Just around the edges."

Rav handed him a sample tube and Adi used the scalpel to transfer some of the dried glue into it. He sealed it and handed it back to Rav, who placed the tube in a case.

"Right." Adi straightened up, the envelope in his hands. He looked at Zoe. "You sure you don't want to do the honours?"

"You carry on."

"The flap has been stuck down, too. Probably licked. We'll take the envelope back to the lab and get a DNA sample from that after we've opened it."

"Good," said Zoe. There was always a chance the DNA they found might not be Albert North's. What if someone else had given him this envelope to hide here?

Adi eased open the flap. The envelope was thick, more than just a couple of sheets of paper inside.

He pulled out its contents one by one, and laid them on the bed. Some of the documents were browning with age. Some had stains. Others were newer and looked barely touched.

Zoe stood next to Adi and scanned the documents laid out in front of them on the bed base. "What are they?"

"They're in Croatian, by the looks of it."

She walked around to the other side of the bed. One of the newer documents was in English. She picked it up.

"Not all of them. This one's from the Home Office."

Her phone rang, making her almost drop the sheet of paper. She placed it back down on the bed, her heart racing.

"Hang on." She moved away from the bed, removed her gloves and placed them in her pocket. She took out her phone. It was Connie.

"Connie, this had better be good."

"Sorry, boss. You in the middle of an interview?"

"No. Adi's found... what have you got, Connie? It must be urgent if you're not going to DS Kaur."

"I'm with her. She told me to call you."

"OK. What is it, Connie?"

"Albert North wasn't Croatian. And his name wasn't Albert North."

"Go on."

"He was Bosnian. His name was Aleksander Nadarević."

"Aleksander?"

"Common Slavic name, according to my research."

Adi pointed at one of the documents on the bed. "Aleksander Nadarević. That's the name on this."

Zoe nodded. She held the phone tighter. "Where did you get this, Connie?"

"A photo of him online. Local news report; rags to riches story."

"You sure it's him?"

A pause.

"Connie?"

"Yes. I'm sure."

Zoe looked up at Adi. "Well. That would explain a few things."

CHAPTER THIRTY-FOUR

Albert North's real name was at the top of the board, next to the one Zoe assumed he'd taken when he'd arrived in the UK.

"OK," she said. "So we have a potential reason for Albert leaving home."

"Aleksander, you mean," said Rhodri.

"Aleksander." She remembered Freya Garside's reaction when she'd tried to find out if the woman knew anything about his past. How would she and her neighbours react when they found out the truth?

"Someone found out his real identity, threatened to expose him," suggested Layla.

"It's the most likely explanation," Zoe replied. "But we can't assume. We need to find out if anyone visited him at home in the days before he left. And we need to know exactly when he did leave."

"I've been onto his electricity supplier," Connie said. "And his phone provider. I've asked if they can look into usage from his address in the last three weeks, see if there's a point at which he stopped turning on the lights or making calls."

Connie's idea was spot on. "He was in his seventies," said Zoe. "He'll still have used his landline. Get all the numbers for calls to and from that line over the last month, too."

"I've already asked for that."

Layla was looking at Connie, a smile playing on her lips. Was she impressed with the DC's initiative, Zoe wondered.

"OK. Unfortunately there's no CCTV on Avenue Road, so we can't find out if he had any visitors that way. Connie, are we anywhere with the CCTV from the Council House?"

"Still waiting on it."

"You asked for it yesterday."

"That was a Sunday."

"And today's Monday. What are they playing at?"

"Sorry, boss. I'll chase it."

"Thanks. OK, so we're going to need to talk to someone with knowledge of Albert from when he was Aleksander."

"The article I found," said Connie. It said he disappeared after the Bosnian war."

"You're sure? What language was it in?"

"Russian, I think. I used Google translate."

"We need to get a translator on this, to be sure."

"I can sort that," said Connie.

"Thanks," replied Zoe. "There's a lot of animosity over those wars. I think we can safely assume that someone was looking for him."

"But he was Bosnian," said Connie. "They weren't the ones committing the war crimes, were they?"

Zoe considered. "There must be a reason he hid that document."

"Yeah."

"In which case, if we approach one of those organisations, we might end up talking to the person who threatened to reveal his identity."

"Or who killed him," Rhodri said.

Zoe felt her heart skip a beat. "You think he was killed in revenge for something he did in the war?"

He shrugged. "What else?"

Zoe blew out a breath. Where to start? They had to find out what they could about Albert's – Aleksander's – history, without attracting the attention of the very people who might be responsible for his death.

She dragged a hand through her hair. She was tired. It was gone seven now and her eyes were sore. She'd left Adi at the house supervising the photographer, making sure they had photos of all the files. Printouts would be on her desk in the morning.

In the meantime, all the agencies they might speak to would be shut and her brain felt like mush.

"OK," she said. "Let's reconvene in the morning. Go home everyone, get a good night's sleep. This feels like a curved ball, but it puts us closer to solving this case." She looked at Rhodri. "In time for Christmas."

He blushed. "Boss."

"Good. Layla, can I have a quick chat with you before you head off?"

Layla's back stiffened but her facial expression didn't budge. "Of course."

"Thanks. Go on, Connie and Rhodri. Rest, and we can crack on with this new lead in the morning."

CHAPTER THIRTY-FIVE

"How are you finding it, settling in to a new team?"

"Fine, thanks for asking."

Zoe and Layla were in the main office, standing next to the board. Connie and Rhodri had left, each of them shooting Zoe a questioning look as they did so. She'd taken plenty of opportunities to chat alone with Mo; there was no reason this should be any different. And her DCs had to get used to that.

"Connie and Rhodri being OK with you? No problems managing their work?"

"None at all, boss. They're good DCs. You're right." Layla's nose twitched.

Zoe pushed back a smile. Layla was trying to impress Zoe, and she knew how close the team was. Whatever her views on Connie and Rhodri, she would flatter them.

Zoe sat in Connie's chair, letting her arms flop on the armrests. She rubbed her forehead; she sensed a headache coming on. "Was it strange being at a post-mortem, after all this time?"

Layla, still standing, flinched. "It hasn't been that long."

"I looked at your file," Zoe replied. "You haven't investigated a murder for over five years."

"Six, actually. One in Longbridge. But no. ACC Jackson's death was investigated by Force CID and by the time his involvement in the corruption around the Canary case was uncovered, that was water under the bridge."

"How did that make you feel?"

Layla frowned. "I don't get you."

"Assistant Chief Constable Jackson was the highest ranking officer in this force ever to be identified as corrupt. But because he died before your team was able to nail him, that fact was never publicly revealed. Did that make you feel as if PSD were being sidelined?"

"It's not my job to judge decisions made by senior officers."

Zoe snorted. "Come on, Layla. This is just you and me here."

Layla turned to look at her. "Surely you can ask DI Whaley what his views are on the subject."

Zoe's eyes widened. "Touché. OK, I'll stop asking you about your time in PSD. I can see how it might be something you don't want to discuss. But I want to clear the air between us."

"So do I, boss. You do know, when I interviewed you, I genuinely—"

Zoe held up a hand. "You were doing your job, Layla. There was good reason to look at the people I was associated with and wonder if I was corrupt too. I'm sure even Carl had his doubts from time to time."

"If you don't mind me saying, boss, during Ian Osman's trial, when you and Detective Superintendent Randle went off in search of Trevor Hamm. It seemed… out of character for you."

"First off, let's not glorify the man by using his title. David Randle was bad news. And yes, maybe I shouldn't have done what I did. But it helped to make the link between Randle and Hamm. I wanted him to think he could trust me, and then he might reveal something he wouldn't have let slip otherwise."

"You'd worked with him for many years. I can imagine it was hard to change your behaviour towards him."

"Oh, he was always a bit dodgy. It wasn't hard at all. And Lesley made it clear I wasn't to trust a word that came out of his mouth. Even if she didn't know I was investigating him for Carl."

DCI Lesley Clarke had been Zoe's boss, until a year ago when she'd transferred to Dorset. Zoe hadn't spoken to her in a while, not since she'd helped her with a case down there that was too sensitive for Lesley to share with her new team. She made a mental note to get in touch, check up on her old mentor.

"Boss, if you don't mind, I'd rather just focus on this case. Not rake over old coals. I won't be in your team for long, and I don't see how it helps."

"No." Zoe hadn't been intending to bring up the subject of David Randle and his links to organised crime. "You don't have any ambitions to stay in Force CID long term?"

"I'm hoping for a transfer to Anti-Terrorism."

"Really." Zoe could see how Layla's skills might be useful there. The undercover experience and other expertise an officer gained in PSD could offer a lot to Anti-Terror. And there wouldn't be many officers in the division whom Layla had investigated in her previous capacity. "Well, if you need a reference..."

"I have one from DI Whaley." Layla blushed, ever so slightly.

Zoe smiled. "Carl never spoke about you to me, but I could tell he thought highly of you."

Layla's blush deepened. "Thanks."

Zoe stood up. "So. I'm glad you're settling in OK. Let's hope we get this case settled quickly. Then we can all enjoy our Christmas."

CHAPTER THIRTY-SIX

Zoe's house was dark as she arrived home. She opened the door to an empty hallway and slung her coat at the hook, missing and watching as it fell to the floor.

"Yoda!" she called as she walked into the living room.

The cat was curled up on an armchair. It yawned, stretched and jumped down to pad across to Zoe and rub itself against her legs.

"Come on you, let's get you some food."

"Miaow."

Zoe bent down to ruffle the top of Yoda's head as the two of them walked into the kitchen, the cat weaving in and out of Zoe's legs as they moved.

She pulled a box of biscuits out of a cupboard and shook them into Yoda's bowl.

"There you go. Yum."

The cat bent over the bowl and crunched noisily. Zoe leaned against the counter and watched for a few moments.

"Where's Carl, eh?"

She knew she couldn't expect him to wait in her house

for her. Maybe he was in his own flat, wondering when she would show up.

Had she said she'd be there tonight? She was losing track of their schedule. When they moved to Cumbria they could get a place together, Carl said. It was just one of the ways he was trying to tempt her. But she liked it here. She'd grown up in Birmingham, built a career and raised a son. Could she just up and leave?

She trudged through to the living room and switched on the TV. She'd check her post and then she'd call Carl.

In the hall, she turned on the light and bent to the doormat to pick up the pile of post. Two circulars, a letter about council tax and an envelope that looked a lot like a Christmas card.

Zoe had long since stopped sending Christmas cards and she knew most of her friends had too. The only likely candidate was Mo.

She checked the postmark: Staffordshire. Not Scotland.

Who was it from?

She wandered back into the living room and used her fingernail to prise open the envelope. Yoda was back in the armchair, licking her paws.

"Hey. That's my chair."

Yoda looked up at Zoe, gave a long, slow blink, then rested her chin on her paws. It looked like Zoe was on the sofa tonight, although she knew that within ten minutes of sitting down, the cat would be on her lap.

She pulled the card out of the envelope as she sat down. It was anodyne; a photo of a snowy scene, no obvious religious references. She opened it up.

She dropped the card like it was on fire.

She sat back on the sofa, her hand on her chest.

Why?

She stared down at the card, which had landed with its back upwards. It was a charity card, for McMillan.

Why are you sending me a Christmas card?

He was trying to mess with her head.

She thought of the postmark: Staffordshire. Was that where he was living? If it was, then he was a fool.

If it wasn't, then…

She shook her head.

"Miaow." Yoda had arrived on the sofa next to her.

"Not now, Yoda."

"Miaow."

She stroked the cat's back and looked down at the card.

Was it evidence? Might it become evidence in the future?

No. Don't be daft. He'd done a deal with the CPS, been offered a place in witness protection. In return for giving them Trevor Hamm and his organised crime associates.

But still…

If anyone from his old world knew where he was, his life could be in danger.

"Miaow." Yoda had a paw on her lap, trying to work her way up. Zoe put a hand on the cat's back.

"Yoda, what should I do?"

"Miaow."

She looked down at the card again. She straightened, pushing Yoda onto the sofa next to her, and went into the hall.

In the pocket of her coat were evidence bags. She opened one and reached down for the card, grabbing it with the corner of the bag and sliding it inside without making skin contact.

She had no idea if she was being paranoid, and she'd already handled the card with her fingers, anyway. But she knew damn well this was one card that wouldn't be displayed on her mantelpiece.

If Lesley was still here, she would have shown it to her. But Frank...

She wasn't going to show it to Frank.

It could go upstairs in her makeshift home office. Holding the evidence bag by the corner, she made for the stairs. Best to get it over with. She certainly didn't want Carl finding it.

Should she tell Carl? He'd been credited with the man's arrest, after all.

She held her breath as she walked up the stairs, the bag with the card inside at arm's length.

At the top she realised Yoda was following her.

"You're clingy today."

"Miaow."

She went into the office and placed the bag in a drawer. It would stay there, in case she should ever need it.

Should she tell Carl?

No. She would pretend it had never arrived.

"Miaow."

Zoe picked the cat up and tickled under its chin. Purring, Yoda rubbed against her face.

"Yoda, tell me something."

The cat continued to purr. Zoe headed down the stairs, her mind still racing. She looked into Yoda's face.

"Why the hell did David Randle think it appropriate to send me a Christmas card?"

CHAPTER THIRTY-SEVEN

Rav from Adi's team had brought copies of all the documents they'd taken from the envelope into the office, and left them on Zoe's desk. She rifled through them, trying to make sense of the Croatian. Or Bosnian, rather. Were the two languages really the same?

There were twenty sheets of paper making up what appeared to be twelve documents. Some were in English: immigration records, correspondence relating to Albert's arrival in the UK twenty-seven years ago. But the rest were in Bosnian. Some of them were typewritten and looked official. One had a stamp on it that looked like it was from the government. Others were handwritten letters.

There was also a passport and a set of identity papers in the name of Aleksander Nadarević. The name Connie had seen online.

So Albert had moved here from Bosnia in 1995, adopted a new identity and carved out a life for himself. Surely he couldn't have been the only person to do something like that? There would have been plenty of others fleeing the war, too.

Zoe had been a teenager when the Bosnian war had begun, oblivious to that kind of thing. She'd had no inclination to keep an eye on current affairs, so had no idea whether the UK had accepted Bosnian refugees.

The outer door opened and Rhodri entered. Zoe checked her watch; not like him to be the first in.

She opened her office door. "Rhod. This is a nice surprise."

He slung his wet coat up on a hook. "I'm motivated, boss. Want to get this case wrapped up for Christmas."

"I know you do. I'm motivated too. But we have to make sure we don't cut corners."

"No." He grinned. "The old DCI would never have stood for that."

He was right. Lesley had been a stickler for doing things correctly. Frank Dawson, not so much.

"She wouldn't," Zoe said. "And nor would I. I've got a job for you."

"Yeah?"

"What's the DS got you working on right now?"

"I've been talking to other units. Trying to piece together Albert's last couple of weeks."

"How's that going?"

"Not great."

"Shame."

"I've worked through everyone I can think of now. They've all got my number. I need to go over some witness statements from neighbours but I've got time if you need me, boss. Where d'you need me to go?"

"Not going anywhere for this one."

"Oh." His shoulders slumped.

"I want you to research the Bosnian war. Did the UK

accept refugees? On what terms? Is Albert on a list of refugees somewhere? Those Home Office documents, they could be the key. Talk to someone in Immigration, see if there's a record of him entering the country. Did he come alone, did he have family? What did he do back home? I want to know the context of Albert moving here. I'm convinced that the reason he left his house is related to those documents under his mattress."

"So why didn't he take them with him?"

She shook her head. "He still had access to the house. Maybe he was worried that if someone caught up with him on the streets, they'd take them from him."

"It doesn't make sense."

"Rhod, in the six years you've been in CID, how many victims or suspects have you seen acting logically?"

He frowned.

"Don't spend too long thinking about it," Zoe said.

"None?"

She smiled. "Exactly. Let's hope we can work out why Albert left his house, and who he was trying to keep away from. That person, if they didn't kill him, will lead us to the person who did."

CHAPTER THIRTY-EIGHT

Rhod was on the phone when Connie got in. The DI and the DS were in the the boss's office, heads down. Connie hurried to her desk, uneasy at being the last in. She'd been out with Rav last night, a gig at the Glee Club, and it had been a struggle to get up this morning.

She had to do better, if she was going to make Sergeant.

"Everything OK?" she hissed across the desks at Rhodri as she sat down. She nodded in the direction of the DI's office. "Something happened?"

He put his hand over the mouthpiece. "Not as far as I know." He lowered the hand. "It *is* urgent, mate. Murder case. Yeah, I know. Thanks. I'll wait to hear from you."

He almost threw the phone onto the desk. "Bloody Home Office."

"What you on to the Home Office for?"

"The boss has got me looking into Albert's past. Wants me to find out the circumstances of him coming here, like."

"What's her theory?"

"She hasn't got one, far as I can tell. But I'm thinking it was something hush hush."

Connie snorted. "You do know your eyes widened when you said *hush hush*? This isn't a Bond movie, Rhod."

His brow furrowed. "I do know that, Con."

Connie winced. It was too late now to tell him to stop calling her that.

"Anyway," he continued. "Can you give me a hand, if you're not busy?"

"I need to chase the council for the CCTV, but apart from that I was waiting to hear what the boss wants us to do." Her gaze flicked to the office. "Or the DS."

"This is for the boss, so I reckon you're OK helping me with it."

"Fair enough." It was ten past eight; nobody would have arrived at the council anyway. "What d'you need me for?"

"I'm looking into the Bosnian War. Trying to find out what Albert was up to when it was all happening."

"You think he was up to something?"

A shrug. "The boss just wants all the background, that's all. Where he lived, which side he was on."

"Which side he was on? He was Bosnian."

"Doesn't automatically follow."

"You think he was working for the Serbs?"

"Yugoslavians, they liked to call themselves back then."

"They were all Yugoslavian."

He eyed her. "D'you know a lot about it all?"

She shook her head. "I wasn't born. But I had a mate at college whose dad was from somewhere else in that neck of the woods."

"Bosnia?"

"Nah. Slovenia, I think. Somewhere that didn't have a war, but was nearby."

"And what did you learn from them?"

"Not much. The whole thing sounds like chaos to me. But there was ethnic cleansing."

"Bosnian Muslims. I know."

Connie rubbed her hands together. It was chilly in the office. On the way in, it had been threatening to snow. She knew how excited Zaf would be by a white Christmas. He might have been nineteen and a good two inches taller than when he'd left for uni, but at heart he was still the same little kid he'd been at primary school.

"OK," she said. "Where should I start?"

"Google. See if you can find records of Albert, Aleksander or anyone in his family. 1990 to 2000."

"No problem." Connie fired up her computer. She'd installed a search engine, one that she was confident was contrary to IT regulations, but which helped her in cases that dated back more than a few weeks. It allowed her to see websites as they would have been at key points in history. And even better, it let her compare different dates, including today's.

"OK," she said. "Those letters, do they tell us when Albert came to the UK?"

"Ninety-five. But we shouldn't be calling him Albert, really."

"I'm not calling him Aleksander until we know what he did that made someone kill him."

"He's just an old fella, Con. You can't think he deserved to die."

She sucked her teeth. "He wasn't such an old fella in 1995."

Rhodri gazed at her for a few moments, then blinked a few times and returned to his screen.

"OK," Connie muttered. "Looks like I've pissed Rhod off." And there was her thinking pissing Rhod off was one of the few things it was impossible to do.

She turned back to her computer and opened up the software. Albert's name was irrelevant; she needed to search for Aleksander Nadarević.

She typed it into the search engine. Hundreds of hits came up, mostly with either the same surname or first name.

She tried again, putting inverted commas around the two names so that only sites that included both of them in the correct order would come up. The list narrowed.

She added Bosnia and hit refresh. The list only lost half a dozen entries. Seemed like Nadarević was a Bosnian name.

She typed in the year Albert had come to the UK. Nothing.

Connie leaned back in her chair, wishing she'd brought some chocolate. She scrolled through what she had: eight hits.

She leaned in, peering down the list. Most of them would need translating. One had a photo of Albert, the same one she'd seen online before.

She clicked through to it. It was in Bosnian – or Croatian, she couldn't tell.

Biting her bottom lip, Connie hit translate.

Her breathing slowed. She leaned in further and read.

Shit.

She looked up from her desk. The boss and the DS were still in the office. Rhodri was on the phone.

Rhodri was always on the phone, while she was always online. Should she be more like him?

CHAPTER THIRTY-EIGHT

Rhodri was smiling, flirting with someone. That was how he got pally with people, encouraged them to tell him things they probably weren't supposed to.

If she wasn't so fond of Rhod, it would really bug her.

She looked back at the screen. None of that was important. This was.

She stood up and walked to the boss's door. She knocked twice.

The DS looked round. The boss looked up and frowned at the sight of Connie.

Connie smiled and knocked again. The boss beckoned her in.

Connie pushed the door open.

"You don't have to keep knocking like that," the boss said.

"Sorry."

"What is it?" asked Zoe. "You look like you've seen a ghost."

"I... I sort of have."

"What is it?" Zoe said.

Connie swallowed. "It's Albert. Aleksander, I mean."

"What about him?"

The DS had risen from her chair and was staring at Connie. Should she have got the two senior officers to come out to the outer office?

"You might want to see what I've found."

The DI stood up. The DS shook her head. "What is it, DC Williams?"

DC Williams. So formal. Connie gestured back towards her desk.

"I've found a news article about him."

"Another one?" The DS had an eyebrow raised. The DI was next to Connie now, a reassuring hand on her arm.

"It's OK, Connie. You look pale."

Connie shook her head. "He was..."

"He was what?" The boss's tone was soft. Was she being sympathetic, or patronising?

"He was a war criminal."

"What?" the DS asked. "You're muttering."

But the DI had heard. Her hand was tighter on Connie's arm.

Connie cleared her throat and looked up at the DS.

"It's Albert. Aleksander. He was wanted for war crimes in the Bosnian conflict."

CHAPTER THIRTY-NINE

The photograph from Connie's website was on the board, together with the crime scene photos and a more recent portrait of Albert from when he'd been living in Avenue Road.

Zoe stood staring at it, arms folded across her chest.

"This changes everything," said Layla.

Zoe nodded. "What else did you get from the news report?" she asked Connie. Rhodri was sitting off to one side, not even behind his desk. She'd given him the research task and he'd asked Connie to help him.

Was he sulking?

"Aleksander Nadarević was suspected of atrocities against Bosnian Muslims in 1992 and 1993. He was part of a unit based near Srebrenica. He was listed as one of over 160 individuals wanted by the international criminal court in The Hague."

"But he was Bosnian," said Layla. "Not Serbian."

"He was a Christian. Sided with the Serbs to rid his homeland of Muslims."

Rhodri whistled. "Nice guy."

Zoe walked to the board and stood with her back to it, facing the team.

"We don't care what sort of person Albert North was. What mattered is that he was murdered and we have to find out who killed him."

"He deserved it, judging by what he did," said Rhodri.

"Rhod, you know our job isn't to judge that kind of thing. No one gets to take the law into their own hands."

"Aleksander Nadarević did," said Connie. Her body language was tense. "Deciding who should and shouldn't live. Massacring innocents."

"Connie. I know it's hard. But try to put what he did out of your mind. He's still Albert North, a pensioner from Kings Heath."

"But he wasn't, was he?" said Rhodri. "He's a butcher."

"Was," said Layla. "And the important thing about this find – well done, Connie – isn't what it tells us about Albert's personality, but what it tells us about whoever might have killed him."

"Aleksander," Connie said. "Let's stop calling him Albert. Makes him sound too nice. Too normal."

Zoe looked at the DC. She could sympathise. Maybe Aleksander had been a war criminal. Maybe he did deserve to be brought to justice. But not without a proper process. And not by whoever had killed him and dumped him in the city centre.

"We need to follow up any leads with regard to vigilantes," she said. "Find out if there were any groups hunting down Bosnian – or Serbian – war criminals. Rhod, you can carry on with your research into Bosnia, expand it to include that question."

CHAPTER THIRTY-NINE

"Right, boss."

"Connie, I want you to go back to the shelters. If anyone made contact with him that way, we need to know about it. And where the hell is the bloody CCTV from the Council House?"

"I'm told it'll be with us before lunchtime," Connie said.

"About bloody time too."

The door to the office opened. Zoe turned to see Frank in the doorway. He jerked his head to beckon her out.

She turned back to the team. "One moment, folks. I need to update the DCI."

She slipped out of the room and closed the door behind her, leaning against it. She was peeved that Frank hadn't knocked; he normally did when he thought he might be interrupting. Not that he needed to; he was her senior officer, after all.

"Frank, you need to know where we're at with the Albert North case." She placed a hand on the wood of the office door behind her. "We have an identity for the victim in addition to the original one."

"I know."

She stopped, her mouth open, the words that were forming there suddenly stuck.

"You know?"

A nod. "I've had a call, Zoe. We've been told to stand down."

"What?"

"We're off the case. Not just you, but Force CID in general."

"On whose say-so?"

"Home Office."

"*Who* in the Home Office?"

"I can't tell you that, Zoe. But you'll need to hand all your case files to me, and be off the case by lunchtime."

CHAPTER FORTY

"I know it's disappointing," Zoe said. "But look at it this way. You'll all be able to enjoy your Christmases."

Connie and Rhodri had long faces. They were both professionals; they didn't like to leave a job unfinished. And the fact that Frank was refusing to tell them why they'd been pulled off the case made both DCs that bit more determined to carry on.

"I guess my time in your team was about as short as it could have been," Layla said.

"Sorry about that," replied Zoe. "What will you do now?"

"Take a long Christmas break, I suppose."

"Paid?"

Layla gave Zoe a *mind your own business* look and said nothing. Of course she'd be paid. She was between assignments, still a member of West Midlands Police.

"He said we can't do anything?" Connie asked. "Nothing at all?"

"You know what it's like," Zoe told her. "The case is too sensitive."

"Someone in the government wants to hush it up, like," said Rhodri.

"It might be nothing like that," Zoe replied. "More likely they want to allocate the proper resources to it."

Connie snorted.

"But in the meantime," Zoe continued, "the DCI has asked us to package up everything we have and send it to him. Adi and his team'll be doing the same."

"How do they feel about it?" Connie asked.

"I haven't spoken to them." Zoe imagined Connie would know the answer to that question later, when she saw Rav.

Connie shook her head and grunted. She checked her watch. "What d'you want us to do for the rest of the day?"

Layla was by her desk, opening drawers. She wouldn't have amassed much in the way of belongings while she'd been here, but she was packing up all the same.

"Thanks for your help," Zoe said to her. "It's been good working with you."

Layla raised an eyebrow, opened her mouth to speak, then hesitated. "You too," she said finally.

Zoe smiled and put out a hand. Layla took it.

"See you again," Zoe said. "Good luck with the Anti-Terror Unit."

"I'm not there yet." Layla put the last of the contents of her desk into a rucksack and made for the door.

"Hang on," said Connie. Layla stopped, her hand on the door.

"What is it?" Zoe asked.

Connie looked up. "It's alright. It's nothing."

"You sure?"

A nod. Connie wasn't meeting Zoe's eye.

"What's up, Connie?"

CHAPTER FORTY

"Nothing. I just thought... I didn't think anything."

"What did you think? If it's something to do with the case, it might be useful for the Home Office investigation."

"I had a hunch about one of... one of the documents. I realised it was wrong. Ignore me."

"If you're sure."

"I am."

Rhodri was gazing at Connie, his expression puzzled.

"Rhod," Zoe said. "Make sure all the leads you've been following are documented. I want a file with the names of all the officers you've spoken to."

"None of those are official, boss."

"That makes no difference. If they can help, they can help."

"I don't want to get anyone into trouble."

"You won't. Everyone's just doing their job."

He twisted his lips together. "If you say so."

"I'm off, then." Layla had opened the door.

"See you around," Zoe said. She wondered if Layla would be on the phone to Carl as soon as she was out of the building, updating him. How close had the two of them been? Not like her and Mo, but they had worked together for a couple of years.

The door closed and Layla was gone. Zoe went to the board and started pulling photos off it. She held them over the bin.

"Don't do that, boss," Rhodri said.

"There's copies on HOLMES. We don't need these."

"Security. Put them through the shredder."

He was right.

"I'll do it," Connie said.

"You sure?"

Connie nodded, standing up from her desk. She tucked her phone into her pocket as she did so. "Sure. I need to get away from this room."

"I'm sorry, Connie. Rhodri too. I know how frustrating this is. But it happens."

"Yeah," Rhodri said.

"Sure," Connie added. She took the photos from Zoe and left the office.

CHAPTER FORTY-ONE

Freya was in her front garden, tending her rose bush, when it happened.

She looked up at the sound of voices, trying not to be conspicuous. There were two men outside Mr North's house, talking animatedly.

One of them wore a white outfit, the kind she'd seen on TV dramas. She imagined he was a forensics person. The other wore a suit. He had pulled up in a large, dark car. She hadn't seen him before.

She moved round so the rose bush was between her and the men. She had a perfect view through its branches.

The man in the suit was pointing at the house. The man in the white outfit turned back and looked at the upstairs windows.

What was happening?

Freya wondered if she should knock on Ruti's door, check that her neighbour wasn't being disturbed.

It was the neighbourly thing to do.

She pulled off her gardening gloves and placed them in

the basket she used for pruning. It was empty. She eased herself up from her crouching position, her back complaining, and took the basket to her house. Quickly, she deposited it in her porch, glancing back at Mr North's house repeatedly as she did so.

The men were still there.

She straightened her coat, a fleece she used for gardening, and made for Ruti's front door. She looked at the men as she approached, but they ignored her.

Rude.

From Ruti's front drive she could make out their voices. Something about transferring the investigation. The white-outfitted man was passing on information about evidence.

Freya stood very still, her gaze on Ruti's front door. She didn't want the men to think she was eavesdropping.

The man in the white outfit went to the front door of Mr North's house and put his head inside.

"Rav!" he called. "Pack everything up. We're to hand over all our evidence to the Home Office."

Freya put a hand to her chest.

The Home Office?

Why was the Home Office taking an interest in the death of her neighbour?

Ruti's door opened. Freya put a finger to her lips as Ruti appeared, willing her new friend to be quiet. She wanted to hear what else the men had to say.

"Freya," Ruti said. "How are you? Come in, I've just put the kettle on."

"Shush." Freya jerked her head sideways, towards the men.

Ruti looked puzzled. "Are you alright? You look... worried."

CHAPTER FORTY-ONE

Freya shook her head. "I'm fine," she muttered. "There's something happening." She jerked her head again.

"Oh." Ruti leaned forward to look around her door frame. "Do they have a suspect?"

The man in the suit had gone back to his car. The man in the white overalls had disappeared into the house. Freya pursed her lips.

"That kettle you've boiled," she said. "Would a cup of tea be available?"

CHAPTER FORTY-TWO

CONNIE SAT on the closed lid of the toilet in the Force CID offices, her phone open in front of her. An email had come in. An email she knew she should tell the boss about, but that she didn't want to.

Not yet.

She opened it up and clicked the link. She sat for a moment while she took it in.

What did it mean?

It wasn't her job to investigate this now. She should send this to the boss, include it as part of the bundle of evidence that was making its way to the Home Office.

But what she'd seen...

It had shocked her.

She clicked on it again. The video was perhaps two minutes long. Not much. But enough for her to recognise the two men.

One of them was Albert North. Aleksander Nadarević.

The other...

CHAPTER FORTY-TWO

She hadn't met him, but she'd seen a photo, on his employer's website. And she'd spoken to him on the phone.

It didn't make sense.

She fired off a text. A reply came back within seconds. *What's up?*

Meet me outside the front of the building. Two minutes.

Connie flushed the toilet, plunged her phone into her pocket and opened the cubicle door. There was no one outside.

She washed her hands and looked at herself in the mirror. Her face was pale. It was time for a break, and Connie knew it. She should be welcoming this opportunity to ease off a little.

But Albert North was dead. He'd been dumped in the city centre, at a time when someone should have been around to see what was happening, yet no one had come forward. And after she'd discovered the kind of man he was...

Connie wanted to know why. And who.

Two minutes later, she was at the front of the building. This wasn't the most private of spaces, but then, she didn't want to be too mysterious.

Rhodri came out of the front doors, his shoulders hunched against the cold.

"Everything OK, Con? You sounded like it was urgent."

She handed him her phone. "Play it."

She watched his face as he did so. His expression went from puzzled, to shocked, to incredulous, and then back to puzzled again.

"Where did you get this?" he asked as he handed the phone back.

"Council House CCTV."

"That was what came in while the boss was telling us to pack up?"

"Yeah."

"You've got to tell the boss."

"She'll hand it over to DCI Dawson. She has to."

A shrug. "That's up to her. But what are you planning on doing, going off and investigating this after being told to steer clear?"

She shrugged.

"You're right." Connie pressed the button on her phone to blank the screen and pocketed it, wishing she'd brought a coat with her. "What d'you think she'll do?"

"She'll do what she's told."

"She doesn't always."

"She hasn't got the DCI to push against any more. The old DCI. She'll toe the line."

Connie wrinkled her nose. "I want to know how he died. And I want an explanation for what's in this video."

"Show it to me again," Rhodri said.

Connie handed over her phone. The two of them huddled over it, watching the video.

It showed Albert North sitting on the steps in Chamberlain Square. A man approached him, holding something. Albert stood up, and the man passed him the object. Albert turned away, his hand going up to his face. The man grabbed him by the arm, and Albert turned back. There was no audio on the recording, but it looked like he shouted something before running away towards Victoria Square and the spot where he'd been found.

"What's the time stamp on this?" Rhodri asked.

"Sixteen minutes past midnight, Sunday morning."

Rhodri nodded. On the screen, Albert was heading

towards New Street, almost tripping over himself in his haste. He looked unsteady on his feet. Drugged, already?

The other man followed him, and grabbed Albert as he slowed next to the stall where they'd found him. Albert turned to the man, his movements jerky, and slumped against him.

"He's drugged him," Connie said. "He gave him the thallium."

"I thought it'd been slipped into his food."

"He gave him something. Maybe food."

Rhodri nodded as, onscreen, Albert stumbled and fell to the ground next to the stall where they'd found him. Connie felt her heart rise into her mouth as she saw Albert stumble for the last time and fall to the ground next to the stall.

The other man lifted his arms and started dragging the older man round the back of the stall.

"How could he have thought he'd get away with it?" Rhodri asked.

"No idea." There were cameras everywhere in that part of town.

The man deposited Albert out of sight, in the darkness behind the stall. He looked up, towards Victoria Square. The area was quiet, no witnesses.

What were the chances of that?

"Wait," said Rhodri.

"I know."

The man lifted his arms over his head as if stretching. Dragging Albert had taken it out of him. Connie and Rhodri watched, Rhodri's hand on Connie's arm, as he walked off down New Street.

"He's going the wrong way," Rhodri said.

"He might have been coming from the shelter, not heading towards it."

"True."

After a few minutes, the man disappeared from view.

"It's him alright," Rhodri said.

"We need to talk to him."

"We need to tell the boss."

Connie shivered. "OK."

Rhodri squeezed her arm. "It's the right call, Con. This is too big for you and me."

"Maybe."

"What d'you think she'll say?"

"She'll be pissed off. Suddenly we have a concrete lead and she can't take it forward."

"She'll want to speak to him."

"Maybe."

Rhodri pulled away from Connie, heading back to the building. "Come on. Let's do it before you change your mind."

CHAPTER FORTY-THREE

"Frank," Zoe said. "We've packaged it all up and it's on the system."

"Thanks, Zoe. I appreciate you doing this so quickly."

"Do you know why the Home Office wants us off the case?"

They were in Frank's office, the room that had once been Lesley's. Frank had removed most of Lesley's clutter from the desk and replaced it with his own, all of which seemed to be football-related. He was clearly an Aston Villa fan.

"Sorry, Zoe. Orders from above. No details. Just wrap up the case, forward the files and draw a line under it."

"OK. There's an aggravated burglary case in Northfield that we haven't completely wrapped up yet. We'll get that finished before Christmas, and then my team can all take the leave they requested."

"The Northfield case isn't finished?"

"It's finished, Frank. We just haven't finalised all the paperwork. We figured a live murder inquiry was more important. Don't worry."

"I won't." He leaned back, fingers laced behind his head. "What are your Christmas plans?"

"Nicholas is back from Uni. It'll be me and him."

"No Carl?"

"He has to go and see his mum and a phalanx of aunties in Manchester."

"Poor DI Whaley. You're not tempted to join him?"

Zoe eyed him. "What are your plans, Frank?"

"Diane and the girls. Diane's mum. The usual."

"Well, I hope you enjoy it."

He blinked at her a few times. "This one will be hard for you."

"'Cos of Carl not being around?"

"Because of your mum."

"My mum never spent Christmas with us."

"Oh. I just assumed…"

Zoe stood up. "Never assume, Frank. It makes for lousy detective work."

"Fair enough. Let me know when the paperwork for the Northfield case is wrapped up, yeah?"

"Yeah." She rounded the chair and left the room.

Back in the office, Connie had returned and Rhodri was looking agitated. The two of them jumped when she entered, both rising from their desks.

"Boss, we need a word," Rhodri said.

"You need to finish early for Christmas? Your mum'll think she's a dragon in shit."

"It's not that, boss."

Zoe looked from him to Connie. The DC's breathing was shallow and she clutched her phone to her front.

"What is it?"

CHAPTER FORTY-THREE

Connie looked from Zoe to the door and back again. "Can we go in your office?"

"Of course you can. What the hell is it? Put me out of my misery, won't you?"

Rhodri had the door open. He all but shoved Connie inside and held out a hand to do the same to Zoe before thinking better of it.

Once in the office, Zoe sat in her chair and faced the two DCs. Connie's fingertips were sweeping up and down the surface of Zoe's desk, while Rhodri tugged at his tie.

"What?" Zoe snapped. If they didn't get to it soon, she would have to shake it out of them.

Connie put her phone on the desk. "CCTV came through. From the Council House."

Zoe looked at the phone. "What's it doing on there?"

"I was the one who requested it, so it came straight to my inbox. I wanted to check it."

"You took it out of the office."

"I... sorry. I knew you were busy wrapping things up."

"The file is closed now. I've handed it all over to Frank."

"Which means that if we do this..." Rhodri began.

Zoe eyed Connie's phone again. *Shit.* The DCs had spent too much time watching her. She needed them to stick to the rules, if they were to have any chance of getting promoted.

"What's on there?" she asked. "What have you seen?"

"We think..." Connie began.

Rhodri grabbed Connie's shirt. "It's Albert North. And his attacker. You can see him being drugged. Keeling over like, then being dragged round the back of that stall."

"You say his attacker," Zoe said. "Who? Can you make them out?"

Rhodri nodded, his cheeks red. "You can."

"Who, then?"

Rhodri looked at Connie, who licked her lips.

"Jimmy Kirk," she said. "It's the bloke from the shelter. He killed Albert."

CHAPTER FORTY-FOUR

"You've put me in a very difficult position," Zoe said. She'd watched the video with them, twice. Connie's phone was in her hand.

"Sorry, boss," replied Connie.

"You knew about this while we were wrapping up the case files, and you snuck out of the building to go and look at it." She looked between the two DCs. "You even got Rhodri to go outside with you."

Rhodri's cheeks were flushed. "Sorry, boss."

"There is one silver lining."

"What?" Connie asked, her eyes filling with hope.

Zoe looked at her for a moment, weighing up whether she should say what was on her mind.

"DS Kaur doesn't know about it," she said eventually.

"No," muttered Rhodri.

"Is that helpful?" Connie asked.

Zoe sighed. "The two of you want to follow this up. You want to go and speak to Jimmy Kirk and find out what he's up to in this video. You want to know if there's an innocent explanation. Although if he can come up with a convincing one I'll be bloody impressed."

"Well...," Rhodri said.

Zoe shook her head. "We've been told to drop the case. Just because there's an important piece of new evidence, doesn't mean we can ignore a direct order."

"The DCI doesn't know about the video." Connie's voice was small.

"*I* do, though," Zoe said. "I do."

She looked at the board. They'd removed the photos but they hadn't yet wiped off the writing. Albert's name was at the top, along with Aleksander's.

"Show me the video again."

Connie pressed the play button. The three of them watched in silence as Jimmy Kirk approached Albert North, handed him something which Albert put to his mouth, then dragged the older man behind the stall after he collapsed.

"We don't know what that is that he's given him," Zoe said. "It might not be the thallium."

The DCs said nothing.

"But the fact that he's dragging him behind the stall..." Zoe ran her hand through her hair, tugging as she went. "It looks pretty conclusive."

"It does," said Connie.

Zoe eyed her. "I'm sorry, Connie. I have to hand this over to Frank with the rest of it."

Connie blinked back at her. Then she lowered her eyes. "I know you do."

Zoe felt a weight lift from her chest. "I'm glad you see it that way, Connie." She looked up. "You too, Rhod."

CHAPTER FORTY-FOUR

"Yes, boss."

"Good. This is on which email account, Connie?"

"Mine."

"Forward it to the team inbox, and to me personally. I'm going to see Frank."

CHAPTER FORTY-FIVE

Avenue Road was quiet.

All the police and forensics vehicles that had been parked along the street had gone, and the front garden of Albert's house was empty.

Freya sat in Ruti's front bay window, watching. Luckily Ruti had net curtains, and Freya could see through them clearly enough; she didn't like to think of herself as a curtain twitcher.

"What do you think's happened?" asked Ruti from her spot on the sofa. She kept checking the clock on the far wall and shifting in her seat. Freya wondered if this was because she lived next door to a murder victim, or because she had things to do.

Things could wait.

"I think we should go round there," Freya said, after staring at the empty front garden next door for more than twenty minutes.

"Is that wise? Last time we – you – did that, that detective turned up."

CHAPTER FORTY-FIVE

Freya sniffed the air. There was something lighter about it, with all those people gone. "Mr North might have dependants. Heirs, even. They'll want to know that the house is locked and secure."

"Do you think the police would have left it unlocked?"

Freya turned back to Ruti. "They've been waltzing in and out for the last twenty-four hours. They didn't seem too concerned about security then."

"But there was an officer standing outside all the time. Surely no one wou—"

Freya put up a hand to stop her friend. "We'll check. Then we'll come back here." She turned in her chair. "I'm sorry, do you have things to do? Christmas preparations, or...? What is it you celebrate, anyway?"

"We celebrate Christmas. Among other things."

"Good." Freya stood up. "Come on then. The quicker we do this, the quicker we can relax. And you can be getting on with your chores."

Freya envied Ruti. She wished she had a large family to cater for at this time of year. Instead, she would be travelling to her sister's on Christmas Eve. Staying for two nights, as short a visit as she could get away with without appearing antisocial. Her sister Charlotte was married to the dullest man Freya had ever met, and her two adult children weren't much better.

"I don't think—" Ruti began.

"Do you want me to go alone again?"

Ruti rubbed her fingertips together. "I'll be lookout, keep an eye on you from here."

Freya raised an eyebrow. "Fair enough. I won't be long." She held out her hand. "Do you have that key?"

"I thought you were just checking that the house was locked?"

"Just in case." Freya flattened her palm.

"Just a minute." Ruti let the room and returned with the keys to Mr North's house. The police had remembered to hand them back to her before they'd cleared out, at least.

Freya gave her a reassuring smile. "Thank you. I'll return them in two shakes of a dog's tail."

Ruti shrugged and looked unconvinced.

Freya drew back her shoulders and walked past Ruti into the hallway. She pulled open the front door and stood on Ruti's front drive, remembering the first time she'd spoken to the woman. It felt like a lot more than two days had passed since Albert North hadn't shown up for his Father Christmas duties.

She shivered. *Poor man*.

Ruti was on her front step. "I'll stay here, keep an eye out."

"Thank you." Freya left Ruti's front garden, slipped onto the pavement and turned into Mr North's garden. It was overgrown, weeds starting to take hold already. She tutted.

At the front door, she pushed the wood and leaned towards it.

"Hello?"

She gave another push. The door was locked. They'd remembered that, then.

But the back door might not be. Or they could have left a window open.

Not pausing to look up at the windows, she brought Ruti's key to the lock and opened the door.

She pushed it open and stepped inside.

"Hello?"

CHAPTER FORTY-FIVE

The house was emptier than it had been last time she'd been inside. Items had been removed and many of the surfaces were bare. Freya wondered if Mr North's family would ever get their belongings back.

Why had they abandoned it so suddenly? Did it have anything to do with what she'd heard? Something connected to the Home Office? Or had they solved the mystery? Was there a murderer under arrest?

Freya shuddered. Extremely inconsiderate of the police not to inform the neighbours, if that *were* the case.

She walked through to the kitchen. The table was empty, no sign of the envelopes that had been here before. Electrical items had been taken from the surfaces and there were patches of fingerprint dust on door fronts, countertops and windowsills. It made the place look grubby.

She turned at the sound of movement behind her. She leaned against the worktop, her heart racing.

Had that come from upstairs?

No. There could be no one upstairs. The police had left the house empty and she had only just come past the stairs.

"Hello? Is there somebody there?"

Freya opened a drawer, hoping to find knives. It was full of utensils and crockery, but no knives. Had the police taken them? Had one of them been used as a weapon against her neighbour?

Another shudder. But that made no sense. He'd died miles from here.

Another noise from beyond the kitchen door, the sound of a door closing. Freya felt her heart jump into her throat.

Where was Ruti? Why had she not sounded the alarm?

Freya scanned the room. There was a door, out to the

garden. She looked down at the keys in her hand. There were three of them on the ring.

Licking her dry lips, she hurried to the back door and fumbled with the keys.

Which one had she used in the front door?

Focus, you stupid old woman. She could do this.

The other keys were a different shape from the one she'd used to open the front door. One was bronze, the other silver.

She tried the bronze one. She jammed it into the lock and turned.

Nothing.

Swallowing, she grabbed the silver key. She slid it into the lock and it turned.

Thank heavens.

She turned the doorknob just as she heard another sound behind her. Glancing round, she saw a shape enter the room.

Freya almost dropped the keys. Her pulse rate had doubled and her hands were clammy. The key was slippery in her fingers.

Drop the key, she told herself. She didn't need it any more. She had to get out of this door, into the garden and then through the alleyway.

She turned the knob further, but it slid against her hands.

Damn arthritis. She hated doorknobs. Why couldn't people have handles?

At last the door shifted. She placed all her weight against it.

"Oh no, you don't." The person was in the kitchen, rounding the table to approach her. She screwed up her eyes, not wanting to look.

A hand fell on her arm. She froze. "I'm just... I'm going... Please..."

CHAPTER FORTY-FIVE

"Not so fast."

She turned to see the man. He'd pushed one of the kitchen chairs to one side and was stumbling over it to get near to her. His arm was outstretched, a firm hold on her own.

She shook her head. *No.* This was not how she was going to die.

She yanked her arm out of his and turned to the door. She threw it open and stumbled through.

Run, Freya. Run.

But her elderly, terrified legs wouldn't do it. She tripped on the step down from the kitchen to the yard outside, grabbing a garden chair to keep herself from falling to the ground. She heaved herself upright and turned towards the alleyway.

"Stop!"

She didn't turn towards the voice. Instead she looked away, in the direction of her escape route. Normally she would want to get a good look at the man, so she could help the police. But she felt somehow certain that if she looked into his eyes, her legs would melt.

Run.

She grabbed the corner of the wall where Mr North's kitchen ended. She pulled herself round, ignoring the scraping of brick on skin.

She could do this.

"No!"

He was outside.

Who was he? Was this the man who'd killed her neighbour?

She wasn't sticking around to find out.

She was round the corner now, making for the alleyway

at the side. There was a gate. She fumbled with the latch, cursing her arthritic fingers.

As she opened the latch and yanked the gate open, she felt a rush of air as the man rounded the corner of the building behind her. She felt her insides seize up.

Run.

"Stop!"

Freya pulled in a breath, ready to pick up speed. To run like she hadn't run for decades. But it was too late. The man was on her. He grabbed the sleeve of her coat and pulled her back and down. Her body twisted, making her gasp.

There was something in his hand. Her vision was blurred and she couldn't work out what it was.

Goodness. She would be no use to the police at all.

Freya blinked as her twisted body slammed into the wall. Shrieking, she slid to the ground.

He was on her. She raised her arms to defend herself but he had a better angle. Whatever it was he was holding came at her from the side.

She screamed, but no sound came out, just as the object hit the side of her head.

Then the world went black.

CHAPTER FORTY-SIX

Frank was in his office, sifting through a pile of paperwork. Zoe thought of the papers she still had on her desk from Albert North's house. She hadn't needed to send them to the Home Office, since they were duplicates. Was she expected to file them now, or destroy them?

"Zoe, how's things? You wrapped up the Northfield paperwork yet?"

"Not quite."

"OK. Please don't tell me there's a problem with one of your officers. DC Hughes?"

Why Frank would assume there was a problem with Rhodri, she had no idea. Zoe shook her head.

"It's about the Albert North case."

He leaned back in his chair. "It's gone, Zoe. Home Office have called us off."

"Another piece of evidence has come in in the meantime."

"OK. What kind of evidence?"

"It's in the team inbox."

"Can't you just tell me?"

Zoe clenched a fist. "It's CCTV, Frank. Best if you watch it."

"Fair enough." Frank took one of the piles of paperwork in front of him and moved it to one side. He pulled his laptop closer. "What am I looking at?"

"Albert North's death, I believe."

His gaze flicked up to hers, his expression surprised.

"Just watch it, Frank."

He scratched his cheek and clicked the trackpad. After a few moments he sat back, hands behind his head, fingers laced together, and gazed at the screen. As he watched, his expression changed: boredom, puzzlement, interest, surprise, disappointment.

He closed the laptop lid. "This has to go to the Home Office."

"I know."

"So why are you bringing it to me?"

She pointed at the laptop. "Rhodri interviewed that man. He runs a shelter in the city centre. He gave no indication of knowing anything about Albert's death. In fact, he denied even knowing Albert."

Frank opened his laptop again. He peered into it and brought up the video. "We can't be one hundred percent sure this is a murder in progress."

"Oh come on. He gives him something, probably the thallium. Then he shoves him to the ground and drags him round the back of the hut."

Frank shook his head. "We can see something change hands. There's no way of knowing it's the poison. And yes, your man pulls the victim round the back of the cabin. But a

CHAPTER FORTY-SIX

good barrister will argue that he was placing him somewhere safe while he called for help."

"But there's no evidence of him calling for help. He just walks away. And that's where Albert's body was found."

Frank nodded. "Either way, this isn't our problem anymore."

"Frank. We spoke to the man. Please, just let me—"

"Zoe. I know what you're like. To be fair, I'm amazed you brought this to me instead of just buggering off and following it up." He cocked his head. "It shows you're maturing as a detective."

Fuck off, she thought. She didn't need Frank Dawson patronising her. But the truth was, the last year with Carl had taught her that officers who carried out unofficial investigations were as likely to get themselves sacked as to solve the case.

"I wanted to do the right thing," she said.

"Cover your back, more like. Send this to the Home Office. Same address as you sent all the other evidence."

"Sir."

Frank chuckled. "First time you've called me that."

"It felt like an appropriate moment."

"You could say that."

There was a knock on the door. Frank looked past Zoe. "Come in." He looked at her. "Go on then. You've got an email to send."

She went to stand up, as the door opened. It was Connie.

"Connie? Everything OK?"

Connie looked from Zoe to Frank. She shook her head, her eyes wide. Her skin had paled.

"It's Freya Garside," she said. "She's been attacked."

CHAPTER FORTY-SEVEN

Every muscle in Freya's body hurt. She squeezed her eyes shut, cursing the bright light.

Was she at home? Who'd brought her here?

She lifted her hand to her face and prodded at her forehead. There was a bandage, a great bulky thing that made her think of Mr Bump. She'd bought the book for her sister's ungrateful daughter when she was a child. Aeons ago.

Her throat hurt. She coughed, her body convulsing. She had to open her eyes, work out where she was.

"She's awake."

Freya stiffened. Who was that?

Could it be the man who'd hit her?

Her throat constricted. If she reached out a hand, what were the chances of her putting it on a weapon?

Slim to non-existent. And even if she did, she was at least thirty years older than her attacker and in pain.

She blinked.

"Miss Garside?" It was a woman's voice. The first voice had been a man.

CHAPTER FORTY-SEVEN

Had the man in Albert's house spoken? She tried to recall. The details were hazy, but yes. He had.

His accent had been Scottish.

"She looks like she's in pain." The man again. He wasn't Scottish. He was Welsh.

She felt her heart lighten.

But... what if he had a colleague? A co-conspirator? That person might be Welsh.

Freya placed her hands down on the surface she was lying on. It was a bed. Hard, but a bed. The man who'd attacked her wouldn't have put her on a bed.

Was she at home?

"Freya?" The woman again. It was that detective, Detective Inspector... some kind of bird. The memory had gone. The man must be a colleague. Maybe her commanding officer.

Open your eyes, damn you.

She clutched at the sheets and blinked again. Gently, her brain protesting against the glare, she opened one eye, and then the other.

It was too bright. All she could see were a handful of shapes.

"Freya? Miss Garside? It's Zoe. Detective Inspector Finch. You're in hospital."

Freya swallowed. She brought a hand up and pointed to her lips, closing her eyes again.

"She needs a drink. Rhod..."

"On it, boss."

Boss. So the man was someone junior, not the senior officer. Freya heard footsteps, then the sound of water being poured She held a hand out, waiting for the cup to be placed in her hand. Freya had done enough hospital visiting in her time to know it would be plastic and flimsy.

She drew the cup to her lips and drank.

That was better.

She tipped it up and downed the last drops, then held it out again.

"I'll get more." The man.

Freya felt better. Her throat was losing the scratchiness. She opened her eyes.

This time, the shapes had become people. She was on a hospital ward. The female detective was on a chair next to the bed, while her male colleague stood behind her.

"I got us a cup of tea, boss… oh."

A young black woman stood at the end of the bed. Freya shrank back into the pillows as the woman smiled at her.

"Hello. I'm Connie. You've had a nasty bump."

Freya lifted her fingertips to her head.

"I wouldn't touch it if I was you," the man said. He was young, wearing a cheap suit and with pale, sunken cheeks. Another child, supposedly protecting the public.

Freya dropped her hand to her lap. She looked at the older woman, DI… Finch. That was it. Zoe Finch.

"Where am I?" Her voice was scratchy.

"You're in the QE. Someone attacked you," said the DI.

Freya nodded, instantly regretting it. "Who?"

"We're hoping you can help us with that."

Freya pulled in a breath and coughed. She felt something touch her hand; another cup of water. She grabbed it and gulped it down.

"A man," she croaked. She shook her head. "Scottish?"

"Scottish?" the young black woman asked. She was Brummie, no trace of a foreign accent.

CHAPTER FORTY-SEVEN

Freya looked at her. "Scottish. About... six foot two. Overweight. He smelled of garlic."

She heard a laugh. It was the man. Freya turned to him, her movements stiff.

"What's funny, young man?"

"Sorry."

"You've just woken up from an assault," the DI said. "And you can remember what he smelled of. It's not what we're used to."

Freya shrugged. *Ouch*. She winced. "I suppose you..." She swallowed. "I suppose you want to know what he was wearing."

"Please." The woman's voice was soft.

"Brown tweed jacket. Harris tweed. Blue jeans." Why did people insist on wearing jeans with everything these days? "Red shirt."

"Any other distinguishing characteristics? Apart from the accent."

"He was pale, ruddy cheeks." Freya breathed in. She would suffer for this; her head was pounding. But she prided herself on always being ready to act as a witness. "Fifty, maybe. Overweight."

"You've said that." The young woman. Freya gave her a look. Goodness, the young were so rude.

"Thank you," the DI said. "You've been very helpful."

That was what they always said. It was how they got rid of you.

The DI turned towards the younger woman at the end of the bed. "Connie, you spoke to him. Rhodri, you met him. Does that sound like Kirk?"

Kirk? Who was Kirk?

"It does, boss," said the man. His Welsh accent intensified. "D'you want me to go see him?"

A pause. Freya felt pain surge through her head. She needed to sleep.

"Are you hassling my patient?" Another voice, brusque and female.

"DI Finch, West Midlands Police. Miss Garside has been helping us identify the individual who did this to her."

"I don't give a flying fig who did this to her. The important thing is you don't make her worse. I need you all out of here."

Freya's eyes were closed. She reached out a hand, falling against nothingness. Finally, a hand grasped hers. She felt movement as someone leaned in.

"What is it, Freya?" the DI asked.

"Find him," Freya replied. "Find him and throw the book at him."

CHAPTER FORTY-EIGHT

"Jimmy Kirk." Rhodri was bouncing as they left the hospital, his eyes alight. "We have to go and see him."

"Not so fast," said Zoe. "All we have is the say-so of a frail elderly woman who's just been attacked."

"Come on," the DC replied. "We've got the CCTV too."

"Rhod. You and I both know that those two things together put Kirk in the frame. But what we also know is that we need more. A witness statement isn't enough, especially not from Freya Garside, however much detail she might have remembered. We need forensics placing Jimmy Kirk at Albert North's house this afternoon."

"He might have visited at an earlier date," Connie suggested. They were at the car now, Zoe standing by the driver's door, Connie on the passenger side and Rhodri beside Zoe at the rear door. "The two men knew each other, through the shelter. Kirk might have had a valid reason to be there."

"He didn't meet Albert until after Albert became homeless," Zoe said. "So he'd got no reason to go to that house.

Even to know about it. And, of course, he denied knowing Albert at all."

"Wouldn't Albert have given his address at the shelter?" Rhodri suggested as he climbed into the car.

"He was homeless," said Connie. "That's the whole point. They won't ask for an address."

Rhodri sucked his lips together, staring out of the side window. Drizzle was falling. Zoe turned the ignition and the windscreen wipers kicked into life along with the engine.

"OK," she said. "We have an assault case to investigate, and a potential suspect. But first I want to see if the forensics from Albert's house show any evidence of Kirk having been there."

"The forensics were all before the attack, boss," Rhodri pointed out.

"Exactly. We examine those first, find out if he was there before it happened. If not, and we find evidence of him from later, then we know he was there when Freya was assaulted."

"Clever." Rhodri grinned at her in the rear-view mirror.

"Or at least at around that time," Connie said.

Zoe glanced across at her. "You OK? You seem restless."

Connie rolled her neck. "I just think we should leave well alone. Maybe Aleksander Nadarević deserved to die. Maybe we *shouldn't* find his killer."

"Bollocks," muttered Rhodri.

"Rhod." Zoe glared at him in the mirror. "Whatever your view of the case, is it appropriate to talk to Connie like that?"

"Sorry." Rhodri lowered his gaze.

"It's OK," said Connie. "I don't need you to fight my battles for me, boss. Besides," she smiled into the mirror, "it's just Rhod."

He looked up and grinned back. "Maybe you're right after all, Con. Maybe it's justice."

Zoe pulled over and stopped the car. She turned in her seat so she could look at the two DCs.

"What's got into you both? Justice doesn't work like that. Vigilantes, revenge. Due process is what it's about."

"I looked into the tribunals at The Hague, after the Bosnian war," Connie said. "They caught everyone. Everyone except Aleksander."

"What difference does that make?"

"He hid out in Birmingham, evading justice. Have you read about what he did?"

Zoe sighed. She had read the reports, but she wasn't about to discuss it with Connie. "What he did back then is irrelevant, Connie. He was murdered, in our city, on our watch. The man who we think killed him then attacked a vulnerable witness."

Connie wrinkled her nose.

"Look, folks," Zoe said. "We can't just go charging into this without more information. Rhodri, I want you to speak to Adi. Find ou—"

"I can do that," Connie said. "I'll speak to Rav."

"No. This has to be done officially. I'm sorry, Connie, but this case is already hot. I don't want any suggestion that we didn't do this properly."

"I wouldn't do that."

"I know." What was up with Connie? "But we need to keep our arses squeaky clean. We're investigating an assault now, not the murder. We happen to have forensics, from the scene, and it doesn't matter that we're no longer involved with the reason they were taken if they can be used to help us rule out a suspect for the crime we *are* involved in."

If Lesley could see her now, she'd be amazed. Zoe had been paying attention, after all. Maybe her old boss insisting she stick to procedure had been the very thing that had stopped her.

"What d'you want me to do?" Connie asked.

"Look into the shelter. Find out what you can about Jimmy Kirk's employment there. Has he been in trouble at all, have there been any complaints by service users?"

"That's all?"

Zoe clenched her teeth. "I'll tell you if there's more."

"We should be doing door-to-door on Avenue Road," Rhodri suggested as they arrived at Rose Road. Zoe waited for the gates to open then drove into the car park.

"You're right, Rhod." She eyed Connie. "Can you do that, Connie? Rhod can look into Jimmy Kirk and the shelter as well as the forensics."

Connie was staring ahead, her gaze not on Zoe. "I've got my bike. I can get back over there."

Zoe sighed. When would Connie give in to the fact that she was a busy detective, and learn to drive?

"Ask Uniform to give you a lift. Then speak to the people on each side. Find out if anyone saw anything."

"Uniform can help." Connie's voice was clipped.

"They can. Get them to assist you, and make your way over there. OK?"

Rhodri raised his hand. They were sitting in Zoe's car, parked in the car park. It reminded Zoe of all the conflabs she'd had here with Mo.

"Rhod, this isn't school."

"Sorry, boss. Wouldn't it make sense for me and Connie to swap? She can do the desk work, and I'll—"

"No. I don't want Connie talking to FSI. You do that,

CHAPTER FORTY-EIGHT

Rhod, and find out what you can about Jimmy Kirk. For the assault forensics, make sure Adi uses a team member who hasn't been inside that house for the murder." Zoe knew that Adi would have thought of this; she didn't need to ask. But it didn't hurt, and could make all the difference.

"Boss."

"Good."

Connie looked at Zoe for a moment. "What are you going to do, boss?"

Zoe gazed back at her, considering.

"Connie, I'm going to speak to someone who might be able to help."

CHAPTER FORTY-NINE

Connie held up her ID. PC Akku Battar, who she'd known vaguely when she was in Uniform, was doing the same thing at the next door along.

"Hi." She smiled. "I'm DC Williams, I'm here about th—"

"Albert North," the man said. "Such a tragedy. I heard they found him at the top of the helter skelter in the German Market."

Connie sighed. "Not quite. But that's not what I'm here about. We're investigating an assault that took place in Albert's house earlier today."

The man took a step back, surprised. "But your lot have been there since he died."

Connie swallowed. "We vacated the house this morning. One of your neighbours, Miss Garside, went to the house and was attacked. She described a man, la—"

"Freya Garside. Nosey old so-and-so that one. Tried to tell me I shouldn't be letting my Dave out on his motorbike late at night."

"Sorry?"

"Dave. My son. Eighteen. None of her business what he does with his bike. She said it was waking her up." The man snorted. He was short, mid fifties, wearing a dressing gown.

"Anyway," Connie continued, "we were wondering if you might have seen anything. Someone leaving Albert's property, maybe by the side alleyway."

"Sorry, love. All the houses face the park along here, so we can't really see what's going on in each other's places. One of the things I like about Avenue Road." He cocked his head. "Not that it stops busybodies like Freya Garside though. Is she OK? Not dead, is she?"

Connie tried not to show her irritation at the man's tone. "She's currently in the QE, recov—"

"Oh, that's alright then. She'll be fine. Made of tough stuff, old Freya. In fact, it's the bloke who attacked her that I'd worry about if I was you." He smiled.

"What makes you say that?"

"She may look like a little old lady, but that woman is made of steel. Maybe a bit of lead, too. I wouldn't want to get on the wrong side of her. She'll get better, you'll see, and then whoever hurt her's gonna have seven shades of hell coming to them."

Connie dragged in a breath, rubbing her hands together. It was cold work, standing on doorsteps. "So you're saying you didn't hear or see anything suspicious."

He scraped his chin. "Depends what you mean by suspicious."

"Anyone going into the alleyways who you didn't recognise as a neighbour. Any of the neighbours behaving strangely."

A snort. "Well there's that kid at number twelve, he acts

strange all the time. And I did see some fella trying the gate round the back of Dawn's house two doors down."

"Dawn?"

He stepped out of his door and turned to face down the street, waving his hand in the general direction of Vicarage Road, which met Avenue Road at its southern end. "She lives along there. Two along from your Albert North. Her and her girlfriend, not sure what her name is. But Dawn's ok, despite everything."

Connie decided not to ask what was meant by the *despite everything*.

"You saw someone trying to access the alleyway at the side of her house?"

"Lunchtime today, like. Jigglin' the padlock. I was putting me recycling out. He gave it a few tries, to be honest I thought it was someone she'd given a key to. But then he gave up and walked off."

"Which direction did he leave in?"

The man pointed. "Down towards the railway bridge."

"Did you get much of a look at him?"

"Sorry, love. Like I say, I was focused on putting me bins out. But I can remember his scarf."

"He was wearing a scarf?"

"Yeah." Another scratch of the chin. "A yellow one. With black lines. I remember thinking it looked like Rupert the Bear." A snort. "What would I go thinking about Rupert the Bear for, eh? Decades since I read those sort of books. But yeah, he was wearing a scarf. Yellow, like."

"Mr Hudson," Connie said as she looked along the road towards Ruti's house, and Albert's beyond. There were more house calls to be made. "Thanks for your help."

CHAPTER FIFTY

"I think I'll be late home tonight, love." Zoe was in the car park, talking to Carl.

"You don't need to tell me."

"We were meeting your sister."

He exhaled. "She won't mind. She's used to it. Anyway, she's a gynaecologist. She does her own share of odd hours."

"Tell her sorry from me, yes?"

"No, I'll tell her you can't stand her and you made up an assault on a septuagenarian just to annoy her."

"Carl..."

Carl laughed. "I'll tell her you're sorry. We'll see her at New Year. Don't worry."

"Thanks. I love you."

"I love you too."

"I'll grab something while I'm working, see you at home later."

"You will."

"Have fun."

"It's dinner with my sister, sweetie. It's not going to be

that much fun. You go, find out who attacked that poor old lady."

Poor old lady. Zoe found it hard to apply that label to Freya Garside.

"See you later." She hung up and stretched her arms out in front, yawning. She was tired; the early morning on Sunday was still taking its toll.

She needed to talk to Frank. She had to square the fact that they were investigating Freya's assault with the fact that they weren't allowed to investigate Albert's death.

She looked up at the buildings, leaning forward to peer up towards the second floor. Was Frank even up there? It was gone 7pm, and since he'd been promoted into Lesley's job, he'd taken to working regular office hours.

Alright for some. Not that Zoe fancied being a DCI. In Force CID it meant sitting behind a desk instead of being out there solving crimes. It meant managing people at arms' length, watching your subordinates getting into the nitty gritty surrounded by their own teams instead of having a tight-knit team you spent all your time with.

She sniffed and leaned back, considering. She dialled.

"Zoe. To what do I owe this honour?"

Zoe grimaced. It had been almost six months since they'd last spoken.

"Sorry. You must think I've forgotten about you."

"Me? Who could forget me? It's alright, Zoe, I know you're a busy woman. Doing Frank's job for him, I'll not doubt."

"Not exactly."

"So. How can I help you?"

"It might be a Merry Christmas call."

CHAPTER FIFTY

At the other end of the line, Lesley snorted. "OK. Let's pretend it is. Merry Christmas."

"Merry Christmas. Will you be spending it in Dorset?"

"Of course. Elsa's got a— you don't need to know what Elsa's doing."

"How is she?"

"Zoe, will you just get to the bloody point? You need my advice on something. Something you can't or won't talk to Frank about. My guess is you're about to get yourself into trouble."

Zoe slumped in the seat. "OK."

"Hit me with it."

"You're sure it's a good time?"

"I'm in Bobby's in Bournemouth shopping for presents. I've left Elsa inside while I take this call. You can bet it's a good time."

Zoe smiled. She'd never seen Lesley as the domesticated type. She was the kind of woman whose Christmas gift shopping consisted of ten minutes in the wine aisle of Tesco, topped up with half an hour on Amazon if you were lucky.

"We've been investigating a murder in the Frankfurt Market."

"I saw."

"You did?"

"I keep an eye on the local news."

Zoe nodded. "So, it turns out the victim was a war criminal. Bosnian war."

A whistle came down the line. "Shit Zoe, you don't do this by halves, do you? Vigilantes, you think?"

"We don't know. The Home Office told us to stop investigating."

"Hang on. You were pulled off the case?"

"It seems it's too sensitive."

"I can see that. Zoe, if you're after my permission to carry on investigating, you know I'm not the right person. First off I'd tell you to stick to procedure. Second off, I'm not your boss."

"I know. But there's been another incident."

"Of course there has. Hit me with it."

"A woman, neighbour of the first victim. She's the curtain twitcher type, fancies herself as Miss Marple. She went into his house after we were pulled off the case and she was attacked."

"By who?"

"We don't have a suspect yet. But I think there's a good chance it's the same person who killed Albert."

"Albert? That's your murder victim?"

"Well, Aleksander, really. He changed his name whe—"

"OK. Here's what I think you should do."

Zoe licked her lips. The front door to the building opened. Two uniformed constables emerged, followed, after a gap, by Frank.

Shit. She sunk lower in her seat.

What was he doing, still here?

Lesley was talking.

"Sorry Lesley, I got distracted. Can you repeat that for me?"

"You sure you want my advice?"

"Of course I do."

"In that case, bloody listen to it this time."

"Sorry."

Lesley grunted. "You need to investigate the old lady's attack, obviously. But you need to keep meticulous records and you need to ensure that any questions you ask witnesses, and any forensics you ask the FSIs for, are specific to this case. No using the case as an excuse to go digging around into the other one."

"What if there's evidence that relates to both cases?"

"Evidence like that still relates to this case, doesn't it?"

Zoe smiled. "It does."

"But remember, Zoe. It *must* relate to this case. You're a good copper, but you have a tendency to go flying off on your own initiative getting everyone into trouble. If whoever killed your Albert bloke is as hot as the Home Office seem to think, they could present a serious threat."

"Albert was the last war criminal to evade justice. They won't be after anyone else."

"You don't know for sure that's why he died. And you don't know that the killer will be content to stop there. There have been other wars in that neck of the woods. Don't assume they're finished."

"OK." Zoe's mouth was dry. She'd sent Connie back to Avenue Road, on door-to-door. What if the killer was still in that road, somewhere they could watch Albert? What if the killer lived there?

No. They'd already knocked on doors and nothing suspicious had come up.

"Anyway. Elsa's in the display window, trying to get my attention. I've got to go."

"Sorry. And thanks."

Zoe sucked in a breath. Should she tell Lesley about the card from Randle? Lesley would have opinions, that was certain.

"That's OK," Lesley said. "You should come down here, sometime. Use some leave, you and Carl. It's lovely."

No. No one needed to know about the card. And Zoe

had never believed that her former boss would describe Dorset as lovely. When she'd first been posted there she'd seen it as an ordeal. Zoe had hoped she was coming back.

Now, with a new team and a relationship, it was obvious she was staying put.

"See you around, Lesley. Maybe when you come up here."

A snort. "I'll hold you to that."

CHAPTER FIFTY-ONE

Rhodri parked his car in the cage and headed down to ground level on foot. He wasn't far from the German Market, from the spot where they'd found Albert North. He also wasn't far from City Centre Gardens, a small green space near the canals that sounded salubrious enough. In reality it was little more than a patch of land behind some tower blocks, fine for people to bring their kids in the daytime, but best avoided by night. His mate Geeta had told him some rough sleepers hung out there.

He dialled Geet's mobile as he walked.

"Rhod. I can't be long with this, mate, I'm on duty."

"That's fine. Where are you?"

"Brindleyplace, just breaking something up in All Bar One. Meet me by the Sea Life Centre, yeah? And hurry up. This'll be sorted in two ticks."

"No problem." Rhodri pocketed his phone and quickened his pace. He pushed through the crowds of Christmas revellers clutching their mugs of weak bier and their glasses of gluhwein. A speaker blared out up by the Council House:

Sweet Caroline. Voices rose around him, joining in, entirely oblivious as to whether they were in tune. At least they had the lyrics right.

Rhodri smiled and kept walking. He loved the market. Sure, it had been a pain when he was in Uniform, but what harm was a bit of fun and a few beers? He'd been one of those lads huddled in the cabins up on Victoria Square when he was a bit younger, downing the bier with his mates and chatting up a few girls if they got lucky.

He made a mental note to head back here before he left for Wales. Evenings weren't the same now he had a copper's eyes and ears, but he could come by in the daytime and buy his mum something nice. Chestnuts, she'd appreciate them. Or maybe one of those necklaces they sold on the stalls down on New Street.

At last he emerged from the crowds, heading over the bridge towards Centenary Square. The area outside the library was busy, people queuing for the ice rink and the big wheel. Kids passed him chewing on chocolate lollipops the size of his arm, parents looking anxious.

At the convention centre, he turned right and headed round towards the canals. It would be easier to get to the Sea Life Centre this way than by going through the centre, especially since it looked like there was something happening in Symphony Hall. He hurried round the back of the ICC, past the modern apartment buildings on one side and high-rise council blocks on the other. He'd be coming back here shortly; it was here that the rough sleepers hung out.

His phone buzzed. "Forget the Sea Life, I'm round the side of the ICC," Geeta said.

"I'm right there."

"OK. Well wait a minute."

CHAPTER FIFTY-ONE

Rhodri stopped walking. His mate would be coming from up ahead. She'd be easy to spot in her uniform.

Sure enough, a figure in a dark police uniform appeared through an archway up ahead and walked towards him. Rhodri put out a hand.

"Geet."

"Rhod. This about the murder in the market?"

"No. An assault in Kings Heath."

"Why you in the city centre, then?"

"We've got a suspect, we think some of the homeless guys might be able to tell us something about him."

"Fair enough. I'll take you down there, they know me. I do this beat four times a week."

Rhodri nodded and followed his friend. They walked down the steps leading towards the canal and around the side of the blocks, their footsteps regular. They didn't want anyone thinking they were sneaking up on them.

Rhodri made out the flicker of a flame up ahead, in the canal basin in front of the Flapper pub. He hunched his shoulders, suddenly aware of the cold, and headed towards it, careful to stay one pace behind Geeta.

"Evening guys," Geeta said. "How's things? Squid, did you go to the drop-in centre to get that sore checked out like I suggested?"

One of the men groaned. "Aw fuck, I forgot."

"You do that tomorrow, yeah? Don't want it getting infected."

The man poked at his cheek. It had a dark patch, indistinct in the light of the flames and the distant streetlamps. Rhodri felt his nose wrinkle.

"This is my mate Rhod," Geeta said. "He wants to have a chat with you about something."

Another man, taller and younger than the first, stepped forward. "What type of somethin'?"

"He can tell you that. I've got to get on, but you'll all be fine with Rhod. Take care, yeah?"

Grunts came from the men. They crowded in on Rhodri, the younger man's eyes bright in the flicker of the flame.

"You a copper?" he asked.

"I am." Rhodri held up his ID, turning it so each member of the group could see. He knew it was risky being here on his own, but felt sure that if they'd come in mob-handed he'd have got nothing useful out of them.

"What d'you want? None of us has done anything wrong."

"That's not why I'm here. I'm hoping you can tell me about someone."

"Tell him to fuck off, Rick," came a voice. Rick raised a hand.

"It's alright, Joe. Give him a chance. Who d'you want to know about? Cos we ain't grassing no one in."

Rhodri tried to smile. "It's not one of you. Not a rough sleeper."

"Who, then? It's not like we spend much time with regular people."

"Do any of you use Greenfields Shelter?"

Rick folded his arms across his chest. "Most of us, yeah. What's it to you?"

"Do you have dealings with Jimmy Kirk, the manager?"

"Course we do, he's in charge. Good bloke."

Rhodri nodded. "How long's he been working there?"

He knew he could get this information from official sources, but he wanted to know what the men said.

"Two years, maybe three. Why?"

"Has he ever been violent towards any of you, or your mates?"

Rick looked back into the group. There was muttering.

He turned back to Rhodri. "Never. What, you trying to get us to grass him up?"

"I just want to know how he treats his service users."

A laugh came from the back of the group. "Service users! That's us, alright. Except it's not much of a service."

"No?" Rhod asked.

"The food's shit and the beds are lumpy."

"Trip, it ain't supposed to be the Ritz, you know," one of the other men said. There was laughter.

"Yeah, you're right. He's alright, Jimmy. Has someone said he did them over?"

"Has he told you guys anything about his history?" Rhodri asked.

"His history? What do you think we are, his fuckin' biographers?"

"Where was he before he was at the shelter? Has he lived in Europe?"

"Have you listened to him? He's from Glasgow."

The man had a point. If Jimmy Kirk had killed Albert North, then Rhodri couldn't see how it could be linked to the Bosnian war.

"Is he married? Got a partner?"

"That's his business, innit?"

"Do you know?"

"He's single. I 'eard him talking to one of the other staff about using a dating app. Poor bugger. Glad I'm too old and ugly for all that shit."

Rhodri considered.

"What about money? D'you think he might have money problems?"

A laugh came from a man who hadn't spoken yet. "He's rich, compared to us. Money problems! Next thing you'll be asking us about his childhood."

If Jimmy had no direct links to the Bosnian conflict, and he wasn't hard up and therefore susceptible to bribes, then what could have motivated him to kill Albert? And to attack Freya in order to prevent her from investigating?

"Do any of you know Albert North? Or did you?"

He shouldn't be asking about this, he'd get himself and the DI into trouble. But he was here now, and these guys were hardly going to report him.

"Poor bastard," said one of the men. Murmurs went round the crowd.

"Albert didn't like Jimmy," came a voice.

"Sorry?" Rhodri asked. "Why not?"

"No idea. But he refused to go to the shelter when Jimmy was working there. Wouldn't say why."

Rhodri looked around the crowd. There were a couple of nodding heads, but most of them looked puzzled. He knew that proper procedure was to separate them out, to question them one by one. But he didn't have time.

"Any of you know why Albert and Jimmy didn't get on?"

"Sorry mate," said the man who'd been at the front of the group from the start. "You'd have to ask Jimmy that."

CHAPTER FIFTY-TWO

"A YELLOW SCARF?"

"Yeah," Connie replied. Zoe was trundling through the evening traffic, windscreen wipers going so fast she thought they might fall off. Trying to get through Selly Oak at the tail end of the rush hour was bad enough, Christmas made it worse, but then the rain gave the impression the entire car-owning population of the UK had chosen this moment to descend on these few streets.

"Has anyone else said anything about a yellow scarf? I don't suppose Jimmy Kirk had one in his office when we went to see him?"

"Sorry, boss," Rhodri said. He and Connie were on hands-free in the office. "Didn't see one."

"It's probably nothing." Zoe glanced in her rearview mirror; the car behind was much too close. She was half tempted to put on her police lights. "Anyway you two, it's getting late. Go home and we'll have fresh heads in the morning."

"If you don't mind, boss, I'd rather—" Rhodri began.

"I know you want to get this wrapped up so you can go home to your mum. I've got Nicholas at home. I understand, I really do. But if you're exhausted, you won't work faster. The opposite in fact."

"She's right," Connie muttered.

Zoe smiled. "See? If Connie says I'm right, then I must be. See you both in the morning."

She hung up and switched her attention to the road. She needed her wits about her if she was ever going to get through this traffic. At least now she only had to drive the quarter mile to her house, instead of the mile to the office in Harborne.

Ten minutes later she'd parked at the wrong end of her road of terraced houses and hurried to her front door. The duffle she was wearing didn't have a hood and she'd forgotten her umbrella. And Zoe's hair was thick and long. Today it was just wet and long.

The door opened before she lifted her key to the lock.

"Mum, you look like shit."

Zoe looked up to see Nicholas standing in the doorway. She felt her heart lift. "Nick!" She stepped up to give him a hug and he backed off.

"Wait till you're dry. Carl's here."

Zoe shook herself out as Nicholas closed the door behind her. The house smelled of cake.

"You're baking." She missed this when he was away; Nicholas was a fantastic cook, a skill born of necessity when he'd learned as a teenager that he could never rely on his mother for home cooked meals.

"I found a bought Christmas cake in the cupboard. You can't do that."

Zoe looked at her son. He seemed to grow taller every term, or was it just that she'd forgotten he wasn't a little boy any more? "You can give me that hug now."

He shrugged, then leaned over her, gathering her in his arms. Nicholas had inherited Zoe's genes for height; she was five foot eight and he was six foot four.

"I thought you'd be pleased to see him."

Zoe turned to see Carl behind her.

"Hi, love. Can we get a curry for tea? I'm in the mood for one."

He exchanged glances with Nicholas, who frowned.

"I was hoping..." Nicholas said.

"You wanted to cook?"

A shrug. "I can cook a curry if you want."

"Sounds perfect. Thanks, love. Mind if I sit down while you get on with it? I'm working a murder case and I'm worn out."

Nicholas headed into the kitchen as Zoe threw off her shoes and slung herself onto the sofa.

Carl stood over her. "Can we have a chat?"

Zoe stiffened. "What about?"

He shook his head. "I don't want Nicholas hearing. How long is that curry going to take?"

"Nicholas!" Zoe called. "We got time to go for a quick drink?"

"Half an hour!"

Zoe looked up at Carl, whose face was expressionless. "Enough time?"

He nodded.

"What is it?" she asked, as she stood up and slipped her shoes back on. "And can I change into some dry jeans first?"

"I'd rather you didn't."

She sighed. "Fair enough." She made for the front door and grabbed her duffel. The rain had seeped through to the inner lining. She shivered.

"Let's walk fast."

Carl ushered her towards the door. "I've got a brolly."

Zoe turned towards the kitchen. "Back in twenty-five minutes!"

"OK!" came the reply.

"This had better be important," she muttered to Carl. "It's not every day I get to spend time with my son."

"Sorry, Zoe. But it is important. And..." He jerked his head towards the kitchen.

"And you don't want him hearing. I get it."

She sighed as they left the house, her mind racing as they hurried along Tiverton Road towards the pub. The OVT, a favourite student haunt. They would raise the average age by about twenty years.

Carl had been banging on about moving to Cumbria for weeks. He was ambitious, and they'd offered him an exciting new posting.

Was this going to be an ultimatum? Move with him, or lose him?

Zoe felt her skin grow cold. And not just because of the rain.

At the pub, he opened the door for her, not making physical contact.

This was it. Carl was about to dump her. The two of them had tried to find a place to live together, but had never managed to agree on the location. Was he fed up with her inability to commit, her attachment to the Selly Oak home where she'd raised Nicholas, and to the job which had been so good to her?

CHAPTER FIFTY-TWO

"What can I get you?" he asked.

Zoe raised an eyebrow. "Seriously?" They both knew what she would want.

"Diet Coke with ice."

"Exactly. I'll find a table."

Zoe pushed through the students, noticing that the crowd was thinner than it would have been a week ago. The students were dispersing, making their way home for Christmas.

She found a table in the corner, thinking of the first time she and Carl had come here. He'd been investigating her old boss David Randle, and she'd been reluctant to help. He'd been undercover in Force CID, something that had shocked her at the time.

Now she knew Carl did that kind of thing regularly. It was the last resort when it came to keeping the police force clean.

A glass appeared in front of her and Carl sat down in the chair opposite. She couldn't help noticing he hadn't brushed the back of her neck as he passed, the way he usually did.

The lump in Zoe's throat grew tighter.

Steel yourself.

It wasn't the first time she'd been dumped. Nicholas's dad, Jim... he'd run for the hills, or at least back to his wife, when Zoe had fallen pregnant. And there had been others before. Men didn't like am ambitious female police officer, not for the long term.

But Carl had been different. He was ambitious too, for starters. And he relished her commitment to the job.

"What is it?" she asked as she sipped the Coke.

Carl leaned on the table, steepling his hands together. "I found something."

Zoe put her drink down. "Found something?" This wasn't what she'd been expecting.

Carl pursed his lips, then placed his drink on the table. A bottle of lager, some kind of local brew.

He gazed at her for a moment. Zoe realised it was the first time he'd made eye contact with her since she'd arrived home.

"What did you find, Carl? Is this something to do with Cumbria?"

"No." He looked down.

"Then what?"

He looked back into her eyes. "Why didn't you tell me you'd had a Christmas card from David Randle?"

Zoe slumped back in her seat. Was this all?

She smiled. "The card? Is that what this is about?"

"What did you think it was about?"

"I thought you were... never mind." She met his gaze. "I have no idea why he sent me a card. I certainly didn't encourage it. And I didn't send him one, if that's what your next question is. I don't know where he is, even if I wanted to." She spotted the look on his face. "And I *don't* want to. Even if I had his address."

"Which you don't."

Zoe pushed her glass across the table, bile rising in her throat. "The man's in witness protection, for fuck's sake. He put me and my team in danger and assisted a gang that abused vulnerable children. Do you really think I'd be voluntarily exchanging Christmas cards with him?"

"Have you reported it?"

"Reported what?"

"That you got the card?"

CHAPTER FIFTY-TWO

"No."

"You should."

Zoe's limbs felt heavy. She'd left David Randle behind. Hiding the card away in her office, she'd hoped, would enable her to forget this.

"What were you doing snooping around my office anyway?"

"I was looking for printer ink."

"That's convenient."

"Oh come on, Zoe. You don't think I was looking for something?"

"No. You're right. Sorry. It's just... It knocked me for six."

"Why didn't you tell me?"

Zoe gestured at the drinks, and the table, and the bar. "Because I knew this would happen. You'd overreact."

"I'm not overreacting. You received a communication from a former officer who was involved in police corruption and is now in witness protection. If the wrong people knew about that, it would make you vulnerable to bribery."

"There's plenty of other things that make me vulnerable to bribery, Carl."

"That doesn't make this any better." He drank from his bottle. "Tell Frank, Zoe. Tell him tomorrow. Take the card in and hand it over. You've already put it in an evidence bag."

The reference to the evidence bag made Zoe's stomach lurch. "I'm busy on a murder case. This will be a distraction."

"You're not; it's an assault case now. And it's necessary."

She downed the last of her Coke and stood up. "Come on, Nicholas will have that curry ready. Let's not talk about this any more."

"Promise me you'll report it."

She had her back to him.

"I promise."

Truth be told, she couldn't be sure if she was lying.

"I promise," she repeated.

CHAPTER FIFTY-THREE

Rav was sitting at a table in Bacchus Bar, in one of a pair of chairs so large it made him look like a child. Connie approached, checking her watch and muttering under her breath. They'd arranged to meet at eight; it was almost half past.

He stood up as she approached and stepped forward to kiss her. She felt heat rise to her cheeks.

"What's this, you didn't think we'd fit in normal size chairs?"

He smiled. "Everything OK?"

"Sorry I'm late. I tried WhatsApping you."

"No signal in here." He held his phone up.

Of course. They were underground, opposite New Street Station. Connie liked this place. It was dark and anonymous and as far as she'd been able to work out, no coppers drank here. At least, no one she knew.

"Sorry," she repeated. "Boss had me checking up on a suspect. I didn't want to bugger off before Rhod did."

"What you drinking?"

"WKD, please."

"Coming right up." He slid out of his chair, shimmied around the table, winking at her as he went, and headed for the bar.

Connie shrugged off her coat and sat in the other giant chair. She should have asked him to wait; she was dying for the loo. She fidgeted in her chair, getting her phone out then putting it back again each time she remembered she had no signal.

That was another virtue of this place: you couldn't be contacted. She knew that as a DC she should be available at all times, just in case. But tonight was for her and Rav, and it couldn't do any harm to be out of communication for a couple of hours.

Rav reappeared with a WKD and a pint of something dark.

"Sorry," Connie breathed, "just need to go to the loo."

She headed for the toilets and hurried into the cubicle. When she emerged, another woman was standing at the mirrors, doing her mascara.

She gave Connie a smile as she washed her hands. "Hi."

Connie resisted the urge to look around. *Who, me?* "Hi." She kept her head down and focused on washing her hands.

"I've seen you somewhere before."

Connie looked up. "Sorry. Don't think so."

"Yes I have. Do you live on Avenue Road? Kings Heath?"

Connie felt her breathing still. "No, but... do you?"

"Yeah. That poor bloke, the one who was killed. I used to get his shopping sometimes."

"Albert's?"

"Yeah. Baked beans and porridge oats. He didn't exactly

have sophisticated tastes. He wasn't in the last time I went round, though."

"You took his shopping round and he wasn't in?"

"Last time I'm doing that. The next time, I made sure I popped round before going to the Co-op. Cost me a fortune, the shop. And I don't eat bloody baked beans."

"When was this?"

The woman had gone back to her mascara. She leaned into the mirror, her eyes wide, her mouth twisted in concentration. "I dunno. Last Monday, I guess?"

"That was when you went to check on him before going to the Co-op?"

"Yeah. The Monday before was when I took his shopping and he weren't there. Always Mondays."

"But he was there the Monday after that? Last Monday?"

"He wasn't. But there were two blokes hanging around."

Connie placed a hand on the sink, resisting the urge to grab it so tight she ended up tearing it from the wall. "Say that again."

The woman plunged the wand back into her mascara and looked at Connie in the mirror. "I shouldn't be telling you all this. Which house do you live at?"

Connie brought her ID out of her jacket pocket, relieved she hadn't taken the jacket off along with her coat. "I'm part of the investigating team."

"Investigating his murder?" The woman gave an exaggerated shudder.

"Yes. Well, no. Actually we're investigating another crime that took place in his house. Do you know Freya Garside?"

A grimace. "Ugh. That interfering old witch. Everyone

knows her. Can't avoid her. What's she blethering about now?"

"She was assaulted, in Albert North's house."

"Poor bitch. Sorry, I mean poor woman. No one deserves that. She dead too?" The woman brought a lipstick out of her bag and started to apply it.

"Sorry," Connie said. "What's your name?"

Lipstick went onto the woman's top lip, then the bottom. She smacked her lips together and leaned back, admiring her handiwork. "Keisha Stanton. I live four doors down from Freya. Miss Garside, as she likes to be called. Why?"

"When you visited Mr North's house and the two men were there, what kind of men? Did you get a look at them? Speak to them?"

Keisha zipped up her bag and wrinkled her nose, considering. "I heard them talking. Scottish guy. And another one, sounded Russian or something. The Scottish guy looked scared."

"Did you hear any of their conversation?"

The door to the toilets opened and two women came in, glancing at Connie and Keisha as they made for the cubicles.

Connie drew herself up. "Keisha, do you mind if I call round and see you in the morning? I think you might be able to help us."

Keisha's eyes widened. "Me?" she chuckled. "Yeah, course. Not sure how much I'll remember, but yeah, if I can help, I will."

"D'you mind giving me your phone number?" Connie grabbed her notebook from the pocket of her jacket and held out a piece of paper.

"Why not?" Keisha wrote a number on the paper with the pen Connie had given her and handed it back to her.

"Thanks." Connie scanned the paper and pocketed it.

"No worries. Hope Freya's alright, like."

She turned away, throwing her bag over her shoulder, and left the toilets. The door banged behind her.

Back at the table, Rav had downed his pint. "You OK?" He looked concerned. "You were... ages."

Connie scanned the bar. There was no sign of Keisha.

Shit.

She looked at her drink. Her mind was racing. She couldn't do this, not now.

"Rav," she said. "D'you mind if we call it a night? I just... I might have had a breakthrough on the case."

CHAPTER FIFTY-FOUR

Zoe yawned and stood up from her desk as Rhodri entered the outer office. Connie was already in, had arrived a couple of minutes after Zoe. But to give Rhodri his due, they were all early; it wasn't long gone 7.30.

Each of them had their own reasons to want this case wrapped up, of course. Rhodri had his trip to the valleys to look forward to, Connie had her brother Zaf at home and Zoe had Nicholas back from university.

Although right now, work was one of the few places she could take refuge from the frosty atmosphere between her and Carl.

"Rhod," she said as he slung his coat over the back of his chair. "Morning."

"Morning boss." His eyes were baggy, but bright with excitement about something. "I've got something for you."

"Good."

"Me too." Connie pulled her chair closer to them. "I was in the Ba—"

CHAPTER FIFTY-FOUR

"Hang on a tick," Zoe interrupted. "Before we do this, I need coffee."

"I'll get it." Rhodri turned towards the door.

"Rhod, you're not my butler. I want coffee, so I'll make coffee. Can I get you both one?"

"Tea for me, please," Rhodri said

"Yeah, me too," added Connie. She reached in her bag. "Can you use this teabag?"

Zoe took the bag from her and sniffed it. "What is it?"

"Strawberry."

Zoe pulled a face. "OK."

"I'm trying to lose some weight."

"Switching to tea that smells like the bottom of my gran's handbag isn't going to help you lose weight."

"It's part of my new healthy eating regime."

"Connie," Zoe told her. "You're not overweight. And Christmas is coming up."

Connie blushed. "My mum stuffs us full of food at Christmas. Now I've got my own place, I'm trying to create a bit of balance."

"Fair enough." Zoe palmed the teabag and made for the kitchen.

Ten minutes later, she was back. She placed the steaming mug of pale pink liquid in front of Connie.

"Good luck with that."

Connie smiled. "Thanks."

"And proper tea for you," Zoe told Rhodri as she handed his over.

"Ah cheers, boss." He slurped it noisily. "That's perfect."

Zoe had never understood tea. The kind of mid-brown builder's brew Rhodri drank was bad enough, but the weak piss in Connie's mug... Ugh.

Coffee was what she needed. She'd added extra granules and a couple of spoonfuls of sugar, to perk herself up. She took a sip and nodded appreciatively.

"So," she said as she approached the board. "Update me. Connie first."

Rhodri opened his mouth, then closed it with a disappointed look. Connie swung towards the board in her chair. If she wanted to get on a health kick, not using that chair like it was a form of transport would be a start.

"So I bumped into this woman in Bacchus Bar last night," Connie began.

Rhodri snorted. "Lucky you."

"Rhod," Zoe said.

"Sorry."

"She was in the loos, recognised me from the case. Keisha Stanton. Turns out she lives on Avenue Road, used to get shopping for Albert. Aleksander."

Zoe frowned. "Surely we've already spoken to her."

"Seems not. I've checked the witness statements and every time someone knocked on her door, there was no answer."

"So if she did his shopping for him, she knew him well?"

"Not really, from what I could tell. But she did say she saw two men visiting his house. After he went missing."

Zoe was about to write Keisha's name on the board. She stopped, pen in mid-air. "Two men?"

Connie nodded.

"What kind of men?"

"One of them was Scottish."

"Jimmy Kirk," breathed Rhodri.

"Yeah," agreed Connie. "And the other one, she said he sounded Russian."

CHAPTER FIFTY-FOUR

"Does Russian sound like Bosnian?" Rhodri asked.

"She said Russian 'or something'."

"I don't imagine the average Brummie knows the difference," said Zoe as she wrote the woman's name on the board. She drew one line from that to Jimmy Kirk, and another to a space in which she wrote *Unknown man*.

The board wasn't as full as it had been. They'd removed anything directly linked to the Albert North case, but carefully preserved anything related to Freya Garside's attack.

"Connie, I want you to follow this up. Did this woman by any chance give you a phone number?"

"She did."

"Good. Call her and arrange a proper interview. Make sure you ask her lots of questions about Freya. It's important this is linked to the fact that Freya was assaulted in Albert's house."

Zoe knew she was on thin ice with this request. But she had legitimate reason to speak to Albert and Freya's neighbours, and a potential witness had come forward.

"Will do," said Connie.

Zoe turned to Rhodri. "You've got something too?"

He grinned. "Yeah."

"Hit us with it, then."

"I went down the canals last night. One of my mates in Uniform told me where some homeless guys hang out. I thought they might use the shelter where Jimmy Kirk works."

"OK. And?"

"They said Jimmy didn't get on with Albert."

"What d'you mean, didn't get on?"

"Albert wouldn't go to the shelter when Jimmy was there. Didn't want to be near him."

"They say why?"

"They didn't know."

Zoe scratched her chin. "That doesn't help us much."

"With respect, boss," said Connie, "it does. If Albert and Jimmy weren't mates, then it makes Jimmy going to Albert's house suspicious."

Rhodri drew in a tight breath, reminding Zoe of a kid in school who'd just worked out the answer to a question. "And if Jimmy was at the house after Albert moved out…"

Zoe pointed the pen at him. "You're right. Jimmy made out he barely knew Albert when Rod spoke to him. But if he was at his house…" She shook her head. "I'm sorry, guys."

"What?" Rhodri asked.

"This is too… we can't paint this as being part of the Freya Garside investigation. Connie, before you make that call I'll have to speak to the DCI."

"But boss—"

"I don't want us all getting into trouble. And if the Home Office are involved, that's bigger than just Frank. Give me an hour." She looked at her watch and sighed. "No, give me a couple of hours. I'll talk to Frank and get back to you."

Connie and Rhodri exchanged irritated looks. Zoe knew how they felt, but she had to make the sensible decision.

The door opened and the three of them turned towards it. Zoe's heart lifted; maybe Frank was in early.

It wasn't Frank.

"Zoe, we need a word."

Connie looked at Zoe. "Boss," she whispered. "What's she—"

Zoe shook her head. "Layla. What brings you back here so soon?"

"Can I talk to you, in private?"

CHAPTER FIFTY-FIVE

Freya gasped, flailing with her hands to grab something. Anything.

She could feel him behind her, the man. His breathing, heavy and ragged. The smell of his clothes, like he hadn't washed for a day or two. And the quiet way he moved, creeping up on her before she'd had a chance to run.

She lashed out, her hand coming into contact with something hard, and shrieked. Her eyes were open but all she could make out were dim shapes, the silhouettes of trees moving at the end of the alleyway.

"Freya? Freya, wake up. You're OK, you're in hospital."

"Hospital?" Her voice was a croak. A whisper.

"You're in the Queen Elizabeth hospital in Selly Oak. You came here after suffering a head injury."

She raised a finger to her head. There was a bandage.

"No. I'm at..." Her mind was playing tricks on her. "I'm at Mr North's house. In his garden."

A hand clasped hers. "Freya. You're safe now. You're in hospital. My name's Di, I'm one of the nurses."

"Oh." The woman had no reason to lie. Freya opened her eyes again to see a slim red-haired woman smiling at her. She sat on the bed Freya was lying in.

"I'm…" She had been about to say she was scared. But Freya Garside didn't get scared. "Thank you."

"Can I get you a cup of tea? Breakfast'll be round in a minute, we've got the urn on."

Freya licked her lips. They were dry. "Please."

The bed shifted as the nurse stood up. "You don't go anywhere, OK?"

Freya attempted to smile. She closed her eyes again. She could see him, the man who had attacked her. Or at least she could make out the dim shape of him, coming at her through Mr North's kitchen.

She'd been a fool, going in there when the owner had been murdered. But she'd been in before, and it had been fine.

She opened her eyes. She had to remember more, so she could be a more effective witness. Help the police catch him. Then maybe the memories would leave her alone.

CHAPTER FIFTY-SIX

"I wasn't expecting you back so soon," Zoe told Layla as she closed the door to her office. "You applying for a permanent job?"

"The DCI wants me back working with you. But not permanently."

"OK. But you were brought in for the Albert North case."

"Which you're still investigating."

Zoe put a hand on her desk. "We were pulled off the case. You were here whe—"

"You're still working the case. You've been seen on Avenue Road."

"One of his neighbours was attacked. We're investigating that."

Layla took a step forward. "I'm ex-PSD, Zoe. That doesn't wash with me."

Zoe took a breath. Her skin felt tight. "Layla, I'd appreciate it if you'd call me boss." She narrowed her eyes.

"Ma'am, even. If you're going to be rejoining my team, then some respect is in order."

Layla lowered her gaze, then brought it back up again. "I apologise. That was inappropriate. But I have to warn y—"

"You're telling me Frank has told you to come back into the team to help us with an assault case? You're that short of things to do between now and Christmas?"

"Can I sit down?"

"Of course."

Layla took the chair closest to the door. Zoe rounded the desk and sat in her own chair. She clasped her hands in her lap, then loosened them and wiped them on her jeans. Her hands were hot.

"DI Finch, you know that we were briefly suspicious of you during the investigation int—"

"And I was exonerated. I did nothing wrong."

"I know."

"So why are you bringing it up now?"

"You have a tendency to... to work under your own initiative."

Zoe laughed. "What's that supposed to mean?" She looked through the glass partition that separated them from the main office. Rhodri was watching them. He turned away quickly.

"You've disobeyed orders to drop an investigation before. You've taken it upon yourself t—"

"Layla. If you're rejoining my team then that's fine. But this," Zoe waved her hand between the two of them, "this is inappropriate. Do you want me to assign a role to you, or not?"

"Of course."

"Good. In that case, I'd like you to go to the hospital and

find out if Freya Garside can remember anything more about her attacker."

"You spoke to her yesterday."

"She might remember more, after a good night's sleep."

Layla looked at Zoe for a moment, as if deciding whether to challenge her. At last she stood up.

"Very well," she said. "I'll need details of where she is."

"Connie can give you those."

Layla's hand was on the doorknob.

"Thanks," Zoe said. "An extra pair of hands will help us wrap this up quicker." She noticed that Layla had asked her nothing about a potential suspect or any leads.

As Layla opened the door, Zoe sat up straighter. "Layla," she said, "are you here to spy on me?"

Layla turned towards her but didn't make eye contact. "Just be careful, boss. That's all I'm saying."

CHAPTER FIFTY-SEVEN

"Bear with me a minute, and I'll see if I can find the appropriate person."

Appropriate person? Rhodri looked at his watch. It was 8am, he was surprised anyone was in at Social Services.

After a few minutes the on-hold music stopped.

"Hello?" came a female voice.

"Er, hi. Is that...? Sorry. My name's DC Hughes, I'm with West Midlands Police. We're investigating an assault and are looking for some background information around a homeless shelter you may have had dealings with."

"Go on."

"Can I ask your name?"

"Pip Newman. I'm the duty officer."

"OK. Thanks, Pip."

Pip? What kind of a name was that?

"So, er, Pip. It's Greenfields Shelter, in the city centre. We need to know if there have been any incidents or complaints relating to the place."

"That shelter is run by a charity."

CHAPTER FIFTY-SEVEN

"Which charity?"

"Er... oh no. It's a social enterprise. Greenfields Homelessness Support."

"Right. And have you had many dealings with them?"

"Not much. Not for a few months, anyway. Why?"

"The dealings you have had, have they involved complaints, or specific incidents?"

"They called us out when a boy we were supporting rocked up there. We took him home to his mum and dad."

Rhodri knew that kids who became homeless often felt unsafe at home.

"Did he run away from home?"

"It was fine, we did a full assessment and he wasn't at risk in the home setting. Is that all you need to know?"

"No other incidents? No complaints?"

"Look, the regulatory body for homeless shelters is the council. You'd have to speak to them."

Rhodri thought of how long it had taken to get the CCTV from the council. "There's a lot of overlap between your service users and those who use shelters."

"Not as much as you'd think. It's hard for us to provide support to someone who doesn't have an address."

"Surely they can use the shelter as their address."

"Greenfields doesn't provide that service. So we don—"

"Hang on," said Rhodri, "why?"

"Why what?"

"Why don't they let their clients use the shelter as an address?"

"It's not a legal requirement, you know. Maybe they can't be arsed with the paperwork."

"OK. Was it you who dealt with the shelter, when you picked that kid up?"

"Let me check the file... matter of fact, it was me and a colleague, yes."

How could someone not remember going to the shelter and making a vulnerable kid go back home?

"Was the guy at the shelter a Scottish bloke? Short, generously built?"

A snort. "Fat, you mean. Yes, that was him, as far as I remember. Bit of a bruiser."

"In what way?"

"Sorry. I shouldn't have said that."

"It's fine. What did he do to make you refer to him as a bruiser?"

"Oh, nothing." A pause. "I guess it was just his manner."

"No specific actions?" Rhodri asked. "You didn't see him threatening anyone? No violent behaviour?"

"No. Is he your suspect?"

"That's confidential. Look, if you remember anything else, give me a call, please?"

"I won't."

"You won't call me?"

"I won't remember anything else. Do you have any idea how many people I've got on my caseload?"

"Anyway, if you do remember anything, call me. At this number. Yeah?"

"Yeah."

The line went dead.

CHAPTER FIFTY-EIGHT

Keisha Stanton worked at a hair salon in Kings Heath. Connie strolled in and looked around. The salon was quiet, the only people present a tattooed man blow-drying the hair of a blonde woman.

She held up her ID. "I'm here to talk to Keisha. She's expecting me."

The man all but dropped his hairdryer and hurried over to her, pushing her ID down. "Don't go waving that around here, if you don't mind. Puts my customers off."

Connie looked around him at the blonde woman. She peered into the mirror, tweaking her hair. She didn't look the slightest bit concerned.

She looked at the man. "Where will I find her?"

"She's gone for a coffee. Place in Kings Court."

"Right." Connie left the shop, unsure where Kings Court was. She soon found it on her mobile; a two minute walk.

Keisha was sitting at one of the two tiny tables inside the coffee shop, an espresso in front of her. She looked up as Connie entered.

"Oh. Sorry, I wasn't in the shop. Sid tell you I was here?"

"He did. Can we have that chat now?"

"We can." Keisha gestured towards the barista behind the counter. "Only Sajid's a mate of mine and this is his business, so if you don't mind..."

"OK." Connie needed caffeine anyway. The strawberry tea had done nothing to allay her withdrawal symptoms. She approached the counter and the man gave her a questioning look.

"Large latte please, extra shot."

"I'll bring it over to you."

Connie thanked him and returned to Keisha's table.

"Thanks for seeing me."

"I'm required to by law, aren't I?"

Connie decided not to contradict her. "I'm investigating an attack on Freya Garside."

"Yeah. Poor old bat. How's she doing?"

"Not sure, sorry. She's in the QE."

Keisha winced. "That's not good. Hope she's got someone looking after her. I can't help you with that, though, I was out all yesterday, working."

"She was attacked at Albert North's house."

"Yeah, you said something about that in Bacchus."

"It's helpful to find out anything we can about that house or the people who may have visited it. One of the men you saw might have been Miss Garside's attacker."

"You think so? I don't see how that makes sense."

The barista put Connie's drink down in front of her. She was pleased to see it came in a mug and not one of those stupid latte glasses she could barely get her fingers into the handle of. "Cheers."

"No problem. Pay at the till before you go, yeah?"

"Course." She turned to Keisha. "If I showed you some photos, could you identify the man you saw?"

"Which one?"

"The Scottish one."

"I didn't get much of a look at him. I saw the Russian one though."

"Can you describe him for me?"

"Tall. Lanky. Thinning hair in a combover, I remember thinking how I could help him not look so bloody daft. Wearing a grey suit, looked like it had seen better days."

"You heard them both speak."

"Didn't catch any of the conversation though."

"Not? You seem quite sure about their accents."

A shrug. Connie sipped at her latte; it was good. The strawberry tea wasn't going to last long.

"I overheard them chatting when I was walking up to the house. They were at the side, coming out of the alleyway."

Connie nodded and drank some more of her coffee.

"D'you think it was one of them that attacked Freya?" Keisha asked.

"I'm not sure, but we want to follow up on anyone acting suspiciously in the vicinity. Had you ever seen them before?"

"No. Sorry."

"And did they spot you? Did they react?"

"I stopped walking when I saw them. Waited for them to go."

Connie nodded. "Here, let me show you those photos."

Connie opened up her phone. She'd gathered together some grainy images of men who looked a bit like Jimmy Kirk, as well as one of him from the CCTV. She handed the phone over.

"Sorry the images aren't all that clear."

"This isn't exactly a photo lineup, is it?"

"No," Connie replied.

"So you haven't arrested him."

"You know a lot about this."

"My half brother's a copper. Uniform, works over in Sandwell."

"So you know what we're up against. Take a look at these images. Do any of them look familiar to you?"

Keisha thumbed through the images on Connie's phone. Connie knew this wasn't a valid photo lineup, the kind of thing that could be used in evidence; to do one of those she'd need to get Keisha into a police station and find a member of staff who knew nothing about this case to administer it. But that only came after they had an arrest.

In the meantime, this might point her in the right direction.

"Him." Keisha held the phone out. "This was one of them. The Scottish guy."

Connie looked at her phone. The photo of Kirk from the CCTV was displayed.

"Thanks. You're sure you didn't see him around Avenue Road at any other time?"

"No. Sorry. What about the Russian bloke?"

"We don't have any photos there, I'm afraid."

"Bet you don't. Jake tells me a thing or two. If he's Russian and dodgy, he'll have buggered off home."

"Let's hope not."

CHAPTER FIFTY-NINE

Zoe dropped Layla off at the QE before heading to Albert North's house. It was a legitimate place for her to attend as it was a crime scene again – but this time for an assault that had actually taken place there rather than a murder that had happened somewhere else.

As she drove away she watched Layla walk into the hospital through her rear-view mirror. She'd spent more time than she cared to remember in and around this hospital; whenever she came now her mind was filled with images of her dad and the times they'd been here when he was having chemo. The hospital had been different then. Now it was a landmark on the south Birmingham skyline, unmissable for miles around. She'd preferred it back when she could find her way around the place.

Fifteen minutes later she pulled up on Avenue Road, three houses away from Albert's. This street of terraces was easier to park on than her own, as most of the houses had front drives. Albert's and Freya's were two of only five that still had gardens instead of tarmac.

She registered the Christmas lights in the windows as she walked to Albert's house. The dead man's house looked sad without them. He would have left his home much too early for that kind of thing.

An FSI van was parked outside the house, and a white-suited tech emerged as she approached.

"Ma'am."

"Hi, Rav." She couldn't be bothered telling him not to Ma'am her. "How's it going?"

"Good. Adi's in the van, he can talk you through what we've got."

Zoe rubbed her hands together, as much from the cold as from anticipation, and made her way to the van. Adi was in the driver's seat, a laptop balanced on his knee.

She knocked on the window. He started then turned to her. When he released who it was, he smiled and gestured for her to join him in the passenger seat.

"I'm not going in there," he said as she closed the door. "Keeping the two teams separate. Rav's been keeping me up to speed."

"Progress?" Zoe asked.

"Lots."

Zoe turned to him, her breath steaming in front of her in the cold van. A tiny Christmas tree hung off the rear-view mirror.. "Go on."

Adi closed the lid of the computer. "We found spots of blood in the doorway out to the back garden, and more in the garden itself. Lots in the alleyway, but that was almost all Freya's."

"What does the spatter look like?"

"Consistent with her being hit with a blunt object. Most of it went up the wall to next door. We've cordoned off the

CHAPTER FIFTY-NINE

alleyway but the sooner we can finish here, the sooner the neighbours can get access to their garden."

"The blood spots in the doorway, were those Freya's too?"

Adi flashed raised eyebrows at her. "No. And they weren't Albert's. They're new, though, from within the last forty-eight hours, and they belong to someone whose DNA we didn't find the first time we examined the place."

"So it's someone who hadn't been here before."

"We can't say that, precisely. Just someone who didn't leave traces of DNA the last time they were here."

Zoe screwed up her face. Connie had spoken to that neighbour, who said she'd seen a Scotsman when she'd visited, long before Freya's assault. If the mysterious Scotsman was Jimmy, he'd have left traces.

"Did you analyse the alleyway last time you were here?"

Adi looked at her. "Sorry, no. It wasn't a crime scene."

"So there might have been traces from this person in the alleyway from earlier."

"It's possible. None in the house, though."

"Have you compared it to the samples we took from the other neighbour who entered the house?"

"It doesn't match those. We'll run it against the database." Adi leaned back, eyeing her. "Are you even supposed to be here?"

"I'm investigating Freya's attack. Not Albert's death."

"Of course you are."

They looked at each other for a moment. Zoe wondered if Adi had something else to tell her, something relating to the murder case. Something he wasn't allowed to mention.

"Adi, you were taken off the Albert North case too. D'you know who's handling the forensics?"

He scratched his face through his mask. "I haven't been informed of who it went to."

"That isn't the same as not knowing. The world of forensics isn't a big one, you must have—"

"I do know, right, Zoe. I do know. But I'm not sure how I feel about passing that information on."

She nodded. "I'm not asking you to break any rules or betray confidences. But if in the course of investigating the attack on Freya Garside you found anything else that might be of use, you'd—"

"I'd send it on to the Home Office. I've got two kids, Zoe. I can't afford to lose my job."

"I'm sorry, I didn't—"

"I'm divorced. Four years ago. Not that you ever took any notice."

"Adi. I'm sorry."

Adi had had what Zoe liked to think of as a crush on her, over a year ago. She hadn't considered it to be anything more than that, hadn't wanted to. Did he resent her lack of interest?

"I'm sorry, Adi," she repeated. "I didn't mean to upset you. And no, I don't expect you to tell me anything."

"Good." He looked past her, at the passenger door. A hint. "I'll let you know if we get a match for those blood spots."

"How long will that take?"

He shrugged, his hand reaching into his pocket. "Not sure. It's Christmas. I'll keep you posted."

He pulled his hand out of his pocket and placed it very briefly on her knee. She flinched then berated herself. Adi gave her a smile then opened the driver's door and left the van.

CHAPTER FIFTY-NINE

Zoe watched him approach Rav outside the house, then realised he'd left something behind.

There was a folded-up piece of paper on her knee, right where Adi's hand had been. He'd been attempting to draw her attention to it.

Zoe smiled and grabbed the paper before opening the passenger door.

CHAPTER SIXTY

Freya sat up in bed, a blanket wrapped around her shoulders. They'd replaced the bandage with the largest plaster she'd ever seen. After a breakfast of soggy toast and strong tea, a doctor young enough to be her grandson had poked and prodded at her, then declared her well enough to go home later.

Go home? She'd spent the night in delirious nightmares. She was hardly fit to go home.

But they needed the bed, and this was the modern NHS. Old women like her were nothing more than a burden.

The nurse was talking to a young Asian woman. She turned in Freya's direction and pointed. Freya frowned; not another visitor. This one would be a junior doctor or maybe one of those busybody social workers wanting to ask how she would cope at home.

Dear God, maybe they'd suggest putting her into care. That would never happen, so long as Freya had breath in her body.

"Hello," the young woman said as she approached the

bed. "I'm Detective Sergeant Kaur." She pulled the curtains closed around them, making Freya feel uneasy. "I work with DI Finch. How are you feeling today?"

"Fine." Freya wasn't about to open up to this woman.

The detective smiled and sat in the flimsy plastic chair next to Freya's bed. "I hope you don't mind, but now that you've had some time to recover, I was hoping you might be able to tell me more about what happened."

"I already told your colleague."

A nod. "I know that. And I'm so sorry to make you go through this again. But your memory will be recovering. And the more you can tell us, the better able we'll be to find whoever did this to you."

Freya sniffed. "I already told your boss, I hardly saw him. He was behind me."

Another nod. The detective pulled the chair a little closer. Freya shifted in the bed, trying to move away.

The detective pulled out a notebook and placed it in her lap. "Can you tell me what happened, from the moment you entered the house?"

"Do I have to?" It hurt to remember it, both physically and emotionally. But Freya wasn't about to admit that. "Surely you can read what your colleague wrote up."

"I already have." The detective looked down at her notebook. "You said he was wearing a brown tweed jacket with blue jeans and a red shirt, is that right?"

"It is."

"And can you describe what happened?"

Freya swallowed. She closed her eyes. "I was in the kitchen. He was in the house before I came in, I think."

"He was in there before you entered?"

"I'm not sure. I think so."

"So you were in the kitchen, and..."

"He came in. Tried to grab me. I ran. Into the garden." She could feel her breath shortening. "He caught up with me in the alleyway. Almost in the alleyway. I think." It was hazy.

"It's OK, Freya."

Freya opened her eyes. "Miss Garside. Please."

The woman smiled. "Miss Garside. Sorry. Did he say anything?"

"I... I can't remember."

"You're sure?"

"Yes." Maybe if Freya gave one-word answers, the woman would go away.

But Freya had always wanted to be a witness in a serious crime investigation. She'd relished being able to help the police with their enquiries into Albert's death.

When she was the victim, things felt a little different.

She took a deep breath, regretting it as she broke into a spate of coughing. The detective grabbed the glass of water on the bedside cabinet.

"There." She held it out, all but pushing it into Freya's hand.

Freya grimaced. *Leave me alone, damn you.* She took the glass, knowing it was the best way to pacify the woman, and drank.

It helped. After a moment the soreness in her throat had subsided and she no longer felt the need to cough.

The detective held out her hand to take the glass. Freya handed it to her. She hated being this helpless. Having complete strangers do something as straightforward as hand her a glass of water...

"You said that he was middle-aged."

"Fifty, I said. Or around that." Freya sniffed. She might

not have seen as much of her attacker as she'd have liked to, but she wouldn't have said anything as vague as *middle-aged*.

"Do you remember anything else now?"

Freya reached into her mind, pushing away the feelings of dread. Trying to remember only made her feel the way she'd felt when she'd woken up from that nightmare this morning.

Her hands were trembling. She shoved them under the bedcovers.

"I apologise," she said, trying hard to make her voice sound convincing instead of pathetic. "I don't remember anything more."

"Did he speak at all? Did you hear his voice?"

Freya closed her eyes, going back over her experience in Albert's house. Under the sheets, she clenched her hands into tight fists.

You can do this.

She opened her eyes. "He shouted."

"What was his voice like? Loud, quiet? Did he have an accent?"

Freya felt woozy. Was it the drugs they'd given her, or delayed shock?

She blinked, hard, three times, then balled her fists even tighter. "He was Scottish."

"Scottish. Can you remember what he said?"

"He shouted. It was... it was unclear. He was a way away from me at that point. But..." Freya forced herself to remember. "*Oh no you don't.* That's what he said."

"Oh no you don't what, do you know?"

"No. Sorry. Get away, I suppose. *Not so fast.* He said that, too. *Not so fast.*"

The detective looked at her for a moment. "Miss Garside, how well did you know Albert North?"

Freya felt heat in her face. She knew she hadn't known Mr North well enough to be entering his house, twice, with Ruti's keys.

"How is Ruti?" she asked. "His neighbour? The man didn't get her, did he?"

"Your neighbour is fine. Don't worry." The detective put a hand on the bed, as if she wanted to grab Freya's shaking fingers. Freya shifted away again. If this carried on, she would fall out of the bed. And then where would they be?

"Good." Ruti didn't deserve any of this. Freya was beginning to regret ever having knocked on the poor woman's door.

"Miss Garside, I asked you if you knew Albert well."

"Not really. Passing acquaintances."

"But you were worried about his welfare when you realised he was missing."

"I wanted to... I wanted to help."

"Is there any chance Albert might have told you something that your attacker didn't want you to know?"

"What kind of thing?"

"I don't know. Something about his past, maybe?"

"His past? What's that got to do with anything? He was an old man, just that."

The detective checked her notes again. "You still don't remember anything more than the man saying 'Oh no you don't' and 'not so fast'."

"No, sorry."

"That's helpful. I'm sorry to have put you through the stress of reliving this."

"It's fine. I just want to be useful."

CHAPTER SIXTY-ONE

Connie was at her desk staring at the screen when her mobile rang.

"Rav," she said as she picked up. "I owe you an—"

"It's OK. So can I take you back to Bacchus another time, then? Maybe stay longer than half an hour."

"I'm sorry."

"I already said, it's OK. Are you alright? You seemed... odd last night."

"It's just this case. It's getting to me. I'll be fine once we've found Freya's attacker."

"You're thinking about the murder case too, aren't you?"

Connie clutched the phone tighter. Rhodri was at his desk opposite, eyes fixed on his screen. She knew he was listening in.

"We've been pulled off that, Rav. You know I can't."

"Yeah. But if it's any help, there's fresh DNA in the house."

"Albert's house?"

"Yeah. Someone was in there who hadn't previously left a trace."

"Who?"

"We don't know yet. We're analysing it, in case we can match it to anyone on the system."

"OK. Let us know if that happens, yeah?"

"Course." Rav hung up.

Connie put down her phone and stared into her screen.

She wasn't sure what to do with this new information, apart from discuss it with the boss when she came back. But meanwhile, she needed to find something to back up what Keisha had told her about the two men visiting Albert. And find a link to Freya, if she could.

Might Freya have visited Albert, come into contact with the men?

The men. One of them Scottish, the other Russian. 'Or something'.

Jimmy Kirk was Scottish. They had CCTV of him with Albert at Victoria Square. Dragging him behind the stall. And Keisha had identified Kirk from the footage as the man she'd seen.

A good lawyer would say that Jimmy saw Albert collapse and then pulled him to a place of safety while he called for help.

But nobody had called 999. And they didn't have access to Jimmy Kirk, not in relation to the murder, so they couldn't check his version of events.

If she had more CCTV, then she might be able to see what happened afterwards. Find out if Albert had visited that spot earlier in the day. If Jimmy had.

But Connie was investigating an assault in Kings Heath,

miles away from Victoria Square, and she had no reason to be requesting CCTV from the city centre.

She leaned back in her chair and yawned. Despite her early night last night and her truncated date with Rav, she'd had little sleep. She'd lain awake all night, thinking about Albert North. Aleksander. About what he'd done.

Did a man like that deserve to be murdered? Was it only fair that he got what he'd dished out to so many others? Or was the boss right, and due process was what mattered most?

Connie didn't know any more. But what she did know was they had a case to investigate. And Freya Garside, annoying as she was, deserved for her attacker to be brought to justice.

So what did they have on him?

The fact that a Scotsman had visited Albert. A Scotsman who, she had to admit, might very well not be Jimmy. Keisha's identification was hardly watertight, after all.

The CCTV. Which had no bearing on Freya's assault.

What else?

She leaned back.

"Shit."

Rhodri looked up from his desk. "What's up?"

"The scarf."

"The one that other neighbour saw?"

Connie nodded. "Freya said that her attacker was wearing a red shirt with blue jeans and a tweed jacket. Old-fashioned, don't you think?"

Rhodri shrugged. "Kind of. I guess."

"Let me..." Connie opened up her browser and started a search.

"What you looking for, Con?"

Don't call me that. She carried on searching.

"Can I help?"

She shook her head. "You just carry on with what you're doing. I'm alright." She wasn't even sure if she should be doing this. But it was Freya's description of her attacker. Freya's assault.

It was fine.

"Whoah." She stopped on the eighth search result, staring into her screen.

"What?" Rhodri rose from his chair. "Con, you're killing me with this."

She nodded at her screen. "Look at him. At what he's wearing."

Rhodri rounded the desks. He put a hand on Connie's chair, making her flinch, and leaned in to look at the screen.

"That's Jimmy Kirk," he said.

"At a fundraiser for the shelter."

"Shaking a tin, drumming up support."

"That's right," she said. "But look at what he's wearing."

"A jacket."

"A tweed jacket."

"And a scarf."

Connie bit her lip as she zoomed in. She imported the photo to her computer and enhanced it. "A yellow scarf."

"And what's that he's wearing under the coat?"

A collar was sticking out, just under the collar of the jacket.

"A red shirt," said Connie.

"Jimmy Kirk's wearing the exact outfit that Freya described."

Connie turned to Rhod. "He is. Plus that yellow scarf."

CHAPTER SIXTY-TWO

"Seriously?" Zoe said into the hands-free. She was driving through Selly Oak once again. This time, thankfully, it wasn't raining. She was even enjoying relatively clear traffic.

"Yeah," Connie replied. "It's on the Birmingham Mail website."

Zoe looked in her rear-view mirror, indicated, then pulled over. She was on double yellows, but she wouldn't be long. A car horn blared as she stopped the ignition.

"Send me a link," she said.

"Done it."

"Thanks." Zoe looked at her phone and clicked the link Connie had sent her. Sure enough, there was Jimmy Kirk, wearing a yellow scarf.

"And you say a neighbour, Darren Hudson, reports that the man he saw at Albert's was wearing this?"

"Yeah. And look at the rest of the outfit. It's what Freya described."

"It is." Zoe pinched the screen to zoom in. She'd have to

take Connie's word for it on the details, but it looked accurate enough.

It was just an outfit. It was circumstantial.

But how many people wore yellow scarves like that? Combined with tweed jackets and red shirts?

She'd certainly never seen it before.

"OK. Thanks, Connie."

Another car blared its horn at her. She had to park, or go back to the office.

The office would be better.

She drove to Harborne, occasionally fingering the piece of paper in her pocket. The information that Adi had left.

DRT Forensics. Working for security services. All I've got.

So the security services were investigating Albert's murder. And they had one of the top forensics specialists in the country working on it.

Fifteen minutes later, she was outside Frank's office, rapping on the door.

"Be in, Frank," she muttered to herself.

"Who is it?"

Zoe felt her muscles unclench. That he was in was something, at least. She opened the door.

"Frank, I need to update you on the Freya Garside case."

He looked up from his papers, taking off a pair of glasses and placing them on the desk.

"Since when...?" she asked, looking at the specs.

"Don't ask. I'm getting old. What is it?"

She sank into the chair opposite him. "We have grounds for arrest. I need a warrant."

"Who?"

"Jimmy Kirk."

CHAPTER SIXTY-TWO

"That's quite a coincidence."

"It makes sense. If he did kill Albert North—"

"Which you have no business speculating on."

"No. But if he did, and Freya was sniffing around, then he might have attacked her to shut her up."

"And why would he have been at the house?"

"Maybe to remove evidence that he'd been there before. We've got a witness who says she saw him there six days before Albert died."

"Zoe, you're not supposed to be investigating the Albert North murder. Both of us could get into—"

"I'm not. I promise. Connie bumped into a woman in Bacchus bar, a neighbour. She recognised Connie and started talking to her." Zoe paused, looking at him in a way that she hoped conveyed honesty. "We didn't go looking for this, I swear to you."

"So what else do you have that links Jimmy Kirk to Freya's attack? Make sure this is specific to the assault, mind. Nothing about the murder."

Zoe nodded. "A neighbour, a Darren Hudson. He saw a man hanging around near Albert's house around the time Freya was attacked. The man went into the alleyway and came out again. He was wearing a yellow scarf."

"A yellow scarf."

"Like Rupert the Bear." She was aware how stupid she sounded. "And Connie has found a photo of Jimmy Kirk wearing the exact same scarf two months ago. Along with the outfit Freya Garside described her attacker as wearing. He fits the physical description too. And Freya says her attacker had a Scottish accent, too."

"You need to check how many of these scarves there are

in circulation. I bet they're common. As are Scots in Birmingham. It's not enough."

"It's not just the scarf."

"Zoe. She's an elderly woman with a head wound. It's really not enough for an arrest."

"You haven't met Freya Garside. She's not what you think." Zoe balled her fists on her knees. "OK. At least let me bring him in for questioning. Under caution."

Frank cocked his head. "I've already told you you can't arrest him. What good would a caution do?"

"I want to find out more about his relationship with Albert." Zoe raised a hand as Frank opened his mouth. "It is relevant to the Freya Garside attack. It gives him motive."

"He only has motive if it can be proved he was involved in Albert's murder. And we're not working that case."

"There's the CCTV. I'm prepared to bet the Home Office or whoever's investigating are watching him."

"You know I don't have any knowledge of that. It's well above my pay grade."

"Who is investigating it? If it's not us, it'll be MI5."

Frank stood up. "I've already told you, I don't know. And given your history, I'd steer clear of sticking your nose in, if I were you."

Zoe stood up to face him. "Frank. All I want to do is interview the man. A caution means he has full legal rights. Give me that, and if it provides me with nothing, I'll pursue other lines of enquiry."

"You will?"

She blinked. "I will."

Frank gripped the desk. His knuckles were red. "OK. But Zoe, you'd better not be lying to me."

CHAPTER SIXTY-THREE

Zoe wished she had Mo with her. The two of them had conducted interviews together for years, decades in fact. They had a way of knowing what the other one was going to ask, of backing each other up at just the right time.

But the one and only time she'd been in an interview with Layla Kaur, she'd been the one on the receiving end.

She'd rather take Connie or Rhodri in with her, but Frank had insisted. Yet another indication that he didn't trust her. And it was increasingly clear that Layla didn't, either.

She tugged at her shirt as they walked along the corridor to the interview room. She'd worked with people she didn't trust, and who didn't trust her, before. David Randle for one. But she'd never been managed by someone with so little respect for her. And she'd certainly never had a team member who spoke to her the way Layla had spoken in her office earlier.

If it wasn't for the history between them, Zoe would have reported her for insubordination.

They arrived at the door to the interview room. Zoe

turned to Layla. She had to stamp her authority on this process, to ensure Layla didn't take over.

"Ready?" she said.

"Of course."

"I'll take the lead. Your job is to stare him down, make him feel uncomfortable."

"If you're sure..."

"You're good at that."

Layla gave her a look but didn't argue. Zoe resisted a smile and pushed open the door.

Jimmy Kirk was inside, sitting across the table with a woman in her thirties next to him. He had a plaster on the back of his hand. He spotted her glancing at it and moved it under the table.

The woman beside him wore a trim blue suit and matching glasses, making Zoe think of Frank and his new specs. Frank would never look as professional as this in his new eyewear.

Zoe nodded at the woman. "I'm DI Finch. You must be Mr Kirk's lawyer."

The woman looked up from her files. "Diane Rees." She went back to her reading.

OK, Zoe thought. So that was how they were going to play it. She hoped this wasn't going to be a *no comment* interview.

She sat down opposite Jimmy, Layla taking the seat opposite the lawyer.

"Jimmy," Zoe said. "You're not under arrest but you are here under caution. Do you understand what that means?"

"Yes."

Zoe looked at the solicitor.

"I've explained it to my client."

"Very well. In that case, I'll start the recording."

Zoe set off the digital recorder, did the formal introductions, explained the caution again, then opened a blank notebook. She had notes beneath the open page, but she didn't want Kirk or his lawyer seeing them.

"Mr Kirk. Can I call you Jimmy?"

"Of course." He sat with an open posture, his legs uncrossed and his hands still beneath the table. He smelt of something Zoe couldn't identify. Zoe could hear movement; were his feet tapping?

"So, Jimmy. We've asked you to come in because the neighbour of a man you knew through your role at Greenfields Shelter was brutally assaulted yesterday."

The lawyer looked up. "Less of the hyperbole, please."

Zoe raised her eyebrows. "Very well. Jimmy, have you heard of a Freya Garside?"

"No."

"She lives in Avenue Road. The same road where Albert North lived. You have heard of Albert North, yes?"

"Your department has been pulled off the Albert North investigation," the solicitor said. "You can't ask my client questions about that case."

Zoe gave the woman a smile, hiding her unease at how this solicitor knew things like this. "I don't intend to. I'm just giving your client some context." She turned to Jimmy. "Freya Garside lives in Avenue Road in Kings Heath, along with Albert North, who I believe was a user of your shelter."

"He was."

"Jimmy, have you ever been to Avenue Road?"

He looked at her, his gaze steady. "I have."

Zoe spotted Layla's legs shift under the table.

"You have?" Zoe asked. "When?"

"I went there nine days ago. Mr North, Albert, had been unwell after visiting the shelter. Following that, he hadn't visited us for a few nights. I wanted to check up on him."

"Really? You make personal visits to all of your service users?"

"If I have concerns, yes."

"But when we first spoke to you, you barely remembered the man."

"I didn't recognise him."

Zoe leaned back. She flicked through her notebook, knowing there was little there to help her.

"Jimmy, Greenfields is a homeless shelter, is that right?"

"It is." He leaned forward. Zoe realised what it was he smelt of: garlic.

"So if you knew that Albert had a home, why did you allow him to use your services?"

"We di—"

The lawyer put a hand on his shoulder. "You don't need to answer any questions about the Albert North investigation. It's outside the scope of this interview."

Jimmy smiled at Zoe. "Sorry."

She pursed her lips. "Did you visit Avenue Road again yesterday?"

"Yesterday?"

"Tuesday. Did you go back to Albert's house?"

"DI Finch, you're asking my client about the wrong investigation again. I would ask you to restrict your questions to those directly related to the assault of Miss Garside, which is what you say you need to speak to Mr Kirk about."

"Miss Garside was assaulted yesterday lunchtime. At Albert North's house. So you can see, Miss Rees, that your client's presence on the premises is directly related to that offence, can you not?" Zoe gave the woman another smile, before returning her attention to Jimmy Kirk. "Jimmy, were you in Avenue Road at that time?"

"No."

"No?"

"I was at work. My colleague Lisa can back that up."

The lawyer frowned. Had she not been ready for this?

"That's odd," Zoe said, leaning towards Jimmy.

He looked back at her, a muscle under his right eye twitching just little.

"Because," she continued, "a man who lives in Avenue Road says he saw you there."

The lawyer placed her hand on the table, in front of her client. "What evidence do you have for this?"

Zoe turned to her. Her heart was racing. Layla stared ahead. Zoe began to wish she'd given the DS something to do.

"We have a witness statement. A neighbour says he saw Mr Kirk near Mr North's house."

"He can't have. Mr Kirk was at work. Can your witness identify Mr Kirk in a line-up?"

Zoe swallowed. All the witness had said was *yellow scarf*. He'd seen Jimmy, if it was Jimmy, at a distance.

She wasn't confident Darren Hudson would identify their suspect in a line-up. But she had no alternative.

"If Mr Kirk consents, then we'll be happy to set up a line-up."

"I'll need to confer with my client before we can agree to that."

I bet you will. Zoe flicked through her pad, wondering where Jimmy had found this lawyer.

"Boss," whispered Layla.

Zoe ignored her. She held her gaze on Jimmy.

"Jimmy, how long have you worked at Greenfields?"

"Boss," Layla repeated, her voice a hiss.

"Sorry," Zoe said. She turned to Layla, flashing her a look.

Layla leaned towards her. She held out her phone under the table.

There was a text.

Tell Zoe need to talk re DNA. Urgent.

"It's from Adi Hanson," Layla muttered.

"I know." Zoe looked across the table. "I'm pausing this interview. Please stay here."

CHAPTER SIXTY-FOUR

Zoe hurried along the corridor. She didn't want Jimmy Kirk or his eagle-eyed solicitor listening in on any of this.

At last she reached a spot in the building where she had some privacy and grabbed her phone.

"Zoe. Where were you? I've been trying to get hold of you."

"Sorry, Adi." She didn't mention the note he'd left her; knew he wouldn't want her to. "I'm in the middle of interviewing a suspect. And before that I was—"

"It doesn't matter. We've got a result for you."

"Go on."

"So we managed to isolate the DNA from the spots of blood around the kitchen door. There's some in the garden that mixed in with Freya's blood, but enough of hers on its own in the alleyway to be able to separate the two. And of course she consented to them taking a sample at the hospital."

"OK. Have you got a match?"

"I tried to call you, but I got Rhodri instead. He ran it through the database."

"OK." Why hadn't Rhodri come to her with this? "Who?"

"Jimmy Kirk. His DNA is on file, Rhodri says he was arrested for affray a couple of years ago. Not charged."

"Jimmy Kirk." Zoe resisted the urge to punch the wall.

"Rhodri's still working on it," Adi said. "He knows DCI Dawson's been reluctant to give you a warrant so he's pulling together an evidence log that should help."

"Good." Not like Rhodri to show such initiative; this case had brought something out in him.

Zoe brushed aside the thought that it was only the prospect of his visit to the valleys that had inspired him. "Thanks Adi. Sorry I was incommunicado."

"No problem."

She hurried upstairs and to the office. Rhodri was inside, at the printer, which appeared to be working now.

"Rhod," she said. "I've just spoken to Adi."

He grabbed the sheet making its way out of the printer and handed it to her. "This should give you what you need."

She looked at it. "Thanks, Rhodri. You've done well."

"Boss." He blushed.

She turned to Connie. "I need you to speak to your witness, the one who saw Jimmy at the house. Ask if he was wearing gloves. If not, did he have a cut on his hand?"

"Boss."

Zoe took a deep breath and pushed the door open.

Frank wasn't in his office. Zoe hammered on the door. Cursing under her breath.

"Shit!"

CHAPTER SIXTY-FOUR

She grabbed her phone and dialled his number. She heard ringing in the near distance. She hung up.

"Frank?"

Frank rounded a corner, dunking a biscuit into a cup of tea as he walked. The new specs were pushed up onto the top of his head.

"Zoe? What's so urgent?"

"I'm in the middle of interviewing Jimmy Kirk, and I got a call from Adi Hanson."

He pulled the specs down onto his face and took the document she was waving in his face.

"Jimmy Kirk's DNA is in the house. It wasn't there when we were investigating Albert North's death, but it was after Freya's attack. He bled in the doorway to the kitchen. He has a wound on his hand. Frank, you have to give me that warrant now."

He shoved the papers back into her hand. "Put this on the system."

"It already is. The warrant?"

Frank looked at her. Zoe could almost see the cogs whirring. "I'll get you that warrant. Now go and make the arrest."

"Thanks." She turned and hurried away.

"Zoe!" he called as she neared the stairs.

She turned. "What?"

"Only for Freya's assault, mind. Nothing to do with the murder."

"Of course not." Zoe might be keen, but she wasn't stupid.

She clattered down the stairs and all but ran to the interview room. Jimmy and the solicitor were still inside, Layla opposite them. The three of them sat in an awkward silence.

Zoe closed the door behind her and looked at Jimmy.

"What's going on?" The solicitor asked. "You should have given my client the opportunity to move to another room whi—"

Zoe ignored her.

"Jimmy Kirk, I'm arresting you on suspicion of assault. You do not have to say anything, but it may harm your defence if you do not mention when questioned something which you later rely on in court."

CHAPTER SIXTY-FIVE

"Thank you, young man."

"Are you sure you'll be alright?"

Freya put a hand on the paramedic's arm. "It's my home. I'll be fine. Thank you for walking me to the door."

Freya watched him walk away and closed the front door. She switched on the light in the hallway and then the kitchen. Freya was normally frugal, but today wasn't a day for that. She'd had twenty-four hours away from home, not turning on lights or using the heating; she could afford to be profligate.

She put just the right amount of water in the kettle and flicked it on. She wished the nurses were here to make her tea. Theirs was a little too strong for her liking, but it made a nice change to have someone else bring it to you. She sometimes went to the so-called Victorian tearoom in the park but it made her feel awkward and old, surrounded by young parents with pushchairs and children running everywhere.

The kettle clicked off and she reached into the cupboard for a cup and saucer. Her muscles felt creakier than usual.

It was understandable. She should be gentle with herself for a little while, allow herself time to recuperate.

She made her cup of tea and left the kitchen, flicking off the light as she went. There was decadence, and there was folly. In the living room, she turned on her reading light in the window, placed her cup and saucer on the coaster and picked up her book. It was where she had left it two nights ago, bookmark in place.

She caught movement out of the corner of her eye; someone outside. She shrank into her chair, suddenly remembering the sound of that man clattering through Mr North's kitchen. The feeling of terror when he'd caught up with her in the back yard and the confusion when she'd woken up in hospital.

She needed to pull herself together. Life was short, and she wasn't about to waste it feeling sorry for herself. Let alone allowing herself to fall prey to such a pointless emotion as fear.

She started at the sound of her doorbell. Had the movement outside been someone coming to her door?

If it was, then that meant someone was watching her. They'd been waiting. They'd seen her come home. They knew she would be in…

Stop it. She was being a stupid old woman.

She pushed herself up, cursing her old bones, and made her way to the door, pausing to close the living room curtains first. She didn't like the idea of people being able to see in, even if she liked being able to see out. But it was too dark to see anything other than the looming shadow of the park opposite.

No, Freya. She mustn't think like that. Being opposite the park was a joy, the thing she loved most about this house. She would not let it become a worry.

She opened the door to find the red-haired detective standing on the path.

"Hello?" Freya said. She hoped the woman didn't have more questions. She was tired. But she wouldn't say no.

The woman smiled at her. "I've got good news."

"Oh." Freya put a steadying hand on the door frame. "I'm sorry, where are my manners? Please, come in."

"It's alright. If you don't mind, I need to get home. To my son."

"I didn't know..."

"I wouldn't expect you to. Anyway. You'll be pleased to know we arrested a man, just over an hour ago."

"A man? The man who attacked me?"

The detective nodded. "We've charged him with your assault."

Freya felt her stomach lift. "Oh, well done. Did my description help?"

The woman smiled. "It did. For someone who had just undergone such an ordeal, you were incredibly detailed with the information you gave us."

"I only wanted to help."

"You did. And you don't have to worry about him now. He's in custody, and no threat to you or any of your neighbours."

"Thank you. Thank you so much."

CHAPTER SIXTY-SIX

"Hello?" Zoe closed the door behind her and slung her coat at the hook. It missed and fell to the floor. Remembering the reactions of both Carl and Nicholas last time that had happened, she stooped to pick it up and place it over the hook, with success this time.

"Miaow." The cat emerged from the living room and stared at Zoe as if she'd done something wrong.

"Yoda? What is it?"

"Miaow."

She stopped to stroke the cat. It turned away and walked into the living room. She followed it through to the kitchen. The cat stopped at its empty bowl.

"Ah, *that's* the problem." Zoe rummaged in a cupboard for a tin of cat food. Yoda purred and began to eat, unconcerned by the food falling onto its head as Zoe tried to spoon it into the bowl.

"Yoda, calm down. It's not going anywhere."

The cat ignored her and carried on eating as if this was the last meal on earth.

CHAPTER SIXTY-SIX

"Hey." Carl was in the doorway.

"Hey." Zoe felt her skin tighten. "You OK?"

He stepped into the kitchen and pulled her to him for a kiss. "I'm fine. Glad to see you. You're early. I assume that means you made an arrest."

She put a hand on his cheek. "You know me so well. We arrested Jimmy Kirk for Freya Garside's assault. I'm pretty sure he's the one who killed Albert North, too."

"You were pulled off that case."

"Doesn't stop me thinking about it." She put a hand on her hip. "Come on Carl love, tell me you've never had a case going round and round in your head after you've finished working on it."

"I suppose so."

"Exactly."

"But I'm worried about you."

"Don't be." She turned on the coffee machine. "Has Nicholas cooked? Is he here?" She stepped into the doorway. "Nicholas? You home?"

No reply.

"He went to the pub with a guy called Fry."

"Fry? What kind of name is that?"

"No idea. But it's what he goes as."

Zoe sniffed. "A new boyfriend?"

"Maybe. I wasn't about to pry."

"Good." Carl had no children of his own, so dealing with Nicholas wasn't entirely instinctive to him. But he was learning.

"Coffee?" she asked him. "Or do you want a beer?"

"I want a conversation."

Zoe rolled her eyes. "Please. I just made an arrest. Told

my team they could go home for Christmas. I'm feeling good. Don't spoil it."

"I'm worried about this card you got from Randle. Did you tell Frank?"

"Not yet. Too busy on the case." She walked into the living room, careful to avoid eye contact.

"Zoe, you have to tell him. Immediately. If he finds out another way…"

Zoe perched on the edge of the sofa. "Tell me you're not planning on telling him yourself."

"Of course not." Carl sat next to her and put a hand on her thigh. She tensed. "But you don't know who else he might have sent one to. Frank himself, for starters."

Zoe had a thought. "Or Lesley."

"Or Lesley."

"Should I call her? Ask?"

"No." Carl sighed. "You need to tell Frank, and not discuss it with anyone else. That card needs to be handed into Force CID or to PSD. It's still in your desk."

"You've been snooping around."

"I have not been snooping around." He caught her expression. "OK, so I checked. But this is for your own good. I worry about you."

"I can look after myself. I did it for a long time, before you came along."

"Don't be like this please, love. I just…" he broke off and looked away. The cat was in front of them, rubbing at their legs. "Hey, Yoda," he said.

"You just… what?" Zoe asked.

Carl turned to her. "Whatever you do here, you'll always be tainted with the shadow of David Randle and what he did. There are people who still think you were in league with him. Layla, for starte—"

"Layla? What's she been saying to you?"

"Nothing. But she never entirely believed you were straight."

"That explains a lot." Zoe slurped down the last of her coffee. "Thank God I don't have to work with her any more."

"She's a good detective."

"There are plenty of those. I'd rather have someone else in my team."

"I understand that. But Zoe, if we moved, went up north, you'd be able to leave this behind you. A fresh start."

"The police force doesn't work like that. Rumours follow you."

He shook his head. "They'd be less likely to follow you to Cumbria than they are to follow you around the West Midlands."

Zoe stood up. "I'm getting another coffee. You need a beer. And let's talk about something else. I'm much too tired for this."

CHAPTER SIXTY-SEVEN

Zoe sat on Mo's old desk and gazed at the board.

"We still don't know if he did it because of her sniffing around for Albert's killer, boss," said Rhodri.

Zoe shook her arms out. She was tired. She'd lain awake half the night, thinking about what Carl had said to her, while Carl lay facing away from her, seeming to sleep but probably doing the same thing.

"Is he still denying it?" Connie asked.

"Denying the assault on Freya, yes," Zoe said. "I haven't asked him about Albert. I can't."

"Still..." muttered Rhodri.

Zoe turned to him. "I can't, Rhod. You heard what the DCI said. Home Office told us to steer well clear. You never know, with the background Albert North had, we might have been in danger ourselves."

Rhodri snorted, while Connie tutted.

"Aleksander Nadarević, you mean," she said. "Don't forget who he was or what he did."

"No," Zoe replied. She jumped off the desk. "OK, we

can clear the board now. File everything away that isn't already on the system, guys. It's time to start thinking about Christmas. I think we've all earned a trip to the Plough after work."

Zoe's phone buzzed: a text from Frank. A summons.

She let out a breath. "I need to speak to the DCI. Back shortly."

She left the office without waiting to see the looks on the two DCs' faces. Fortunately Layla hadn't come in this morning; it seemed that she was no longer required to spy on them.

"Frank," Zoe said as she opened the door to his office.

"Will you at least bloody knock?" he said. "I've just about learned to put up with you refusing to call me sir, but—"

"You asked me to come and see you. I assumed you'd be waiting for me." She looked at him. He was fidgeting, the specs on his desk and his hair standing on end. "What's up?"

"The Detective Superintendent has had a call."

"What kind of a call?"

"Sit down, Zoe."

She did as she was told. "What kind of a call?" she asked, again.

"From the Home Office. They aren't best pleased."

"Why not? We handed over the files. You'll know from Layla that we stuck to investigating Freya's attack."

"That's not the problem."

"What is, then?"

"We've got their prime suspect in custody."

"Jimmy Kirk?"

Frank nodded.

"Well we couldn't exactly *not* arrest him once we had proof he'd attacked a vulnerable old woman."

"I thought you told me Freya Garside was tough as old boots."

"That's not the point."

"Still. I think he might be taken off us."

Zoe was aware that this happened from time to time. A suspect wanted by one investigation was occasionally poached by another, more influential, agency. She thought of the note from Adi.

"Who in the Home Office is investigating this? I mean, it's clearly not the civil servants."

"I haven't been told. But based on Aleksander Nadarević's history, I imagine it's not Home Office at all, but MI5."

"That's what I thought."

"They'll take him off us, Zoe. So if you want to speak to the man about the assault on your little old lady, I suggest you do it asap."

"OK. I will. Thanks for the heads-up, Frank."

"It isn't a heads-up. Just a statement of fact. And to be fair, I wanted to pass their anger down to you."

"If that was your goal…" She considered. "You haven't achieved it. Quite the opposite, in fact."

Frank smiled. "Well I failed there then, didn't I?"

"Oh, I wouldn't beat yourself up about it." Zoe smiled and stood up. "I'll tell the team to do what they need to quickly and then wind down for Christmas."

There was a knock on the door.

"Come in!" Zoe and Frank said in unison. He glared at her.

"Sorry," she muttered.

The door opened and Connie appeared. She looked from Frank to Zoe. "Boss, there's something you need to know."

"What? I'll come back to the office with you."

CHAPTER SIXTY-SEVEN

"DC Williams, you can tell me too," Frank said. "What's happened?" He gave Zoe a look. She wondered if he was thinking what she was; that Jimmy Kirk had already been snatched from under them.

"It's Jimmy Kirk's computer records," Connie said. "I've found evidence of him communicating with a Bosnian vigilante group."

CHAPTER SIXTY-EIGHT

"I TOLD you that your team were not to work on this case," Frank said. His specs were in his hand, being squeezed to within an inch of their lives.

Connie stepped inside, closing the door. "I didn't mean to, Sir. I was investigating his social media profile to help build a case in the Freya Garside assault. I thought maybe it would help us trace his movements on that day."

"And you accidentally stumbled on evidence relating to the Nadarević case."

Connie looked from Frank to Zoe and back again. "I'm sorry. It wasn't—"

Frank waggled his hand at Connie. "You've done it now. Sit down and tell me what you've found."

Connie glanced at Zoe, who gave her a nod. She took the seat next to Zoe, who sat back down next to her, resisting the urge to clasp her hand in encouragement.

"Go on then," Frank sighed. "Tell me what you found. And how."

"Well..." Connie licked her lips. "I've been checking out Kirk's Facebook profile, to see if I could find out what he was doing on the day Freya Garside was attacked."

"But Facebook is private."

"His security settings were light, Sir. It's a standard practice, when a suspect is arrested—"

"OK. So you looked at his feed."

"His profile page, yes. But then I thought I'd access his account *as* him, see if there was anything else that might connect him to Miss Garside, or to Avenue Road."

"That's convenient."

"Frank," Zoe interrupted. "Connie was doing her job. This is what she excels at. Please, let her continue."

He gave her a look and gestured to Connie to carry on.

Connie took a breath. "So I found some groups he was a member of. Nothing too dodgy, just some pressure groups relating to Bosnian politics. I found a friend who he kept chatting to in these groups. Who it turned out was his brother-in-law."

"So his brother-in-law is Bosnian?" Zoe asked.

"Yes. That could be why he took such an interest."

"Not for money."

"No."

"What are you two on about?" huffed Frank. "You're not working on this case, so why have you been discussing Jimmy Kirk's potential motive to kill Albert North?"

"That was before we were taken off the case," said Zoe. "It was a legitimate area of investigation at that point."

"I'll choose to believe you." He nodded at Connie.

"So I found some messages between Kirk and another individual. Founder of a vigilante group, goes under at least six names and almost as many nationalities, if you believe social media. He and his associates chased down war criminals from the Balkan states, and informed The Hague of where they were."

"Why didn't they just do that with Albert?" Zoe asked.

"I dug into the brother-in-law's past, and it seems he had a child who died. At Srebrenica."

"Which Albert was involved in," Zoe said.

"Aleksander," corrected Connie.

They all sat in silence for a moment. Zoe dug her fingernails into her palm.

"How old?"

"That's not relevant," said Frank.

Zoe turned to Connie. "How old was the child?"

"Eleven." Connie's voice was small.

"Poor bastard. That gives him motive, then." She pulled her shoulders back. "Is that everything you found?"

"Pretty much."

Zoe looked at Frank. "I think we should give this to the Home Office."

"I think if they have half a brain they'll have worked it out for themselves by now."

"Connie's good at this stuff. They might not have."

He snorted. "Leave it with me, both of you. And Connie," he looked her in the eye, "leave this alone now, will you?"

"Sir." Connie looked down at her hands, clasped in her lap. Zoe put out a hand then retracted it before patting Connie's fist. She wasn't a child, and she didn't need protecting.

"Now leave, both of you," said Frank. "I'll see you in the

New Year, and there'll be no talk of vigilantes, or Bosnia, or Albert North."

"Aleksander Nadarević," muttered Connie. Zoe shushed her as they left the office.

CHAPTER SIXTY-NINE

"I can't believe the DCI just stamped on it like that," Connie said as they walked back along the corridor.

"Not here," Zoe replied, glancing behind them. "Wait until we're in the office."

Connie sniffed and said nothing.

Once they were in the office, Connie flung herself into her chair, her gaze on her screen.

"Have you still got it up?" asked Zoe.

"Yeah."

"Well get rid of it. You heard what the DCI said."

"Boss. That's not like you to—"

"Don't talk like that, Connie. We've been given orders. I'm sure whoever's investigating Albert's death will be more than capable of finding the evidence you're referring to."

Connie humphed.

"Hang on," said Rhodri. "Come over here."

Zoe hauled herself over to Rhodri's desk. Connie stayed where she was.

CHAPTER SIXTY-NINE

"I'm on Twitter," he said. He looked across the desks. "Con, you'll want to see this."

She shook her head and slapped her computer monitor. Zoe frowned; she didn't like the way this case was getting to Connie.

"They've arrested someone," Rhodri said. "Look."

Zoe leaned in to see a series of tweets. The first was a BBC journalist: *Birmingham man arrested for murder of suspected Bosnian war criminal.* The comments were piling up and a thread was building. *Shelter owner taken into custody. Vigilantes tracked down after killing homeless man in German Market.* Then the comments: *he got what was coming to him. How come the authorities didn't track him down?*

She stopped at another tweet from the journalist: *Now learning that two men arrested. One a Bosnian national.*

"Bosnian?" Zoe breathed.

"The brother-in-law, maybe." Connie had got up from her chair and was behind Zoe, reading the tweets.

"Who arrested him?" Rhodri asked.

"It doesn't say," Zoe replied. She scrolled down. "Hang on... looks like security services. Shit."

"D'you think it was the social media evidence that made the difference?" Connie asked.

"It's too quick for that, Connie," Zoe replied. "But if Frank passes it on, it'll help them build a case."

"If they don't have it already."

Zoe looked at Connie. "Does it matter?"

"Sorry?"

"So long as they have the evidence and arrest the right person, does it really matter where they got it from?"

Connie opened her mouth then closed it again. She clenched her fist. "I suppose not."

Zoe put a hand on her fist and Connie unfurled it. "I spoke to emergency control. They got the name of the person who dialled 999, after Freya was attacked."

Zoe had been assuming that was a neighbour. "Oh?"

"It was Jimmy Kirk. I don't get it, boss. He tries to kill her, and then he calls an ambulance for her."

"His motive for attacking Freya wouldn't have been as fixed as the one he had for killing Albert."

"Aleksander."

"Aleksander. Maybe once he'd done it, he wanted to make it right, somehow."

"She should have left well alone. We all should have."

"Aleksander Nadarević did some awful things, Connie. But there's nothing you can do about that. Freya Garside was assaulted, and she has the security of knowing that the man who attacked her is in custody."

"Not here, though," added Rhodri.

"It doesn't matter where he is."

"So he thought she was onto him and wanted her out of the way?" he said.

Zoe nodded. "It looks that way. Let's hope he confesses to that crime, at least. But he isn't our problem now. And the fact is, Freya is safe. We did our job."

Connie grunted.

"Take that home for Christmas, you two," Zoe said. "You did a good job, and brought a criminal to justice."

CHAPTER SEVENTY

Zoe raised her mug of hot chocolate and Carl chinked his gluhwein to it. They were huddled in one of the wooden stalls outside the Council House, within view of the spot where Albert North had been found.

"Congratulations," Carl said. "You solved the case in time for everyone to go home for Christmas."

"I'm not sure it was appreciated in Connie's case," Zoe replied as she blew on the surface of her drink. "She's sick of Zaf already."

"Ah, she'll be fine. And Rhodri'll be in his element."

"I know." Zoe smiled. "Can you imagine Rhodri's family? That would be quite something."

Carl laughed and wiped wine off his top lip. "I owe you an apology," he said.

She put her drink down. "How so?"

"I've been too hard on you, the last few days. About that card. About the case."

"You haven't said anything that wasn't correct."

"Yeah." He paused, considering. "But maybe I could have been... gentler."

Zoe grabbed his hand. "I grew up with an alcoholic mother. Gentle isn't something I've come to expect.,"

"Your dad was gentle though."

"Until he died."

"Sorry, Zoe. I didn't mean to make you think about him."

She looked into his eyes. "It doesn't work like that. I'll think about my dad whether people remind me of him or not. I'll think about my mum, too. Whether I want to or not. I like thinking about my dad. Yes, it's shit that he died when I was in my twenties. But there were happy times. It's good to remember those. And to talk to Nicholas about them."

"Even if he does ignore you half the time these days."

"It'll pass. Uni has given him some independence. That's good."

"So..."

"Yes?" She drank from her mug, wishing she hadn't blown on it. It was cooling quickly.

"Have you had a chance to think any more about Cumbria?"

"Carl, you're like a stuck record. Shut up about bloody Cumbria, will you?"

"I have to make a decision by the middle of February."

"Which means I have until the middle of February to make my mind up."

"I'd rather know before the deadline."

She tightened her grip on his hand. "I know, love. And I'll give it some serious thought over Christmas. I'm not as averse to the idea as I was."

His eyes brightened. "You're not?"

CHAPTER SEVENTY

"No."

The music from the tannoy switched to *Delilah*. The crowd sang along.

"Can we go home?" Zoe asked. "I'm too knackered for this."

Carl stood up and downed his wine. "Of course."

"Don't forget to return that," she told him. "Get your deposit."

"Yeah." He looked at the mug. "I could keep it as a souvenir of Birmingham."

"Carl..."

"I know, I know. Don't assume anything."

She stood up and put her arms around him. He was as soft as she was, bundled up in layers. "I'll need to talk to Nicholas."

"He's at Uni now."

"I still need to talk to him. I'm not saying I need his permission, but I want to know what he thinks. And I'll need to find a job up there."

"You're going to go for it?"

"I didn't say that, Carl. I'll do the research, then I'll make my mind up."

"So—"

She silenced him with a kiss. "Stop it, Carl. Just enjoy Christmas and forget about work for a minute."

I hope you have enjoyed reading the Zoe Finch series. Zoe isn't done though: she's moved to Cumbria and has a new team and a new set of challenges. And the taint of the

Canary case might just follow her north... You can read about her move north in the novella *The Castle*, which is free to members of my book club at rachelmclean.com/the-castle-book.

Happy Reading!
Rachel

READ A FREE PREQUEL NOVELLA, THE CASTLE

DI Zoe Finch has a big decision to make

Will she stay in Birmingham, clinging to the wreckage of her beloved team as it breaks up and leaves her behind? Or will she follow her partner Carl to Cumbria, a new job and a new life?

Carl's already decided. He's heading up north, revelling in the lakes and fells and excited about his new job chasing down dodgy coppers.

And Zoe's future colleague DS Aaron Keyes is perplexed. A man has been found dead at Egremont Castle – a man who left a voicemail for him just before he died.

Can Aaron track down the killer? Will Carl be able to work out exactly why members of Cumbria police are acting strangely? And will Zoe decide to make the move up north?

Find out by reading *The Castle* for FREE at rachelmclean.com/the-castle-book.

READ THE DI ZOE FINCH SERIES

Deadly Wishes

Deadly Choices

Deadly Desires

Deadly Terror

Deadly Reprisal

Deadly Fallout

Deadly Christmas

Deadly Origins, the FREE Zoe Finch prequel

Buy from book retailers or via the Rachel McLean website.

ALSO BY RACHEL MCLEAN

The Dorset Crime Series – buy from book retailers or via the Rachel McLean website.

The Corfe Castle Murders

The Clifftop Murders

The Island Murders

The Monument Murders

The Millionaire Murders

The Fossil Beach Murders

The Blue Pool Murders

The Lighthouse Murders

The Ghost Village Murders

The Poole Harbour Murders

...and more to come

The Ballard Down Murder, the FREE Dorset Crime prequel

The McBride & Tanner Series – Buy from book retailers or via the Rachel McLean website.

Blood and Money

Death and Poetry

Power and Treachery

Secrets and History

The Cumbria Crime Series by Rachel McLean and Joel Hames – Buy from book retailers or via the Rachel McLean website.

The Harbour

The Mine

The Cairn

The Barn

The Lake

...and more to come

Read the London Cosy Mystery Series by Rachel McLean and Millie Ravensworth – Buy from book retailers or via the Rachel McLean website.

Death at Westminster

Death in the West End

Death at Tower Bridge

Death on the Thames

Death at St Paul's Cathedral

Death at Abbey Road